TO CAPTURE HIS HEART

TO CAPTURE HIS HEART

NANCY CAMPBELL ALLEN

SHADOW
MOUNTAIN
PUBLISHING

To Mark

How glad I am we are on this journey together.
Thanks for being my person.

Visit us at shadowmountain.com

Library of Congress Cataloging-in-Publication Data
Names: Allen, Nancy Campbell, 1969– author.
Title: To capture his heart / Nancy Campbell Allen.
Other titles: Proper romance.
Description: Salt Lake City : Shadow Mountain, [2022] | Series: Proper romance | Summary: "Photographer Eva Caldwell and Detective Nathan Winston fall in love while working together to capture a criminal at Nathan's mother's summer matchmaking party"—Provided by publisher.
Identifiers: LCCN 2022019502 | ISBN 9781639930517 (trade paperback)
Subjects: LCSH: Man-woman relationships—Fiction. | Photographers—Fiction. | BISAC: FICTION / Romance / Historical / Victorian | FICTION / Romance / Clean & Wholesome | LCGFT: Historical fiction. | Romance fiction.
Classification: LCC PS3551.L39644 T58 2022 | DDC 813/.54—dc23/eng/20220603
LC record available at https://lccn.loc.gov/2022019502

Printed in the United States of America
Lake Book Manufacturing, Melrose Park, IL

10 9 8 7 6 5 4 3 2 1

CHAPTER 1

Evangeline Caldwell finished developing the last of Sir Henry Blake's family photos and wiped her hands on a cloth. She surveyed the results hanging across the darkroom with satisfaction, knowing the family would be pleased despite their notoriously fussy expectations. She glanced at her assistant, ten-year-old Sammy White, and smiled. The formerly homeless orphan was surprisingly effective at his position, which she had initially offered as a means of keeping him out of trouble. Now, she well and truly depended on his help.

"Almost used all the developing liquid," Sammy said as he took the clean towel she offered.

She nodded. "I'll be purchasing several items tomorrow in Town." She picked up a pencil and paper and added the liquid ingredients to the list.

"'S a good thing we keep runnin' out. Means we're busy as bees." Sammy grinned, and she tousled his hair.

"A good thing, indeed," she agreed. "I cannot imagine how I would do this without your help."

"Nor can I."

She looked at him askance as they left the room, and he

laughed. "I suppose we ought to add *humility* to your list of lessons from Mrs. Burnette."

"Ain't bragging if it's a fact."

"I doubt that to be true." They climbed the stairs out of the cellar, and she closed the door at the top. He dashed into the kitchen where the delicious smell of freshly baked scones hung in the air. Eva heard the typical slap and scolding from the cook, Mrs. Peters, as Sammy must have snatched a warm scone from the tray. For all that Mrs. Burnette and Mrs. Peters complained about the boy's incorrigibility, however, their consistent chastisement lacked any real sting.

"I'm off to meet Charlotte at Amelie's house," she called to Sammy. "We'll develop another batch tomorrow. Behave yourself and mind your studies with Mrs. Burnette."

Sammy rolled his eyes but mumbled, "Yes, miss," around a mouthful of scone.

"Geography and maths today, young man," Mrs. Burnette said as she descended the staircase. "We've fallen behind, what with you spending so much time making pictures downstairs."

Eva smiled as the brusque housekeeper-turned-tutor-turned-caretaker lectured Sammy while she joined him in the kitchen. She heard Sammy's voice rise in protest at the reminder of his pending bath later in the evening. It was an argument that had become a veritable ritual twice weekly. " . . . should be glad I don't insist on nightly bathing," Mrs. Burnette was saying now.

Eva had placed her new springtime pelisse on the coatrack near the front door, and she now shrugged into it, buttoning the front. She secured her new hat at just the right angle atop her dark curls and retrieved her valise and gloves from the side table. Then she made her way out the front door into the brisk spring afternoon.

The cab ride to her cousin Amelie Hampton Baker's house took ten short minutes, and as she paid the driver, another cab pulled alongside the curb. Eva smiled at her other cousin, Charlotte Duvall, who was returning from a visit home to the countryside. Charlotte hopped down from her cab, paid the driver, and grinned at Eva, her green eyes bright and her deep auburn curls shining like burnished fire in the sunlight.

Charlotte clasped Eva close in a warm embrace and said, "Mercy, I missed you! Have you taken loads of photographs in my absence?"

Eva laughed and pulled back, squeezing Charlotte's arms. "Loads and loads. And what have you done for one long month at home with your brothers and father?"

"Oh." Charlotte rolled her eyes and linked an arm through Eva's. "Survived, but only just. Convincing them I'm no longer their infant sister is a task by itself."

They approached the front door of Amelie's tidy townhome and Charlotte knocked briskly. "Our darling cousin is no longer a young maiden," Charlotte said as an aside with one brow raised. "Do you suppose she'll share any secrets?"

Eva laughed and bumped her hip against Charlotte's. "Silly, we aren't supposed to know there are secrets to be shared." Eva was genuinely amused but also had to admit, if only privately, that she doubted the existence of any secrets she might find interesting. She had squelched that curiosity nearly six years earlier when her heart had been spectacularly broken. She'd been exceptionally leery of anything resembling vulnerability ever since.

The door swung open wide to reveal Amelie, who squealed and leaped on them, and the three women wrapped together in a tight bunch. "I've missed you so much!"

"And how is your new husband?" Eva asked, placing her hand alongside Amelie's cheek.

"Wonderful, of course!" Amelie beamed. "He's just inside, but once he's said hello, I've made him promise to leave us alone in the parlor so we can gossip."

Amelie looked well and whole, and Eva was relieved. Seven months earlier, Amelie had narrowly escaped death at the hands of a man under investigation by Scotland Yard's Criminal Investigation Division. Last month, she married Michael Baker, the detective conducting the investigation, and was apparently flourishing.

Eva and Charlotte followed Amelie into the house, past the stairs, and down a corridor to the parlor they'd helped her decorate before the wedding. The walls were papered in soft tones, the furniture a lovely counterpart, and a small fire glowed in the hearth. Catching Eva's eye, however, was a gentleman who rose with Michael as they entered.

Detective Winston, Michael's partner, was as handsome a man as any Eva had seen. The cousins had worked closely with the two detectives during their investigation the year before and had developed genuine friendships. There was something about Detective Winston that caused Eva's heart to thump, whether because of his tall stature, thick blond hair, or tawny-colored eyes, she was unsure. Or it might have been the smile that crossed his face whenever he saw her, or the fact that he enjoyed conversing with her about photography, even welcoming her as a stand-in for crime scenes when the police photographer was unable to document for them. She genuinely liked him and considered him a true friend. It was because of these things that she refrained from allowing any feelings to deepen. She couldn't bear the thought of history repeating itself at the hands of a man she so admired.

"Ladies," Michael said, his grin extending to his bright blue eyes. "Wonderful to see you." He clasped Eva's hand and then Charlotte's. "I would say Amelie missed you dreadfully, except I'd then be obliged to admit I did as well."

"That would never do," Charlotte said, chuckling. "Would tarnish your reputation as a fearsome detective."

"Precisely." Michael nodded once, still smiling. "I'll trust you not to breathe a word of it to anyone."

Eva mimed locking her lips closed with a key and tossing it over her shoulder.

"Ladies, lovely to see you again," Detective Winston said, edging forward as Michael stepped to one side and placed a hand under Amelie's elbow.

"Detective." Eva smiled at him and placed her hand in his larger one. It was firm, and she felt the warmth of it through her thin glove.

"Miss Duvall," he now said, taking Charlotte's hand, "I trust your vacation was delightful?"

Charlotte's lips twitched. "'Delightful' would be stretching the truth a bit too far, but I did enjoy the bulk of it, yes."

"We shall vacate the room and retire to the study," Michael said. "Nathan has much to tell me before I return to work in the morning."

Nathan. Short for Nathaniel. Eva had heard Michael using the familiar version of his partner's name for months, and she felt what her mother had often called "a little case of the envies." She didn't envy Michael his professional relationship and friendship with Detective Winston, but she did wish it within her purview to be on such familiar terms.

Detective Winston tipped his head and met Eva's eyes once more before heading toward the door with Michael. There was an element to the glance, a certain something Eva couldn't define, but lately, she'd noticed it more. A half smile played on his lips, and there was something in his eyes, as though he knew a secret he might eventually be prevailed upon to share. Whatever it was, it had her heart thumping again, just once.

She watched his retreating form before finally turning her attention to her cousins, who both watched *her* with interest. "What?" she finally asked them as they all sat together on the long sofa.

"Has it gotten worse in our absence, I wonder?" Amelie asked Charlotte, tapping her lip with her fingertip.

Charlotte lifted a shoulder. "Time will tell. Hopefully, old wounds have healed by now. She may require a nudge, so our return is timely, no doubt."

Amelie nodded. "No doubt." They both regarded Eva again, who couldn't say she liked the look of their scrutiny.

"Whatever you're thinking, I need nothing of it."

"Of course, of course, certainly not," both cousins answered on top of each other.

Eva was relieved when Charlotte placed both hands on Amelie's knee and said, "Now dearest, you must tell us all of the secrets. Every last one, if you please, and leave nothing out. We," she continued, placing one hand on her chest modestly, "your humble spinster cousins are at your mercy. If you do not impart of your newly acquired wisdom, we may find ourselves wallowing in eternal ignorance. So, you see, our happiness, or lack, rests squarely on your shoulders."

Amelie tipped back her head and laughed. "Well," she managed as she sobered and dropped her voice, "I will say this. Had

I known what I was missing, I would have made an earnest effort to evade my chaperones."

Charlotte's eyes sparkled, and Amelie's cheeks flushed a becoming pink. The sound of the gentlemen across the hall as they laughed together during their own conversation had Eva feeling a bit flushed herself. Her mind wandered, and she wondered if she would see Detective Winston again before he left the Baker residence; she hoped so. He laughed again, and she felt warmth unfurling in her midsection. He really was such a lovely man and a dear, dear friend.

CHAPTER 2

"Nathaniel Joshua Winston, I'll not hear another word of protest. You were unable to attend last year, and I understand." Mrs. James Winston, Christine, widowed for two decades but still handsome of face and figure, pointed her pen at her son. She sat at her parlor writing desk, making a list. Christine was a consummate list maker, a habit that served her well. She was efficient and ruthless in her efforts to run a well-organized life, and Nathan realized with sinking clarity that his protestations would get him nowhere.

Every summer, his mother hosted a house party at the family property in Seaside, on the southern coast. It was different than most, however, because it served as a fundraiser for special projects Christine supported. This year, the money would benefit a girls' school in desperate need of funds. Potential guests received an invitation to apply for the event, along with proposed donation amounts. Because the guest list varied each year, the party was unpredictable and entertaining. Christine had a waiting list for people wishing to be considered.

He tried again. "Mother. Mama. I do not have time to devote to the house party this year either. It lasts for ten days." He sat on a yellow-and-red-brocade settee and rested his elbows on knees, weary to the bone. He had just concluded a significant arrest in a grueling case, and he was tired.

"I know you've finished that nasty business in Wickleston; I read the dailies. Consider yourself fortunate I held off until that investigation was complete. Nicely done, incidentally." She flashed him a smile and turned back to her journal, which was thick with papers, invitations, photographs, household accounts, and lists upon lists. A record of a full life. Any other time he'd have looked upon it with affection; now, the logbook represented what was surely to be an event he'd rather avoid at all costs.

"Thank you. I have finished that 'nasty business,' yes, but that does not mean I am free of obligations. I have new cases, of course."

"Of course, but you surely must sleep sometime. You may as well rest your head at the holiday house in Seaside. With the recent rail addition, we are an accessible ride from Town."

"Wouldn't that be a waste of time? If I'm only sleeping there, I may as well remain at my flat. Besides, my absence would free the use of my bedchamber to another guest. I'm certain you'll have plenty."

She shot him an arch look. "I will indeed have plenty—this year, the list is curated to include mostly single young people."

Nathan held his breath. His argument was falling flat. The beachside home accommodated their entire family plus twenty guests easily, with room to spare.

"Mother," he tried again.

"No 'Mama' this time?"

"Would it help my cause?"

"Not if your cause is anything other than agreeing to be present for this gathering."

He leaned back against the arm of the settee with a sigh and closed his eyes. "You do not need my presence at the summer holiday fundraiser."

"On the contrary; your presence is very much required."

A fissure of worry settled uncomfortably at the base of his spine. It had been a handful of years since his mother's last attempt at matchmaking, and he'd grown complacent by assuming she had given the matter up as a lost cause. He would court someone when he found the time, and time was not an item he possessed in luxurious amounts. He couldn't even say he possessed any in frugal amounts.

"I'll not be party to any endeavor that sees an end to my bachelorhood. You know I haven't the time nor inclination for it." Unbidden, an image flashed in his mind, a woman with black hair and brown eyes, achingly beautiful and incredibly witty. He blinked, recognizing the yearning that accompanied it.

Evangeline Caldwell was one of society's rising stars in the realm of independent women. As the world approached a new century, opportunities and attitudes were shifting, and what once had been considered scandalous now seemed plausible. Before long, a woman may have the luxury of professional pursuits or education that would allow her to postpone marriage until a time of her own choosing. Eva would have her choice of suitors when she decided she wanted them, and as far as Nathan could tell, she hadn't much more time on her hands than he did. His mother would understand—she was a fixture at suffragette events, with his four younger sisters usually in tow. Eva and his family would get along famously, he was sure of it. The thought left a feeling in the pit of his stomach, but it wasn't nausea-inducing.

Interesting.

He would pull that thought out for later examination. Much later.

His mother sighed softly, and he angled his head to look at her. She watched him quietly for a moment before saying, "I would be thrilled to see you married, but additionally, your sisters need this, Nathaniel. I cannot assume they'll each choose an independent path. I'll not force anything upon any of you, but I must provide a wide variety of opportunities for success. The girls need to spend more time socially with eligible gentlemen, and they need their elder brother with them."

Nathan's father had married Christine, an heiress, and stepped into the family textile business with ease. However, James Winston had died young, after siring the five children, leaving behind a son too young to take the reins. Christine had slid into the position and, with the help of trusted solicitors and advisors, handled the family business. It was unconventional, but her talents for it were clear. Legal maneuvering before her father had died insured the business and assets would revert to her, the only child, upon her husband's death.

Nathan often wondered if the brilliance behind his father's business acumen had actually been his mother's quick brain all along. When Nathan had reached the age of majority, they decided together she would continue in the role, and his responsibilities would include annual meetings and signing papers she put before him. It was a system that served them well, and Nathan had been free to choose other ventures.

Sometimes, his choice to pursue a vocation seemed like a guilty indulgence. His mother would never say it outright, but he knew she must think it. His childhood fascination with Edgar Allan Poe's Inspector Dupin had led to a career in police work that she had encouraged, but she'd never really asked anything else of him. He could stomach one house party.

"I'll arrange my schedule with Director Ellis," he said, massaging tired eyes with his thumb and forefinger. The director had only yesterday suggested Nathan take a small holiday now that Michael and Amelie had returned from their wedding trip. He may not appreciate Nathan taking an entire week away from the Yard, but a few days certainly wouldn't be a problem.

"Thank you." He heard the smile in his mother's voice.

"I do apologize for being scarce lately," he said quietly. "Work has been—"

"Do not apologize, darling. I appreciate you indulging your mother in this one thing."

"Ah, yes. Speaking of which, do not worry about social machinations for my benefit. I'm happy to be there with you and the girls, and I'll do my best elder brother routine for potential suitors."

"It is not a bother at all! In fact, I've already sent invitations to several young women, a few of whom you'll remember from years past, and some new friends of your sisters as well."

Still reclining his head against the settee, Nathan's eyes now opened wide in alarm, and he stared at the paneled ceiling. Already sent the invitations? He could hardly imagine a fate worse than spending several days with friends of his sisters who would be ardently on the matrimonial hunt. He had already experienced a near disaster because of one of those friends, but, desiring to keep the peace, had remained silent concerning it. He should have kept his mother informed.

He cleared his throat and bit back an angry retort. "If there's no chance of recalling the invitations, perhaps you'll put out the word that I am . . . I am not available." The room grew warmer with each imagined scenario. Parlor games. Beach games. Scavenger hunts. Cave explorations. Each guaranteed to produce a scene more fraught with drama than the last.

He didn't believe in the probability of a couple falling in love during such manufactured events. To Nathan, it seemed far more preferable that a compatible couple become acquainted in a work setting, perhaps, where conversation about professional topics filled the space if other conversation ran dry. Women were attending university in greater numbers, thanks to the Queen, and working in offices and shops with regularity. Courtship was a tricky affair, riddled with rules and innuendo and the continual possibility of putting one's foot right in a pile of—

"And how would you explain the reason that you are suddenly 'unavailable'?" His mother had turned the full effect of her regard in his direction.

He slowly sat up and loosened his tie. "I am . . . I am . . . " He cleared his throat again. "I am interested in someone else." There! It was the perfect excuse. He wondered why he'd not thought of it sooner.

"Splendid!" Christine's brows raised high in delight. "Tell me her name and address; I'll send an invitation to her straightaway. She need not pledge a donation—consider it my gift to you." She sifted through cards and papers on her desk until she found an extra invitation and poised her pen above it. At his silence, she looked at him again, blinking once. Twice.

He also blinked twice, and slowly rose to his feet. "Oh, she is quite—that is, she has a very full schedule."

"What does she do with her time?" Another blink.

He blurted the first thing that came to mind. "She is a photographer. She takes pictures, many of them, all day. Sometimes into the evenings." He began making his way to the door.

"Oh!" His mother stood, her smile huge, and she followed him across the room, card in one hand, and pen gripped in the other. "Excellent! You'll never believe the coincidence, but my list includes the very phrase, 'Hire a photographer to attend the house party'!"

He tried for a smile, but it felt sickly. "Imagine that!"

"Wait." Her eyes widened. "Wait! Is it Miss Caldwell, who photographed Inspector Baker's wedding last month? Cousin of the bride, is she not?"

He winced at his own lack of foresight. Why had he not manufactured a bakery hostess? Or a shopgirl? His mother had *met* Eva. He stopped moving and faced her, one hand palm out. "Mother, she is incredibly busy. She is scheduled weeks in advance with clients. We are fortunate to acquire her help on the spur of the moment when the crime scene photographer doesn't show up."

Her mouth gaped. "She photographs *crime scenes?*"

He closed his eyes briefly, cursing his stupidity. Eva's sometime involvement with the Yard wasn't a secret, but he didn't want to be the reason her reputation suffered if unseemly gossip spread. "I oughtn't have mentioned it," he said, increasingly uncomfortable.

"I'll not say a word; you know I do not indulge in gossip." She looked highly offended, and to her credit, he did have to agree that his mother was not one for idle chitchat bent on harming an innocent person. She moved closer and lowered her voice, as though a throng of onlookers may overhear. "Is she aware of your interest in her?"

What on earth had he just done?

A bead of sweat formed at his brow.

Christine waved a hand at him and returned to her writing

table to scribble something on the card. She folded it and sealed the invitation closed before handing it to him. "I need a photographer, and who better than someone we know and trust? The party is five weeks away, and I'll compensate her in triplicate to offset any scheduling issues."

He took the invitation, feeling light-headed.

"I shall be clear to party attendees that you are not to be pursued because you're otherwise engaged. I am certain it will become obvious enough exactly where those interests lie once we are all together in Seaside." She smiled brightly.

"Well . . . I mean to say . . . we are hardly betrothed, there has been no talk of courtship after all, and—"

One brow shot up. "So, you *are* interested in other potential courtship options?"

"No! No, I only—"

She took his arm and slowly propelled him from the parlor and into the front hall, speaking soothingly the entire way. A buzzing in his ears prevented him from hearing half of it. He forced himself to focus as the butler handed him his hat and overcoat before opening the front door.

" . . . will know straightaway you did not deliver the invitation if I do not receive a response from Miss Caldwell. As a professional woman of integrity, I believe she would not allow a significant amount of time to lapse before contacting me. And as you said, scheduling is of paramount importance to her work, so you mustn't delay in delivering it."

"Mother—"

She reached up and kissed his cheek, grasping his hand in both of hers. "Thank you, darling, for removing one very large task from my list!" She smiled broadly. "You've no idea how happy you've made me today."

As he left the house and stepped into a drizzling rain, he placed the invitation in his inner coat pocket, next to his chest. He had no doubt he'd just made his mother deliriously happy. Regrettably, he'd just complicated his own life to an unbelievable degree, and in only a few short moments.

He firmed his lips and shook his head, shoving his hat in place. His mother was a master, and he'd allowed himself to forget it. He walked down the street, thinking he ought to have brought his carriage rather than be dropped off by a fellow officer on his way to an interview. Some time passed before he was able to hail a hansom cab, but he figured it was just as well. He'd yet to work out how he would possibly approach a young woman he'd admired from a distance—albeit a short distance—with the notion that to avoid a ploy from his matchmaking mother, he'd stepped straight into a snare of his own making and would now require help.

He needed Eva Caldwell to pretend an interest in him so other marriage-minded friends of his sisters would leave him alone at the house party. And it must be managed in a way that kept her good name intact throughout the process. *If* she agreed at all. Perhaps her schedule wouldn't allow it, and all problems would be solved. Except that he would then be at the house party as available prey. The circle came back round again, and his frustration grew.

The fog in his brain cleared enough to realize he'd given the driver the address to Hampton House, the mansion in Bloomsbury where Eva resided with her cousin and an odd assortment of other residents. As the cab pulled to the front, he sat for so long the driver eventually called out to him.

For the first time in a very long time, Nathaniel Winston was utterly flummoxed.

CHAPTER 3

Eva and Charlotte had just left the dining room when a knock sounded at the front door. Mrs. Burnette was at the back of the house debating something with the cook, and both maids, Katie and Sarah, were busily clearing the dining table. Having never taken issue with the social indignity of answering one's own door, Eva shrugged at Charlotte and opened it. Her heart tripped at the sight of Detective Winston, who seemed slightly breathless, as though he'd just dashed through the rain from the carriage now pulling away from the front gate.

He removed his hat and smiled, but he seemed awfully pale.

"Detective? Is something amiss?" She opened the door wider and motioned him inside.

"Thank you, Miss Caldwell, and no, nothing is wrong; however, I wonder if I might have a word with you."

Charlotte smiled and held out her hand for his hat, which she hung on the rack next to the door. "May I take your coat?" she added.

"Oh, I . . . I suppose," he mumbled. "I can hang it myself; I'd hate for you to get all wet."

"Nonsense." Charlotte chuckled. "We are down one butler, and the housekeeper is otherwise engaged in a very serious debate about tomorrow morning's breakfast. You may call me Duvall, and I shall manage the door this evening."

The detective blinked at them both, as though trying to process Charlotte's quip.

"I jest, of course," Charlotte finally said. "Mrs. Burnette has yet to interview butler prospects that are to her liking. But do let me take your coat."

He handed the coat to Charlotte with an awkward smile. Eva watched him, growing concerned. Was the man ill?

"Come," Eva said, extending a hand to the parlor. "Warm yourself by the fire and collect your thoughts."

He cleared his throat and looked at her with a weak smile. "My behavior certainly must suggest a gathering of thoughts would be in order. Forgive me." He inclined his head for Eva and Charlotte to precede him into the parlor.

"You go," Charlotte said. "I'll warm some tea."

Eva nodded and led the way to the parlor's cozy fire, and he took a chair opposite hers. "Now, detective," she said, placing her hands on her lap. "What brings you to Hampton House this evening? I hope nothing untoward has happened, but I fear you bring unpleasant news."

He sighed and rotated his head, as though suffering from stiffness in the neck. "Miss Caldwell." He paused and half-smiled. It was sheepish and genuine and removed the edge from her rising anxiety. "I am wasting your time and have decided I must simply do the brave thing and stand up to my mother."

Eva wondered if her confusion showed. "Perhaps you might elaborate."

His eyes wandered over her face, lingering, and her breath caught. Again, he smiled, and she noted his color had returned. He seemed much less alarmed and more like his confident self.

"I cannot apologize enough for encroaching on your time this evening. Forgive me."

He shifted in his seat as though to rise, so she scooted forward in her chair and held out her hand, unintentionally brushing his knee. She pulled her fingers back but said, "Wait, if you please. Charlotte will have warmed the tea for nothing."

He slowly settled into the seat and offered another quick smile. Eva studied him for a moment, eyes narrowing in speculation. He did not bear bad tidings, he appeared to have collected himself, and yet he bore the look of one caught in an embarrassing trap.

He mentioned his mother . . .

She tapped her fingertips lightly against the armrest, still watching him and not feeling one grain of regret when he shifted slightly under her regard. She would throw herself prostrate in front of the door before allowing him to leave without explaining the reason for his sudden arrival. She considered telling him as much but opted for a subtler approach.

"Your mother—how is she? In good health, I hope." Eva smiled. "It was so lovely to meet her last month at the wedding."

He nodded, raising his eyebrows in what he probably hoped was an innocent manner. "Very well, very well. Healthy as an ox, that one." He winced, as though regretting his choice of words.

He had said something about standing up to his mother. Eva turned the statement over in her mind. "I was amazed at her mastery of a difficult situation when she arranged for Detective Baker's family to be kept safely hidden away from that awful business last year."

"Certainly." He nodded. "Mastery of situations is her specialty."

"I find it admirable. A strong woman, she must be. Strong in her opinions, I should think."

He tilted his head slightly to the side and studied the fire in the grate. "An understatement," he muttered.

Eva sensed victory on the horizon. "Perhaps you and she have encountered a difference of opinion lately."

He looked back at her, now narrowing *his* eyes at her in speculation. The half smile returned, and her heart tripped. "Perhaps."

Drat. He seemed disinclined to continue. "The topic must be quite serious to require you to stop here on your way home. That is, I presume you were headed for home . . ."

He pursed his lips, still watching her. After a few prolonged moments, he inhaled and exhaled quietly. Deliberately.

"Miss Caldwell, my mother is hosting a house party in the family villa at Seaside. It is a fundraising event occurring annually. Perhaps you have heard of it."

"Oh, yes! I have indeed. Aunt Sally was a guest two years ago."

He nodded. "She asked that I deliver this invitation to you, but as well as being a guest, she hopes you'll be amenable to acting as the party photographer. It would be a professional arrangement, for which she is willing to pay handsomely in hopes that any scheduling conflicts might be resolved."

Eva blinked. *This* was the cause of his consternation? Perhaps he was uncomfortable discussing money or matters of finance. Society considered such topics of conversation gauche, at best. "I am flattered and honored to be your mother's event photographer." She accepted the sealed invitation he handed her. "I shall consult my schedule straightaway and have an answer for her in the morning's post." She smiled. "You needn't have been concerned to bring this matter to me, Detective, I assure you. I am accustomed to discussing matters of business. I hope you are not unduly uncomfortable."

He scratched his temple, a wry smile crossing his lips. "There is more to the invitation, I fear."

"Oh?"

"I shall attend the gathering at my mother's request, as male head of the family. The guest list includes many of my mother's friends' adult children who are yet unattached. I believe she is hopeful one of my sisters might find a suitable match."

Eva nodded. It was a sound notion—house parties often spanned a weekend, and in such proximity, guests were afforded a longer stretch of time to make acquaintances. The thought of spending a couple of days and evenings under the same roof as the detective was a heady one, and her cheeks warmed. She slid her finger under the sealed flap and opened the invitation, scanning the dates.

Her eyes widened. "Ten days? My goodness, such an extended amount of time!" She glanced up at him, noted his slightly pained expression, and attempted to soften her reaction. "Have no fear, however; I am certain I can manage it." She looked down again at the dates in question, nodding. "I believe this may conflict with two scheduled sittings, but if my clients are unable to adjust, I can simply return to Town for the mornings in question." She paused. "Should that meet with your mother's approval."

He chuckled softly. "I am certain such an arrangement would meet with her approval."

Eva had to admit surprise that the normally unflappable Detective Winston had been so apprehensive about approaching her with the prospect. Did he find her disagreeable or difficult?

21

She saw a flash of fabric at the doorway, signaling Charlotte's arrival with the tea.

"I fear there is more," the detective said, and Charlotte did an about-face, mumbling something about forgetting the sugar.

Eva waited patiently as the detective appeared to choose his words.

"My mother has a habit of introducing me to conveniently available ladies. Naturally, she hopes to see me wed—yesterday, if she had her way. In order to prevent matchmaking on my behalf at the house party, however, I told her—" He paused and cleared his throat. "I told her that she needn't go to such lengths for my sake, as I am already interested in someone."

Eva felt a stab of disappointment and, to her dismay, realized silence was stretching between them. She ought to say something, but now she found herself irrationally frustrated that he would tell her of an interest in another. Why shouldn't he? They were friends, after all. But what had it to do with their discussion?

She pulled in a quiet breath and managed a smile. "I see. And this mysterious someone else—is she someone of my acquaintance? I fear I do not follow the relevance."

He rubbed the back of his neck and shifted in the chair. A rueful smile accompanied the movement. "I would say she is definitely someone you know well. I told my mother the woman who holds my regard is a photographer."

Eva's brows drew together. She was, quite literally, the only female photographer of her caliber in Town and beyond. She leaned forward, head tilted, wondering what she was missing.

"I told her the woman is a photographer, to whom she then insisted I deliver an invitation for the house party."

"Oh." Eva sat back. Then, her eyes widened, and her heart thumped once, hard. "Oh!"

"Yes." His smile tightened at the corners. "Oh."

With an effort, she closed her mouth. "Detective, I am . . . I am—"

"I panicked," he interrupted, hurrying to explain, "and I blurted the first thing that came to mind. I cannot apologize enough, and I fear my mother could say something awkward. It was only fair that you be forewarned."

Eva felt as though her brain were submerged in jelly. She could not maintain a train of thought for the jumble of emotions that warred for her attention. She'd known a small glimpse of joy at the thought that he was interested in her, only to have it hurled back down spectacularly with his admission that he'd said it only to keep his mother from playing matchmaker with the single party guests.

She sat very still in her chair, feeling the weight of the moment. As he studied her, his expression one of growing concern, she figured she must appear either stony or angry. Neither was a good option for the sake of her pride. She sighed and waved a hand at him, trying for a laugh that sounded hollow.

"Think nothing of it, Detective. Surely, since you clarified to your mother that we are only friends, I don't imagine her saying anything awkward to me. She is a woman of exacting manners and bearing."

He frowned and turned his attention back to the fire. "I did not exactly disabuse her of the notion."

She leaned forward subtly again, uncertain she'd heard him correctly. "I beg your pardon?"

He also leaned forward and lowered his voice. "My mother is still under the impression that I am interested in courting you, to the exclusion of any other female in the whole of England. When you arrive at the house party—if you still wish to—you will be in the company of a mother who sees you as a potential daughter-in-law. A mother who very much wants to see her son married."

He hadn't told his mother the truth.

He must have been desperate to avoid her machinations. Eva's brain slowly ground back to life, the cogs turning and fitting together nicely. "Tell me one thing honestly, Detective Winston." She lowered her voice, and he leaned closer still. Their knees were close enough that she felt the warmth of him through her skirt. "You do not have even the slightest interest in any of the women on your mother's guest list?"

He swallowed. "I do not have an interest in any of the women on my mother's written guest list."

She sensed prevarication but chose to leave it for the moment. "Do any of the women on the list have reason to expect special attention from you? This is important—I'll not be party to breaking a fellow woman's heart."

He shook his head once, looking very confused. "I do not believe anyone expects special attention from me."

Without asking him bluntly whether he'd ever flirted outrageously with anyone on the guest list, it was the best she could hope to glean from him.

"What has this to do with anything?" he asked.

She realized how closely they'd leaned together, and her fingers itched to brush through his thick, honey-colored hair. He also smelled wonderful, though she couldn't put a finger on the nature of the scent.

"You clearly wish to exit your mother's holiday with your bachelorhood still intact, or you would have told her the truth.

Having not done so, I imagine the situation requires an amount of playacting on our part."

He was slow to respond, and his only reaction was a tightening at the corners of his mouth. "What—" His voice was hoarse, and he cleared it. "What would you suggest?"

She relaxed back into her chair, a germ of an idea forming. They would pretend to be enamored of one another, but for her part, her feelings would be, regrettably, genuine. She could view it as an enjoyable diversion; she was not brave enough to overtly express her interest in him anyway. That was a road that had led her once before to heartache. She would simply guard herself carefully, and she would be no worse off than she was now.

She hoped she would be no worse off.

She smiled. "I propose we feign an interest in each other for the duration of the gathering. You are then protected from your mother's clever wiles."

He raised his mouth in a half smile. "And the benefit to you, Miss Caldwell? Seems rather one-sided in my favor, I fear."

The benefit to her was his attention for ten days. She would hardly admit it to him, however. "The value is to my business, of course. My reputation will only be enhanced by association with your mother's exclusive gathering."

"You are generous. I shouldn't think your reputation needs help at all, from my mother or otherwise." He also settled back into his seat, regarding her now with the same measure she bestowed on him. She suddenly had the impression of a chess match but was uncertain of her opponent's true skill.

He smiled. "I've told you before to address me as Nathan."

"And I have given you permission to address me as Eva, yet you refrain."

"I refrain because *you* still refrain. I would not like to be considered anything but a gentleman."

"Perhaps I am shy." She lifted the corner of her mouth.

He chuckled. "Reserved, yes. Shy? I would not categorize you as such."

Charlotte finally entered with a tea tray, and Eva was grateful for the timely distraction. She turned her attention to her cousin but was conscious of the detective's gaze, which lingered on her. Charlotte's eyes moved from Eva to the detective, and he finally said, "Miss Duvall, thank you kindly for the tea." He smiled, and Eva quietly exhaled.

Awareness hung in the air, and she knew something was different. Shifting. When she had moved to Town to live with her cousins at Hampton House, she had felt the occasion directly alter the course of her life. This moment felt the same. If she did not exercise the utmost care, Mrs. Winston's house party would change everything.

CHAPTER 4

Nathan sucked in a breath of cold air and it caught in his throat as he walked quickly away from Hampton House, prompting a coughing spasm that added to his sense of embarrassment. He'd fallen very neatly into a trap of his own making, and he'd acted like a fool in the process. He was now going to *pretend* to be enamored of Miss Caldwell, and he was concerned he'd play the part all too well.

She was so lovely she took his breath away. He could watch her every movement for days, and if not for the fact that it would brand him a lunatic—and likely a perverse one at that— would never tire of observing each expression that crossed her face.

He was torn between wanting to wring his mother's neck and kissing her cheek in gratitude when he realized the boon she'd handed him. She had unwittingly provided him with an opportunity to indulge in his daydream of watching Evangeline Caldwell as she went about her work, and he would be allowed to stare at her in lovelorn fascination without drawing undue criticism. The guests would expect as much from a gentleman who was enamored of a woman to the point of expressing said interest to his own mother.

The benefit, he supposed, as he rounded the corner, lost in thought and ignoring the falling rain, was that he would not be obliged to hide his interest. His detective partner, Michael Baker, had made a sly comment not long ago about Nathan's clear awareness of Eva. They had built a friendship, but lately his sense of urgency to see her had increased. He found himself fabricating reasons to be wherever she was. With Eva's proposed plan, he could avoid scrutiny by sinking into the charade.

Shivering, he finally realized he was soaked to the skin. He hailed a cab to Euston station and took a train farther into Town, alighting at his stop and making the rest of the way to his flat on foot. As he walked, he categorized the cases currently occupying his time at work, deciding to whom they could comfortably shift, thereby squeezing as much holiday time as possible out of Director Ellis.

His suite of rooms was located in a respectable boarding establishment that housed four other gentlemen. He preferred it to staying at the family townhouse in Steepington Square, which was large, pretentious, and full of his mother and sisters all the time. As much as he loved them, he craved occasional solitude.

Rent for the boardinghouse came with maid services, weekly laundry, breakfast, and supper. The latter he typically missed or preferred to take in the privacy of his own rooms so that he might enjoy a quiet hour or two before taking advantage of the washroom facilities that were usually unoccupied by the time he finished his long day.

Now, he shrugged out of his wet outer coat and hat, hanging them on the tree near the door. He made his way to the parlor, removing articles of clothing as he went, until he stood in the room in trousers and shirtwaist. He held his tie and waistcoat in one hand, his suitcoat in the other, and finally tossed them onto his favorite reading chair with a sigh. He didn't imagine that evening would afford him any sense of relaxation, even with a book by a warm fire.

He rolled back the cuffs of his sleeves and went to the small stove where he set a kettle to boil. Brow furrowed in thought, he reflected on the first time he'd seen Evangeline Caldwell. They had met at an odd event the year before. Two eccentric octogenarian twins, Margaret and Ethel Van Horne, had hosted an "Evening of Entertainment" that ended in murder and mayhem. Eva had been in attendance, along with her cousins, Amelie Hampton and Charlotte Duvall.

The event began pleasantly enough, and Nathan had found himself paired with Eva and another guest in a scavenger hunt through the eclectic mansion. Eva was clever and quick, with an engaging wit and easy conversation that masked a subtle spirit of competition—she had been determined to beat her cousins to the punch and win the scavenger hunt. He'd quite forgotten he was at the gathering in an official capacity, investigating another of the guests, as he slowly fell under her spell.

Then the body had been discovered. Eva had eventually stood in as an emergency crime scene photographer that night, leaving Nathan flabbergasted and intrigued. He'd thought of few others since then and had compared every woman of his acquaintance to her and found them wanting. Amelie and Michael Baker had married several months after the Van Horne debacle, and because of their circumstances as first an engaged couple, and then married, Nathan frequently found himself at events where Amelie's cousins were in attendance.

He often noted Eva's attention fixed on him for lingering moments, wondered if the subtle blush in her cheek had presented because of a smile from him. He hoped her tendency to situate herself near him wasn't only his imagination. And yet, she was lovely and friendly and conversed easily with any who might join her circle. He was not the only recipient of her subtle wit and easy smile.

It was for those reasons he'd not formally asked her for a carriage ride through the park or to join him at a tearoom for dinner. She was gracious to all, and knowing that continued proximity to Michael and Amelie would see Nathan and Eva attending the same events for the foreseeable future prevented him from introducing an element to the friendship that could prove awkward later. He hadn't been willing to risk the friendship, but additionally had no stomach for courting someone else. How could he when everyone else placed a distant second to her?

He sighed and rubbed the bridge of his nose with thumb and forefinger. His bumbling prevarication with his mother may have undone months of careful maneuvering around Eva. While he couldn't deny the prospective thrill the house party prompted, if he wasn't careful, he could destroy the balance of *almost* flirtatious communion with her. He was about to leap into the fray of deliberately unveiled interest and must do so convincingly enough that his mother's marriage-minded invitees would give him a decent berth, but not so boldly that Eva would emerge from the party with a bruised reputation. It would require extreme care.

He really hadn't a clue how to manage it.

His only consolation now was that Eva, herself, was amenable to the plan and would behave accordingly. She would understand better than he the importance of creating the façade of a woman on the cusp of courting an interested gentleman but not throwing herself so fully into it that she would damage further prospects for herself.

The thought of those "further prospects" tied his stomach in knots, and he found the notion most disagreeable. He couldn't imagine seeing her on the arm of another man. She would marry for love, and she was not necessarily facing a midnight death squad. She was becoming a woman of independent means, with a lucrative, budding career and resources of her own. While she might face self-imposed deadlines for beginning a family—and he was ignorant of her thinking on the matter—she was not in as much of a hurry as her mother or grandmother likely had been.

Marriage had been the only option once a certain age was reached, and the farther one had drifted from it, the dimmer society's view of a woman became. Some pressure remained; he saw as much in his sisters' desire for a good match, but the panicked sense of urgency had lessened for many women, especially those who were embracing careers.

In short, he did not have the luxury of hoping Evangeline Caldwell would settle for anything less than true love in her choice of husband material. She could afford to be particular. If she did not love him, it was of no use to propose a marriage of convenience for the purpose of forwarding mutual goals.

He shook his head and retrieved the tea tin. He'd never imagined himself as one who would entertain the notion of being satisfied with a woman's hand in marriage if she did not love him wholly. With Eva, however, he was beginning to think he'd take whatever she might throw his way.

The kettle whistled, and he poured the boiling water through the strainer. A thump sounded just outside his door, and thinking his landlady, Mrs. Engleberry, was delivering his laundered clothing, he crossed the flat and opened the door, peering into the darkened hallway.

A flash of clothing caught his attention as someone fled down the stairs. A distinctive scent of cheap cologne lingered in the air, pulling him with sickening clarity to a time two years past. Images of a traveling carnival, a ring of kidnappers, an abducted child, and an undercover assignment fraught with danger for himself and the victim flashed simultaneously through his mind. He had solved the case, rescued the child and returned him to his family, and apprehended the perpetrators—a family well entrenched in a vast underworld of crime and debauchery.

All except for one.

The thirty-year-old middle son of the Toole family, Bernard Toole, had managed to escape the trap Nathan and his fellow officers had set and then sprung. An elusive figure, Bernard had been scarce—coming and going in secrecy, so much that Nathan had been surprised to realize Bernard had been the brain behind the operation, the driving force, and the organizer. He toyed with people as a cat with a mouse. His aim was to watch the mouse suffer rather than swiftly cut down enemies with one fatal blow.

Nathan had known the man would return to the criminal enterprise, and the sense that someday he might come for revenge had lingered in the back of Nathan's thoughts since that fateful night. Continued intelligence gathered from informants never yielded any new leads, however, despite Nathan's diligence. A year ago, he had been transferred to work under Director Ellis and the Criminal Investigation Division, and the matter had become an issue for the department he'd left behind.

He dashed to the top of the stairs in time to see the front door slowly close. Perhaps he was mistaken, and the stranger wasn't Toole at all. It might have been anyone. Nathan ran back into his flat to the front windows and looked down onto the dark street that was lit with gas lamps affording slight illumination but little real help. A man in dark clothing ran into the street, stopped short to avoid trampling by a passing omnibus, and looked back up at Nathan's windows.

A hat sat low on the stranger's head, hiding his face in shadows, and rain distorted the image on the glass. It might have been Bernard, but he couldn't say for certain. Nathan knew that Toole was a nondescript sort who blended well into a crowd. When Nathan had been in the man's presence, it was only from a distance, and Bernard had sported a full beard and kept his hair long then. Nathan didn't know if he'd recognize him without those elements.

The cologne, however, he would know anywhere. All of the men in the family wore the scent, especially prepared by Hortence Toole, the youngest sister. Even now, the scent had seeped into the flat from the front door. What was the man's game? If it was vengeance he sought, Bernard could have simply plunged a knife in Nathan's gut and run.

Just as Nathan reasoned he might be able to catch Toole before he made his escape, the moment passed, and the omnibus rattled out of the way. Toole tore across the street and disappeared into the darkness. Nathan could give chase, but experience had taught him the advantage was not on his side with the man. He was clever and dangerous, with savvy street knowledge that served him well. Without a plan in place—and even a good plan was no guarantee of success—Nathan would find himself rushing headlong into an ambush.

He exhaled, heart beating quickly, and made his way back to his still-open entryway. He scanned the hallway, and his eye caught on an item just outside the door. He flicked a clean handkerchief from his pocket, knowing what the item was even before he bent to retrieve it. A box of cigars, emblazoned with the Toole Family Carnival logo, sat ominously in his hand. Remnants of the cologne still clung to the box, bringing with it a fresh surge of memories he'd rather leave permanently in his past.

He elbowed the door closed and locked it, and then he placed the box on a small round dining table in his parlor. Slowly lifting the lid, not trusting the gift giver to have abstained from delivering a baited trap, he noted the signature item Bernard had chosen to include in the carnival logo in an attempt to reinvent the business. As a fan of Edgar Allan Poe, Nathan had subtly resented Toole's use of the image. A single, black feather, in honor of "The Raven."

Inside the box was an actual black feather. Carefully setting that aside, Nathan reached for a folded piece of paper nestled atop the neat rows of cheap cigars organized within. Opening the paper slowly, taking care to touch only the corners, he recognized it as an article from the prior day's newspaper, about the death of Toole's sister Greta while in jail. She'd succumbed to an illness that was spreading through the facility.

Nathan rubbed the back of his neck where tension had gathered and settled. Security for his mother and sisters, always in Nathan's thoughts, would need to be increased. Toole hadn't made an overt threat, but he didn't have to. The meaning of the feather was clear enough. Bernard was inching his way out of hiding, and Nathan was already a step behind.

CHAPTER 5

The Winston family holiday home in Seaside sat on a plateau near the town and boasted a breathtaking view of the water. Equally breathtaking was the property itself; the home was an enormous Georgian-era mansion, previously owned by landed gentry possessing a temporary title. When the original owner passed, and the tangential family did not have the resources to maintain it, James and Christine Winston had purchased it. The grounds were extensive and included two formal gardens, a pond stocked with fish, a manicured eight-foot-tall labyrinth, a man-made forest, and a path on the property's edge that wound down the hillside to a private stretch of beach nestled in an alcove.

Mrs. Winston had told Eva about the property as the time for the party drew near. They had discussed details for photography sittings, and the descriptions alone had made her head spin. Now, as the carriage carrying her and young Sammy White rocked to a stop in the circular drive, she realized her imagination hadn't done the place justice. It was breathtaking and enormous.

And as she considered Detective Winston, she was amazed at his choice of profession, indeed his desire for *any* profession, and wondered at his easy modesty. For all of his family's wealth,

Detective Nathaniel Winston ought to have been insufferably stuffy. At the very least, arrogant.

Sammy scrambled out of the carriage and flipped the stairs down for her. "Like ta get lost in a place like this, Miss Eva," he said, eyes wide. "Don' know how I'll find you when you need me."

Eva smiled at the boy and put her hand on his shoulder. "No fretting now, Sam. Once you've been shown the property, you'll remember what's where." She tried to be reassuring, but she'd overheard Sammy asking Mrs. Burnette about where he would sleep while on assignment at the house party. Since taking him in as a homeless orphan the year before, the Hampton House occupants had noticed a general sense of wellness about the boy that had been absent upon arrival.

He'd bounced from workhouse to alleyway all his life, and his trust was not easily won. He'd adapted to his life on the streets and was savvier than most adults Eva knew, but the security of his past year with her, the cousins, and Mrs. Burnette had rubbed off some of the edge he'd acquired as a means of survival. He'd suffered a setback when an abduction at the hands of a criminal had rattled his newfound sense of security, but the steady company of the no-nonsense housekeeper had proved his salvation. Now, the prospect of spending ten days in the company of strangers was unsettling, and Eva wondered if she should have left Sammy at home.

"I can arrange for your return to Hampton House if you wish it," she said gently. "Certainly, no shame in bowing out of this assignment."

He looked up at her, frowning, his expression clearly showing his dissatisfaction with her statement. "Who will look after you if I go back? An' who would be yer assistant? Nobody understands photography like me."

"I mean no insult, of course. You are absolutely correct; you know this business of ours better than anyone I could hope to find—I could certainly never replace you as my assistant." That much was largely true. He had become her right hand when photographing and developing. He often anticipated her needs before she expressed them. "I would manage, however, if you would rather look after Mrs. Burnette and Mrs. Peters."

He shook his head. "They'll get on well enough with Mr. Frost and Mr. Roy," he said, speaking of the house's elder residents. "An' the Wells sisters are always there to help."

Eva's lips twitched at the thought of the elderly gentlemen providing any sort of protection for the female staff, but she held back a chuckle. The earnest expression on Sammy's face prevented her from any show of humor he might mistake as criticism.

"Very well. Alert me immediately should you change your mind, and please remember that although I would miss you, I would soldier on. Are we clear?"

He nodded, and she gave his shoulder a squeeze. "Good man." She looked up at the sound of footsteps descending the front stairs, and her heart skipped a beat at the sight of Detective Winston in a casual, lightweight linen suit. She felt a subtle shift in Sammy's attention and glanced down to see a smile spread on the boy's face. Since the mess of danger the year before, the detective had paid special attention to the boy to be sure he was doing well. What the detective likely did not realize was that he'd gained a loyal protector for life.

"Miss Caldwell, a pleasure," the detective said, and when she offered her hand, he inclined his head and placed a kiss on her knuckles. Rather than relinquish her hand, he smiled and placed his other atop it with a gentle squeeze, causing her breath to catch. Murmuring quietly, his back to the house, he said, "My mother is on her way to greet you."

Ah, yes. The charade had begun in earnest. She'd best not grow accustomed to the thrill of his holding her hand. They would soon have an audience, and his attention was solely for that purpose. She smiled up at him, prepared to play her part when she noticed subtle tension in the lines around his eyes. Was he so very worried?

"Everything will go as planned," she reassured him quietly, and with a smile, added, "I'll protect you from the matrimonial wolves."

He paused for a moment, and then a flicker of comprehension crossed his face. "Oh, I've no worries on that count."

"What sort of worries have you?"

He was still holding her hand between his, and she fought to concentrate. "Detective sort of worries. Nothing to mar the festivities here." He smiled, but it left her feeling unsettled.

Sammy cleared his throat, and the detective turned his attention to the boy, releasing Eva's hand.

"Young Mr. White," he said, extending his hand, which Sammy took. "A pleasure to welcome you to my home."

"'S a big home," Sammy said, and Eva noted his concentration returning the handshake in a firm grip, as Amelie had taught him.

Detective Winston looked back at the imposing structure and massive gardens. "It is, rather," he agreed, "and truth be told, there's a caretaker's cottage not far from here that I find much more to my liking. Perhaps we can convince your merciless taskmaster here to photograph it in the days ahead."

"Ha ha," Eva said. "Merciless taskmaster. I've spoiled this

boy for any other profession. He is earning more money than any other ten-year-old in London, I wager."

The detective chuckled, but Sammy nodded. "Miss Eva is quite gen'rous. Even with Mrs. Burnette taking a portion for rents and Miss Eva makes me save some, I've shillings left over to spend how I likes."

Eva smiled at him. She had developed a small financial plan for him, complete with a record book where Mrs. Burnette had him faithfully notate every debit and credit in neat columns.

A few footmen approached the driver and began the process of unloading their luggage. Eva turned to Nathan and asked about her item of greatest concern for weeks. "You sent word that the portable darkroom carriage arrived without incident—once we're settled, will you take me to it?"

"Of course. It's just there, on the side of the house. I thought to set it there as it will see the best sunlight for processing the photos. Additionally, Mrs. Snow, the cook, has arranged several deliveries of eggs for the treatment of your plate edges or your paper, should you need to create more."

Eva smiled. Nathan had spent enough time with her at events—sometimes crime scenes—to understand the process and had even observed once as she and Sammy had created an albumen wash, used sometimes as a border for holding the collodion solution in place on the plates and also used for creating special photographic paper.

"You would make a fine photographer's assistant," she said.

He inclined his head. "A position for which I may someday apply." Small lines appeared at the corners of his eyes as he smiled.

She bit her tongue rather than return the banter and suggest she knew a photographer who might hire him. Sammy was quite literal and would worry he would be ousted from his position. As the footmen and carriage driver continued carrying boxes and trunks, she wrinkled her brow in concern. "Perhaps I ought to have instructed the driver to drop us at the servants' entrance at the rear," Eva began.

"You're a guest," the detective interrupted.

"I am also paid help, and I understand—"

"You're a guest." His tone was firm and final.

Sammy busied himself with aiding the driver, piling their luggage and equipment by the stairs. Eva glanced at the front door, but still did not see Mrs. Winston.

"I hope our early arrival doesn't inconvenience the household. We are nearly thirty minutes ahead of your mother's requested time. I fear I misjudged the distance from the train station."

The detective offered a wry smile, placing his hands comfortably in the pockets of his tan trousers. "As it is, my mother's 'requested time' for *you* is an additional two hours ahead of the rest of the party. She has yet to show her face out here, which leads me to suspect she is hiding behind the glass near the front door and observing our every interaction."

Eva laughed and pointedly did not look at the house. "I certainly hope our charade meets with her satisfaction."

He chuckled. "As long as she is unaware it is a charade, I believe she will, indeed, be satisfied."

Silence stretched for a moment, and Eva found the courage to ask, "What will you tell her when the holiday is finished?" She also found the courage to look at his face and was met with an expression she couldn't define.

"A bridge I will cross when I reach it." He watched her, as though gauging her reaction.

Uncertain of what he hoped to see, and equally uncertain of how she felt, she pasted on a smile and gave him a nod. "A sound enough plan."

His expression remained enigmatic. "Thank you, Miss Caldwell."

"My pleasure, Detective Winston."

"Nathan."

Her breath caught again, and the corner of her mouth turned up. "Eva."

He sighed dramatically. "Finally."

She rolled her eyes but smiled. "We won't seem too familiar?"

"As we have been friends for some time, I should say not." His smile warmed her from the inside.

"Are we to imagine you've approached my father for permission to court me?" She spoke as though teasing, but tightness in her abdomen belied her tension. She placed a hand there and lightly exhaled. For goodness' sake, she'd been with him less than ten minutes and was wound tighter than a clock. Eva was the smooth, polished Hampton cousin, rarely ruffled, effortlessly at ease in company of all stripes. She made a conscious effort to pull her wits together.

He appeared to consider her question. "I have met your parents—we dined at the same table after Michael's and Amelie's wedding. Perhaps that association will be enough."

She nodded. "I had forgotten that. Good. You have an idea of my father's nature. The implication that you've spoken with him, regardless of subject matter, should suffice."

He'd opened his mouth to respond when they were interrupted by a call from the front door. Mrs. Winston approached with a smile, and they walked forward to meet her. She extended her hands to Eva's and took them, kissing the air on either side of her face.

"Miss Caldwell, I am so delighted you are able to attend our little gathering! And more delighted still that you've agreed to help me document the entire thing."

Eva felt herself relax by small degrees. Finally, a situation she felt equipped to handle. "The pleasure is mine, Mrs. Winston, truly." It was an event she would likely otherwise never have occasion to attend; her pockets were not deep enough for substantial donations.

"Now, my dear," the stylish matron said, tucking Eva's hand in her arm and walking slowly toward the house, "you must avail yourself of anything you need, anything at all. Nathaniel was very specific about securely positioning the carriage containing your portable darkroom at the side of the house, where you will find it easily accessible. Should you require any other supplies, please do not hesitate to tell me or Turner, my housekeeper. She is most efficient. Runs the place like a seasoned general."

They ascended the steps to the wide front landing. Nathan walked just behind them, and in her periphery, Eva saw him shake his head. To her relief, however, she sensed a smile.

"I don't mind telling you," Mrs. Winston continued, "that I've given you my favorite guest suite in the entire house. I call it the Blue Room because, well, it's blue. And my favorite shade of blue. You will understand when you see it. I am certain you would agree with me that toile is timeless, regardless of fashions that come and go. The paper in the Blue Room bedchamber is exquisite."

"I shall love it, I'm sure. You're too kind, Mrs. Winston."

They reached the massive front doors, and Mrs. Winston paused, clasping Eva's hands again. "Not at all, dearest. Believe me when I say that the favor you're providing me is far beyond compare. I was quite at my wits' end locating a photographer with the right sense of style. When Nathaniel told me you might be available for the party, I was over the moon. I have seen your work, and it is just the thing I am looking for."

Eva felt a twinge of guilt. She genuinely hoped the poor woman's enthusiasm was indeed because of Eva's photography skills and not because she believed her son truly fancied Eva. The eventual disappointment would be crushing, given her current level of apparent euphoria.

Eva put her hand to her heart. "I am flattered and honored. I shall do my very best to meet with your approval."

Mrs. Winston patted Eva's free hand affectionately and smiled widely. She then turned to a man who opened the door to the front hall, which boasted soaring ceilings, ivory-colored marble, and lavish floral arrangements on side tables.

"Jansen, please direct the staff to deposit Miss Caldwell's belongings in the Blue Room. Oh! And she mentioned her little assistant—that must be him speaking with the coachman. Jansen, please show him to the servant's cottage and have Turner direct him further."

Eva looked at Sammy, who watched her with wary eyes. She was torn between wanting to fight the boy's battles for him and knowing he could stand on his own well enough. He'd done it his entire life thus far. She hesitated.

"Eva," Nathan said, "as it happens, I promised to provide my aging valet, Swearington, a helper for errands and such. I wonder if I might employ your young Mr. White when he is not otherwise engaged in assisting you?"

Eva looked at Nathan, so grateful she exhaled a breath she

hadn't realized she'd been holding. "I am certain he would be delighted with such an arrangement."

He offered her a half smile, his eyes warm, and stepped back onto the front landing. He called for Sammy, who ran to him, and Eva saw the boy's eyes widen. Sammy nodded rapidly as Nathan spoke, and a smile twitched at the corners of his mouth. Eva recognized it as the expression that habitually tried to manifest itself when Sammy was doing his utmost to look very mature and not like a giddy, delighted child.

She realized the hall had grown quiet, and she pulled her gaze from the scene unfolding outside. Mrs. Winston was observing her, and in that moment, Eva wondered how much the woman knew. Was she aware that her son was trying to pull the wool over her eyes, and that Eva had agreed to help him do it? Eva was not a cruel person, and as much as she relished the thought of playacting affection for Nathan—which would be considered "playacting" only in the loosest of terms—the subterfuge rested uneasily upon her.

She swallowed, and Mrs. Winston smiled. "I am very glad you are here," the woman said gently. "I—" She paused, searching for words. "You are an elegant young woman, with talent and intelligence. I do not know what the future holds, but please know I appreciate you."

Eva was stunned at the open, candid expression. Most women of her acquaintance through Aunt Sally who were extraordinarily wealthy or socially well-connected had little use for sincerity or genuine affection. There was too much at stake to enjoy the luxury of lowering their collective guard; others waited in the wings to mar the reputations of any unsuspecting lady or her daughters. An offensive approach was the smartest, one that left a potential rival without a doubt as to her position. Eva was beautiful and had suffered insults covering the spectrum from veiled to openly hostile. She was always perceived a rival, regardless of setting or class structure.

Mrs. Winston was an anomaly.

Eva cleared her throat of the sudden emotion that gathered there. "Thank you, Mrs. Winston, for your kind words." She repeated what she'd said before, but now felt the weight of the words extending beyond her role as photographer. "I shall do my very best to meet with your continued approval."

"I have no doubt of it." Mrs. Winston reached for Eva's hand and put it again through her arm. "Come, come. Let Nathaniel work his magic with the lad." She moved them toward a sweeping staircase. "Known some trauma in his young years, that little one?"

Eva nodded. "Very much so."

"I thought as much. Nathaniel has always been a champion for those to whom life has not been especially kind."

"You must be very proud. He is an exceptional man." Eva meant every word.

Mrs. Winston smiled, but it was a bit misty. "Very much like his father. I could not be prouder."

The front door opened, and Eva looked down over the banister to see Nathan and Sammy enter. Sammy's eyes bugged at the immense room, while Nathan's found Eva. He smiled and winked, and Eva wondered how she would possibly survive ten days of the man's attention and emerge unhurt on the other side.

CHAPTER 6

Ten days would be the death of him.

Nathan leaned against the windowpane and looked out his bedroom window onto the back gardens. He had made a comfortable makeshift room for young Master Sammy in his large dressing room that adjoined the bedroom and then sent the boy outside with a sweet roll and the two family dogs. Sammy now tossed a ball for them, laughing when they scrambled to beat each other to it and return for another round.

Nathan's exchange with Eva on the front drive, innocent enough, had felt intimate. They shared a secret, and it bonded them, even if only temporarily. He had another secret, of course, and that was he'd wanted to embrace her so badly he'd had to shove his hands in his pockets to keep from reaching for her. It was as though all sense and reason had fled his brain when he realized that she was truly there and would be spending time in his home while pretending to be enamored of him.

He sighed, thinking of his mother and her transparent placement of Eva in the Blue Room. Her favorite room, was it? His mother's favorite color was yellow. For all he knew, she despised blue. The relevance of the Blue Room was, of course, the proximity to *his* room. The family suites were located in the second-floor left wing, and the guest suites were in the right wing. The hallways were separated in the middle by a large landing with a grouping of settees and comfortable chairs. His was the first suite to the left of the landing, and the Blue Room was the first suite to the right. Entirely appropriate and respectable, but suspiciously close, all things considered. His mother could easily have put her matronly friends in the Blue Room.

He wasn't about to complain, however. In for a penny and out for a pound. He was committed, the architect of his own demise, and had only himself to blame. He could have told his mother the truth seven times over by now. He'd pushed forward with the mad scheme, so he would enjoy it while it lasted.

The only thing dimming the delightful prospect of seeing Eva leave her room each morning was the ever-present specter of Bernard Toole lurking in the back of his thoughts. Nathan kept a small security force employed year-round wherever his mother and sisters were residing, whether at the country estate or in Town, and for this holiday, he'd added half again as many men to dress as servants and provide extra protection for the family and guests. The case involving the Toole carnival abduction was still an open one because of Bernard's escape, and Nathan's recent sighting of the man provided his colleagues with the freshest lead. Toole was slippery, however, and Nathan would not fully relax until the man was caught.

He'd told his mother to be vigilant but hadn't shared so many details that she would worry to the point of distraction. She was a practical woman and knew what his job entailed, but he wouldn't have her feeling as though it was her responsibility to keep them all safe.

Before long, Eva joined Sammy in the garden and scooped up the ball one of the dogs had dropped at the boy's feet. She tossed it beyond a row of bushes and laughed when the dogs vaulted over the greenery to retrieve it. She'd changed from her travel clothing to a light-blue day dress and pelisse. She looked beautiful, but then he was likely biased concerning her. She could wear a feed sack and he'd find it the most attractive piece of the season.

Her thick, black hair was twisted and braided, piled, pinned, and lovely. She'd not brought a maid, probably because his mother kept several on staff during parties and multiday gatherings. Christine would have explained as much to Eva in their exchanges of recent days as they solidified their plans. To his knowledge, and the smug admission of his sister Grace, their mother had communicated more with Eva than anyone else in the weeks leading to the holiday. She had apparently maintained it was necessary because they had to arrange the photography plans, but each of his four sisters, once they'd learned from their mother that Nathan had designs on the photographer, understood her motivation all too well.

His sisters had peppered him with questions he'd answered only in the vaguest of terms, even as he realized it would be to his advantage to share as many details as he could manage with them. That way, they would help carry the tale throughout the party that their brother's heart was unavailable for the taking. He'd held back, however, for no reason he could ascertain. He wasn't willing to lie about Eva and create anecdotes they'd not actually experienced. He was grateful she had agreed to help him, but he resented the false version of himself that would enjoy the charade. He wanted it all to be true, and he wanted to savor each genuine moment.

Eva and Sammy turned around, and Nathan's sisters and mother came into view. The five women surrounded Eva, looking like a bundle of hothouse flowers. His sisters—two sets of twins—were nearly identical in appearance. They stood at Eva's same height, but in contrast to her black hair, the Winston girls sported variations of dark blonde. He didn't hear what they said and wouldn't risk drawing attention to himself now by opening the window. Alice, twenty years old, was effusive, clasping Eva's hands and kissing her cheeks as his mother had done; Olivia, her twin, was more reserved but friendly. Grace and Delilah, twenty-four, exchanged greetings with Eva and made easy conversation.

Nathan had no doubt his family would treat Eva well. For that, he was especially grateful. Each of his sisters was comfortable in her own skin and had either enough confidence or pride to refrain from catty or petty behavior. They were as different in personality as they were identical in appearance but were well-mannered and free of envy or spite. They occasionally engaged in squabbles amongst themselves, and he'd known more than one occasion when they'd switched places to fool a nanny (or attempted to fool their mother), but they had grown into lovely women, and to the world at large, they were kind.

A knock at his door took him from the window, and he received a letter from a housemaid who curtsied and dashed off. The message was from Michael Baker, informing Nathan that two fellow investigators with the Criminal Investigation Division had tracked Bernard Toole definitively to a flat near the docks, only to find he had vacated two days earlier. They *had* found him, though; that was something. Nathan told himself the news was positive, despite Toole slipping away yet again.

Michael had signed off the letter with best wishes and a note that he would keep him apprised of every detail of the investigation. Nathan wished the party included their small circle of friends, and he could escape to one of the local pubs with Michael for a pint and a break from the socializing a house party entailed.

He heard carriages clattering on the front drive, eventually rolling to a stop. Shouts from carriage drivers and servants rang out, and as his mother, sisters, and Eva left the back lawn and entered the parlor below, he turned away, resigned to the noise and chaos that would soon fill the house.

He made his way down to the front hall, hanging back as his mother and sisters spilled out onto the front drive. Squeals of excitement rang high and loud, and Nathan was relieved to hear a few male voices interspersed in the melee. He was acquainted with a few of the gentlemen guests, who, for the most part, were the decent sort. Only two irritated him to the point of head pain.

Movement to his right drew his attention to one of the massive hall's entryways, and he spied Eva awaiting the inevitable bustle of activity. She whispered something to Sammy, who nodded and disappeared, presumably to return to the back garden and safety of the dogs. Outside the front doors, chaos ensued, but around Eva was an element of calm. It was one of the traits that had initially snagged his attention; the night they'd first met, mayhem had abounded, but she'd been a steady beacon of efficiency. Even as she'd fetched her photography equipment and documented a scene complete with a bloodied corpse.

Nathan smiled and joined her, almost regretting what he had subjected her to. "Feel as though I should apologize in advance. Do you favor large gatherings? There's a question I ought to have put to you earlier."

"I knew fully what I was agreeing to," she laughed. "I've attended enough house parties to appreciate the perils." She seemed tranquil enough, but he wondered if he imagined a telltale tightness in her expression. She motioned to the front door. "You ought to join your mother as the host, no?"

He cast her a sidelong glance. "I prefer to remain right here, if you don't mind. My mother is in her element and requires no help from me in the least. Besides, my sisters have things well enough in hand."

"Your sisters are lovely. And I must confess, I have never been in the company of four sisters who so completely resemble each other! I'm certain you can tell them apart, but other than faint variations in hair tone, the only difference I noted was eye color."

He nodded. "Very astute of you." He leaned closer, conspiratorially. "Now the trick is to pair them with the correct twin. Grace has green eyes, like my mother, and Delilah has brown eyes, like my father. As for the younger two, Olivia has green eyes, and Alice has the brown."

"I shall try to remember that Alice and Delilah have eyes that match yours. *Tawny* is the word I would use to describe them. Or *amber*, perhaps. *Gold*, at times." She searched his eyes, looking deeply, as though studying a specimen under glass. She must have realized her scrutiny because she blushed and cleared her throat.

"I am not surprised to hear astute observations from a person who has such good sense of color and design. If you say my eyes are tawny, then tawny they are. I prefer that descriptor to plain brown, certainly."

Her lips twitched. "There is nothing plain, about you, Detective."

He raised a brow and affected surprise. "Why, Miss Caldwell, what a lovely compliment! Unwarranted, but lovely. I must insist you elaborate, of course, otherwise I shall never agree with your assessment."

"Oh, shall I convince you?" She grinned and tipped her head in thought. "Perhaps you'll answer a question: what entices a man of wealth to pursue a career in investigative work?"

He smiled, feeling self-conscious. Heat began beneath his collar, and he wondered if he were actually blushing. "Have you ever heard of Inspector Dupin?"

Eva's eyes lit up with her smile. "Of course! Edgar Allan Poe's detective! Charlotte reads his work voraciously, but I confess, some of his stories terrify me."

"I read him as a young man and was immediately enthralled. I wanted to be that one who solved the mystery and righted the wrong. I'd no idea at the time that reality is different, but I feel I've accomplished some of it."

Her expression softened. "Of course, you have. You continue to do an admirable job of it. You and Detective Baker captured the villain last year and saved Amelie in the process. I am eternally grateful for that alone."

"That was a combined effort, was it not? Neither Michael nor I would ever have been at the right place and at the right time if not for you and your cousins' quick action. Truthfully, I am still in awe of all three of you."

She laughed. "It would seem you and I have formed a Mutual Admiration Society."

"I am glad to know it is mutual." He returned her smile, and the moment stretched. He held her gaze and she didn't look away, even as light color again touched her cheeks. He sought for something profound to say but was interrupted by a mass of humanity spilling into the hall. He took note of a few of his sisters' friends, exchanged head bows with gentlemen he recognized, and didn't realize until he looked down again at Eva that he'd drifted closer to her.

Her dress brushed his leg, and he caught a light scent of rosewater she must have used to wash her hair. She clasped her hands loosely at her waist, fingers gently intertwined, but her subtle fidgeting was betrayed by a slight bounce of one of the curls resting against her temple. He realized she must be tapping one foot quietly, hidden beneath the length of her skirt.

She was apparently not as calm as she appeared. As he glanced again at the gathering throng, he fantasized about snatching Eva from the house and running with her down to the beach. He continued looking at her, noting the shrinking distance between them as she leaned closer to him. He rested his hand lightly on her back and said, "Perhaps we can still escape. Nobody has noticed us yet."

She smiled tightly, observing the crowd. "The moment has passed, regrettably. Besides, that would quite defeat our purpose, would it not?"

"I am beginning to doubt the wisdom of our purpose," he muttered. He felt as though he were throwing her to a pack of wolves.

She arched one brow and looked up at him. "Oh? It is not too late. We can certainly call a stop to the charade before it begins. You'll be free to court to your heart's content, and nobody need believe you harbor an 'interest' in me."

"Continue saying such things to me and I shall drop to one knee this very moment and profess my adoration." He meant it as a jest. Of course, he did.

Her lips twitched, and a small laugh escaped. "Fair enough, we shall continue as planned."

The banter was always easy, effortless. It felt as natural as breathing, but also thrilling. "What shall I do if I find myself besieged by the throng and you are nowhere in sight?"

She folded her arms and tapped one finger in contemplation. "You must do your best to escape said throng and then find me. You've built a career on investigative techniques, and I should think you'd accomplish the task in no time." She turned slightly toward him, and his hand brushed her waist before he reluctantly moved it away. It was familiar in the extreme, and he knew he trod on shaky ground. For her sake, he shoved his hands into his pockets.

"If *you* are besieged by the throng," he continued, "I shall ride into the fray on a steed."

She laughed curtly and shook her head. "A woman must hold her own ground in the company of other women or face certain annihilation. You must know this from having sisters."

He frowned, barely registering the conversations flowing around them—the serving staff bustling to see to coats and hats, his mother giving instructions to freshen up and meet in the parlor in an hour's time. He considered Eva's statement and realized his sisters were not mistreated because they enjoyed an amount of status. Other women might be catty, but they were obliged to treat the Winston family well, lest they be removed from invitation lists.

"I do not believe my sisters have been unduly . . . attacked," he admitted finally.

The shadow he questioned earlier again flitted across her features. "They are fortunate, indeed."

They were bumped back into the corridor by a quickly moving footman, who stammered a quick apology. Laughter, exclamations of delight as friends found one another, and general sounds of merriment continued to grow with the gathering crowd. Looking out into the hall, he spied his sister Grace. He would need to speak with her, and soon. Eva's cousins weren't there, and Nathan only belatedly realized he couldn't be with Eva every moment. She would need an ally.

CHAPTER 7

Eva entered the empty parlor, smoothing her hands over her gown, and looked at her photography equipment. She'd already checked it a dozen times—everything was in place, the plates were ready and waiting, and for the first time in her short photography career, she wished something would break so she'd have an excuse to leave and fix it.

Her nerves had churned with the gathering guests, who would soon descend on the parlor for Mrs. Winston's welcome while tea was served. Suddenly, she felt the weight of the charade pressing down on her, and it wasn't because she was concerned about lying or subterfuge. She had taken in the view of other party attendees gathering in the front hall and known a fierce stab of possession of the man standing next to her. She'd caught one young woman, in particular, eyeing Nathan, and then Eva, in speculation. The smile the woman gave Eva was tight. Calculating.

The parlor was a large room, with multiple seating areas and long window seats along the far wall that looked out over the back gardens. She recognized classic and current works of art, along with the latest trends in fabrics and furnishings. It was understated, but elegant, very much like the home's matron.

Mrs. Winston entered the room and gave an exclamation of delight when she saw Eva. "Oh, excellent! I ought to have known you to be a consummate professional. I was prepared to send Turner to fetch you."

Eva smiled. Turner, the housekeeper, was every bit as taciturn and no-nonsense as Mrs. Burnette at Hampton House. "I should have hopped to it straightaway, in that case. Turner strikes me as one who brooks no excuses."

Mrs. Winston laughed. "Right, you are, Miss Caldwell. I do not know how I would accomplish anything if not for that woman."

Sammy dashed into the room, brushing crumbs from his jacket and dragging his sleeve across his mouth. "'Pologies, Miss Eva. I was helping Mrs. Snow in 'change for a tea cake."

Eva was relieved to see the boy appearing much more at ease than he'd been upon arrival. She tried to look stern as she motioned Sammy closer. She straightened his collar and wiped a hand down his waistcoat. "I can appreciate a tea cake as much as anyone; however, you mustn't be tardy when an appointment is set." She smiled. "Also, next time, please make use of a napkin." She examined the sleeve where he'd wiped his face, satisfied he'd not transferred anything to the fabric.

"Snow is as severe as is Turner," Mrs. Winston remarked, a smile playing on her lips as she regarded Sammy. "You must have made a favorable impression on her, young man."

Sammy nodded and seemed to be searching for an appropriate response. He settled for, "Thank you, madam," and gave her a bow.

Voices sounded in the hall, and Mrs. Winston looked toward the door where the butler, Jansen, had taken his position.

"Show them in," she said, and then motioned to Eva. "Miss Caldwell, do sit over here closer to me, if you please."

Eva was surprised but followed the instructions and took a seat near Mrs. Winston and the hearth at the far end of the large room. She'd been planning to remain with Sammy near her camera, unobtrusively standing in the corner. No sooner had she situated herself than Nathan's sisters entered, and one of them plunked herself next to Eva with a bright smile. Alice, Eva remembered; she was one of the younger twins, had been most effusive in her welcome earlier, and her eyes were "tawny," like her brother's.

"Miss Caldwell, I am ever so eager to see you taking photographs and handling the equipment!" Alice's eyes shone, and Eva couldn't help but smile at the genuine enthusiasm.

"Please, do call me Eva. And I hope my picture taking will prove as exciting as it seems."

"Will you show me? I mean, not now, of course, but when we've a quiet moment?"

Delilah, the other tawny-eyed twin had sat next to Alice and now nodded her agreement. "If you've no objection, I should love to learn as well."

"I am happy to show you, of course. If you're interested further, perhaps you'll join me for the processing and development phase. It truly is astounding, every single time. I never tire of it."

Grace, Delilah's twin, settled across from them, and the final Winston daughter, Olivia, sat next to her. Referring to Eva's comment about photo development, Grace added, "I imagine it must seem like magic." She offered Eva a smile, and while seeming genuine, she also appeared to possess a level of scrutiny, as though perhaps reserving judgment.

Eva nodded and smiled, remembering a comment Nathan

had once made about Grace; she was straightforward and reminded him of Charlotte. Eva managed to keep her smile in place, even as she fought an urge to loosen her collar.

Guests continued to file into the parlor, and the air was filled with excitement. Friends laughed and sat together, and most of the gentlemen stood, exchanging greetings and hearty handshakes. The ensemble included a mixture of ages and styles, ranging from brightly dressed young adults to a more conservative pair of women who were clearly Mrs. Winston's friends. A quick assessment of the numbers showed a rough equality of men and women, which Eva presumed was entirely by design. Nathan had said his mother was attempting to play matchmaker, after all, and she appeared to have considered every last detail.

The young woman who had caught Eva's eye earlier now sat next to Olivia Winston. She was truly stunning, with bright blue eyes and rich blonde hair, the color of spun gold. Olivia looked at her in some surprise but recovered well enough and offered a smile.

"I trust you do not object to my joining you?" the woman said to Olivia.

Olivia blinked. "No, of course not, Blanche. Lovely to see you."

"I presume you may have been saving the seat for my sister, but her delay is my boon." Blanche smiled brilliantly. She paused, a light frown crossing her brow, before adding, "You *are* Olivia, I hope?"

"Yes, I am Olivia."

"Oh, splendid!"

Alice Winston, seated next to Eva, sighed quietly. "Are you acquainted with the Parkers?"

Eva shook her head. "I've not had the pleasure."

Alice lowered her voice further. "The pleasure would be in meeting Miss Ann Parker, who is the younger sister and friend to me and Olivia. *That one* is two years older. She has fancied Nate for years, and I suspect she now hopes to use Ann's friendship with us to maneuver her way closer to him."

Alice's eyes widened as she looked at Eva, as though regretting the admission. "But Nate has no use for her either, I assure you." She patted Eva's hand.

Eva felt an odd combination of foolishness and curiosity. She wondered if Nathan's impulsive statement to his mother about his supposed interest in "a photographer" had been prompted by his awareness of Miss Blanche Parker on the invitation list. If she had set her cap for him in the past, and he was aware but not amenable to the prospect, that would certainly account for his fateful pronouncement to Christine Winston several weeks prior.

She felt eyes on her, and she glanced at Miss Parker, who was assessing Eva and, apparently, finding her wanting. Eva knew, if nothing else, that her clothing was impeccable and of the newest fashion, and her face and hair were pleasing to the eye. She straightened in her seat and smiled at the young woman. Alice, following the silent exchange, said, "Miss Blanche Parker, this is our dear family friend, Miss Evangeline Caldwell."

Eva and Blanche murmured hellos, and Delilah Winston added, "Miss Caldwell is a photographer! We're fortunate to enjoy her company and talents for this little holiday."

"Oh, of course!" Recognition and something like relief settled over the young woman's pretty face. "Your reputation precedes you, Miss Caldwell." She smiled. "I believe you provided your services to my family friends, the Robertsons? You would remember, their family estate is of the most impressive in Town. My bosom friend, Miss Agatha Robertson, mentioned the photographer was a woman, and of course that would have been you."

Eva nodded. "I do remember the Robertson sitting. Lovely home, indeed." She also remembered spending twice the normal amount of time catering to Mrs. Robertson's highly repetitive demands.

"You will hardly believe it, but Miss Robertson confided that her father very nearly cancelled the sitting when he realized the photographer was a woman." Blanche laughed lightly. "Mrs. Robertson was obliged to go to some lengths to convince him that they were not allowing a woman of questionable character into their home."

Before Eva could respond, Alice interjected, "I cannot imagine why such a thing would indicate questionable character."

"Why, because she is a young woman, *earning money*, plying a man's trade, of course. Venturing into people's homes and the like." Blanche's eyes widened. "Of course, I would never hold with such archaic ideas. We are all modern women, are we not? It is perfectly respectable for women to step outside the factory realm if they find themselves in circumstances of want. Gone are the days when a girl's only option is either factory work, domestic help, or governess positions." She shuddered. "Thankless tasks. I am certain it must be a relief for one with no family connections to make her way in the world without being obliged to while away her life in drudgery."

Eva managed to keep her mouth from falling open at the backhanded insult. Alice, again, jumped to her defense. "You may be correct, but such is not the circumstance for Miss Caldwell. *She* is a *Hampton*."

Eva was, unfortunately, unable to stop the involuntary wince that crossed her features. She was of the Notorious Branch of the Hampton family. The only respectable members there were Aunt Sally, Amelie's father, Charlotte's late mother, and Eva's own mother. Two generations back and beyond had been little but scandal.

Blanche's expression was subtly shrewd, her smile tight. The house party was fewer than five minutes into the first actual tea, and Eva clearly saw the lay of the land with the beautiful woman. She had met her kind before; the cutting personality was reminiscent of an uncomfortable association from years earlier. Eva reminded herself that she was a mature woman of twenty-four. She was nothing if not calm and collected. She did not stoop to pettiness or insults, and she would handle Miss Parker with her usual grace and dignity.

Before anyone else could add to the conversation, Mrs. Winston tapped a wineglass to gather attention. "Ladies and gentlemen, if you please! I am thrilled to have you all here in attendance and will leave you to your socializing soon enough, but I must explain some of the scheduling for the next ten days. I'll not reveal many of our activities, however; you may know that this special gathering is meant to surprise and delight."

Her pronouncement was met with scattered applause, laughs, and eventually relative silence. Eva looked over her shoulder to find Nathan, but he was absent. *Odd*, she thought. Did he plan to avoid nearly everything and leave her to somehow manage the ruse on her own? She did not like that prospect in the least and resolved to tell him as much when he finally showed his handsome face.

Two more young women entered the parlor, and Blanche waved, scooting closer to Olivia to make space available. Olivia, in turn, bumped Grace, who shot a dark look at Blanche but squished herself against the arm of the sofa. Eva wondered how both newcomers were supposed to fit into the spot, but it was a moot point as the one Blanche beckoned planted herself onto the sofa and the other one was left standing, looking awkward.

"Ann," someone whispered, and the young woman, blushing, gratefully sank onto a seat beside another girl who put an arm around her shoulders.

Ann? The girl left standing had been Blanche Parker's sister? Another piece of the woman's personality clicked into place.

As Mrs. Winston continued her welcome speech, Alice leaned over to Eva and whispered in her ear, "That's Blanche's bosom friend, Mathilda Dilworth. Peas in a pod, those two."

Eva did her best not to grimace at the news. Blanche had a duplicate. She wondered why, when the Winston sisters seemed to have no clear affection for Blanche Parker or Mathilda Dilworth, their mother would have included them on the guest list.

As Mrs. Winston outlined the massive itinerary for the party, Eva began formulating a plan to avoid Blanche and her bosom friend whenever possible. Uncomfortable memories from school days years before again crowded in and she shoved them aside, impatient with herself. She was a woman grown, for heaven's sake. She was no longer affected by churlish behavior at the hands of peers. She had endured it once and then matured beyond it.

She smiled as Mrs. Winston introduced her and provided the guests with details about her role and waxed about the amazing boon it was to have the celebrated Miss Caldwell among them. "She is a dear family friend and an occasional colleague of my son, Nathaniel." She paused. "Where is Nathaniel? Well, never mind. He will show himself soon, I am certain."

Where was he, indeed? Eva blamed the surge of irritation on the fact that Blanche Parker had put her all out of sorts. A glance at the young woman showed her whispering to her friend, Mathilda, and side-eyeing Eva. Blanche paused to give Eva a small smile, and then straightened, attention again beatifically focused on Mrs. Winston. Eva felt her nostrils flare, but also returned her focus to their hostess. Miss Parker seemed to be throwing down the gauntlet, and Eva was undecided whether to pick it up or step straight over it. Either way, the woman's presence could stretch ten days into a very long time.

CHAPTER 8

Nathan left the large stables after meeting with his security team. One of the men had noticed fresh footprints near the dining room window for the second day in a row, and the groundskeepers denied knowledge of anyone working in the area. The footprints clearly showed someone had looked directly into the house and then walked away. He was inclined to believe the gardeners, as the footprints did not lead anywhere else, especially to the rosebushes nearby. Someone had peered inside and hadn't even bothered with the pretense of working on the garden.

If he hadn't been so concerned about Bernard Toole's threat, he might have written the footprints off as something innocuous, but he didn't have that luxury. Stafford, his head security man, was loyal and trustworthy, and Nathan had worked with him for years. He promised Nathan he would send a message straightaway if he noticed anything else out of the ordinary.

Next, he visited with a small group of extra security he'd hired to dress as footmen and house servants. They were to be his eyes and ears on the inside, and they were each trusted individuals. He felt marginally better after speaking with them and learning that none of them had noted anything suspicious among the guests or the staff. The house was packed full of people, and he wished he could be fully at ease.

He checked the time and cursed, quickly heading to the house. He'd promised his mother he would be available and visible at her welcome tea, and he was now thirty minutes late. He circled around to the parlor garden and ran a hand through his hair, making note through the large windows of the people gathered inside. They sat in small groups, balancing tea cakes and teacups, laughing and chatting. Eva was somewhere in the mix, and he frowned, trying to find her. He caught sight of his mother, who was directing maids carrying trays of food. He tried the door, only to find it locked. He waved at his mother, but she didn't see him. He hoped to catch the eye of someone—anyone—close by who would open the door.

Regrettably, he did finally catch the eye of a guest and was instantly leery of Miss Parker's quick smile. She made her way across the room and unlocked the door, opening it wide and offering him both of her hands. He took them and sketched a quick bow, steeling himself for the flirtation he suspected was soon to follow.

He did not trust the young woman. He found her insincere and calculating, and knew she was at the party only because her younger sister, Ann, was a good friend to his sisters, and also that the Parkers had pledged an unseemly amount of money to his mother's cause.

Blanche had attempted to corner him on more than one occasion and had even tried to orchestrate an encounter at a ball that would have found them in a compromising position, alone in a garden, when one of her friends "chanced" upon them. He'd taken Grace into his confidence over it, insisting she remain vigilant when they all happened to be at a social event where

Blanche Parker might strike again. His intentions in sharing the incident only with Grace had been to protect the reputation of a foolish girl who had probably made a one-time error in judgment. Perhaps, if he'd informed his mother, she'd have found a way to keep her off the guest list.

"Why, Mr. Winston," Blanche Parker cooed, "it is so good of you to join us. What if I'd not noticed you trying to catch my attention? You'd have been left out here all alone for possibly ages." She affected a pout on his behalf.

His lips twitched in what he hoped would pass for a smile. "I would have gone around to the front," he said. "No harm done."

He dropped her hands and cleared his throat when she still blocked his entrance.

"There you are." Grace, bless her, marched over and reached around Blanche, pulling him into the room. "Mother will likely wring your neck for this bit of rebellion."

"I've not been rebelling," he said, pulling her hand into the crook of his arm. "Pressing matters of business." He allowed her to direct him around guests and staff to the hearth, where Eva sat, conversing with his sisters. Blanche Parker had followed close behind, and took a seat not far from Eva, who now looked up at him with a tight smile.

He released Grace's hand and made a point of going directly to Eva. He bowed lightly and, deliberately using her first name, said, "Eva. How lovely you are this afternoon."

Her lips quirked. "Am I not lovely in the morning hours, as well?" She lowered her lids and smiled, offering her hand. He nearly gaped in surprise. Eva Caldwell on a normal day as his friend was incredible. Eva Caldwell pretending a romantic interest in him was staggering. She tightened her fingers when he bowed over her hand, placing a soft kiss on her knuckles. "Gauche of me to tease, of course," she murmured. "You must forgive me."

"My dear friend," he said softly and very much *not* for their audience, "you are lovely every minute of every day." He met her eyes, still holding her fingers, but paused at the strain he saw on her face. "What is it?" he whispered.

She shook her head fractionally and took back her hand, smoothing her features with a smile. "Several of your gentlemen acquaintances have wandered by, quite wearying your sisters with questions as to your whereabouts. You simply must make the rounds."

"Of course, of course. I was unavoidably detained. Telegram from work, you see." He caught Blanche Parker and Mathilda Dilworth eyeing him like cats, and Blanche's eyes flickered to Eva, narrowing slightly as Eva answered something Alice asked her.

"I wonder, Miss Caldwell, if you care to accompany me? Mr. Jacobson will be most interested in your photography work. He is an avid arborist!" Nathan reached for Eva's hand without giving her an opportunity to respond. She had turned from Alice and now frowned lightly as if in question as he tugged her to her feet.

"I shall return her straightaway, Alice," he said with a wink at his sister, and pulled Eva through the room. They stopped short when his mother stepped directly in his path.

"Hello, son," she said, and turned her cheek to the side for him to kiss.

"Mother." He smiled. "Apologies for my tardiness. It couldn't be helped."

"I do hope it can be helped in the future." She returned his smile. She then glanced down at his hand, which clasped Eva's as though she were a lifeline on a sinking ship.

He hurriedly released it and pulled it through his arm instead, patting it rather awkwardly. Christine smiled brightly and moved, allowing them to pass.

"Apologies," he muttered to Eva. "Miss Parker and her ilk rattle my nerves. I am sorry you must bear a moment of their company. I'm afraid at this point it cannot be helped."

"I hope everything is well with work?" she asked, sidestepping any comment on Miss Parker and her ilk.

"Work?" He glanced down at her. "Oh! Yes. Work. Everything is fine."

She studied him for a moment as they progressed slowly to a group of gentlemen on the other side of the room. "So, if you were not engaged in 'work,' what on earth could have kept you from a timely arrival at this first event of the party?"

"I said everything is fine at work."

"I am certain it is. I admit, while awaiting your arrival, I found myself wondering if you might be found in your chambers, reading a good book, or perhaps playing a round of billiards."

He chuckled. "You believe I was merely avoiding afternoon tea with guests?"

"I confess I was growing concerned that this entire multi-day event would comprise me standing in for you while you are . . . answering correspondence from work."

He looked at her in surprise, his already slow step slowing further. One corner of his mouth quirked in a smile. "Eva, you are out of sorts with me."

She started to shake her head, a light frown marring her brow, but then stopped and nodded once. "I am. Solitary efforts on my part for the duration of this thing are not what I agreed to do."

"I can assure you, leaving your side for even a moment of this thing pains me."

"Pains you." She looked at him flatly.

"Why, yes, as a matter of fact. I pulled you into this, and I have second-guessed myself ever since."

She narrowed her eyes. "You are concerned I'll not perform to an appropriate standard?"

He stopped walking altogether, wanting to take her out into the hallway but conscious of several pairs of eyes on them. "A conversation awaits us, but not now." He smiled. "Allow me to introduce you to a few friends, a few acquaintances, and a few cads."

The gentlemen reacted exactly as Nathan had known they would. Some were reduced to stammering schoolboy status, despite Eva's grace and charm. Or perhaps, he considered, because of it. Some of them, however, were all too willing to make her acquaintance.

"Miss Caldwell," Jens Sorenson, son of the Swedish ambassador, bowed elegantly over her fingers. "The pleasure is mine. Allow me to introduce my friend, Mr. Peter Meyer, visiting my family from Germany." Mr. Meyer, likewise, sketched a courtly bow and dripped charm. Nathan had met both men briefly earlier in the season and wondered if one day he might call either of them "brother-in-law." Alice, at least, had shown avid interest in both.

Nathan took Eva's elbow and introduced her to the others. "The Honourable Mr. John Smythe," he said, motioning to the aristocratically handsome son of a baron, who had recently come into his inheritance. Mr. Smythe greeted Eva with less flair but no less interest. If memory served, Mr. Smythe was a snobbish sort who likely wouldn't entertain a formal pairing with Eva, although she *was* a Hampton; he would certainly, however, entertain a dalliance, and Nathan mentally redoubled his intention to keep an eye on the man.

Eva, for her part, seemed to view the gentlemen with subtle humor, and her murmured pleasantries showed a woman used to a gentleman's theatrics.

"Mr. Davis Jacobson, a longtime member of the London Society of Avid Amateur Arborists," Nathan continued, and felt a softening in Eva's demeanor as Mr. Jacobson blushed and offered his greetings in a quieter voice than the others. Mr. Burton Handy, shorter and slighter than the rest, was classically polite and as far from flamboyant as one could be. He and Mr. Jacobson were the ducklings to the other swans.

"And finally, Mr. Franklin Frampton, without whom no gathering is complete." Nathan smiled when Frampton, the proverbial life of the party, placed a hand on his chest and bowed to Eva.

"Your servant, Miss Caldwell. I do hope occasion will permit you to offer a photography demonstration while we're gathered here." Frampton smiled.

The others murmured their assent, and Eva nodded. "I should be delighted, gentlemen, and it is a pleasure to make your collective introduction." She smiled. "With such a wide variety of personalities, this holiday promises to be splendid."

As the men mingled with the ladies, Nathan took a moment to study Eva, who had been drawn into conversation with the Swede and the German. He'd never seen her irked, and had certainly never been on the receiving end of her displeasure. He mused, and certainly not for the first time, that she was not a woman who would have to settle for anyone. What little advantage he might hold over the other gentlemen because of his friendship with her could be easily eclipsed. She laughed softly at something Jens Sorenson said, and Nathan made a conscious effort to keep a scowl away. Easily eclipsed, indeed.

Nathan dressed for dinner, his thoughts a mass of concern about whoever had been spying outside the dining room window and worry about how Toole might infiltrate his security around the property. He reflected on the afternoon with his mother's party guests; he was annoyed to recognize a mad, irrational sense of jealousy over Jens Sorenson, the handsome Swede who had charmed Eva out of her irritation, and Peter Meyer, the Sorensons' German visitor who seemed to enjoy the novelty of being one of two foreigners in the midst of other Englishmen who could boast of little else but being merely English. There were those, however, who would never desire to be anything but, and even the Honourable John Smythe, who was a snooty cad of the first order, had also elicited smiles from Eva.

Nathan told himself he was a million times a fool as he stood before the mirror and tried, for the third time, to fix his cravat. Swearington, his valet, was already abed for the night. Sammy might have been some help, if the lad had been available, but he had been tasked with prepping the photography equipment for supper photos.

"You are a fool," he muttered to his reflection, "to be jealous over a false pretense." The cravat was now wrinkled beyond repair, so he threw it on a bench in his dressing room and grabbed a fresh one. He had no claim on Eva's smiles, would have no claim on them even if theirs was a true arrangement. She could smile at whomever she pleased. The woman was achingly beautiful, and her smile was ready and equally bestowed on any in her company deserving of it. He knew that much from observing her in their casual interactions over the past several months. That she smiled now at gentlemen in the party who might actually be competition for him was the rub, he supposed. He was used to seeing her turn heads wherever she went. He was not used to the sudden surge of possessiveness that he knew could not be healthy.

He was going to be late meeting her on the landing just outside his door, and he cursed at himself again. His cravat hanging loose around his neck, he shoved a pair of cuff links into his pocket and left his room in a huff. Noting the empty landing, he crossed to Eva's door. The Blue Room was actually a suite, with a sitting room and a bedchamber beyond it. He knocked lightly, hopeful a maid might be with her and perhaps willing to tie a cravat.

Eva opened the door, and he dropped his jaw. Her dress was formfitting emerald satin with elbow-length gloves. Her hair was piled high on her head and woven with a strand of ribbon and tiny pearls. He finally remembered to suck in a breath when he felt light-headed.

Her eyes widened, and she looked past him down the empty hall. With an exclamation of clear frustration, she pulled him into the room and then quietly closed the door. "What are you doing?" she hissed. "We were supposed to meet on the landing, and you're not even dressed!"

"You are . . ." he managed, and cleared his throat, trying again. "You are exquisite."

She stilled, taking in his shock and his compliment. "You

have seen me dressed in evening attire several times. This is nothing new."

"The dress is new. I would have remembered that dress."

"We do not have an audience, Detective—even my maid has left to help other guests. You needn't . . ." She looked away and then down at her gloves, picking at one fingertip.

He inhaled, slowing his pace of both movement and thought. "I am not playacting," he said, reading her vulnerability in her clear discomfort. He took her elbow. "You are the most beautiful woman I have ever known."

She looked up, then, and her dark eyes flashed with anger. "That is not true, and I'll thank you not to patronize me."

He slowly shook his head. "I am not patronizing you. Evangeline Caldwell, you are the most beautiful woman I have ever known. And easily the smartest and most talented. That you are here with me, *because* of me, at this farce of a party, quite takes my breath away."

"You'll forgive me for questioning the truthfulness of that statement. I cannot count the number of times you have told me you regret this arrangement of ours, or how you are 'second-guessing' it. I am beginning to feel an insult."

There was the reason he had insisted they take a moment to talk before dinner. Just before he'd introduced her to the gentlemen at tea, she'd implied, erroneously, that he found her inadequate to the task. He took her elbow and led her to a small settee. He lowered the flame on one of the sconces to soften the glare permeating the room and sat next to her.

"I have insulted you, and I am not certain I understand how. My only reservations about this whole arrangement have been for your sake. I do not, for one moment, believe you incapable of your part in this. I feel horribly guilty for trapping you into it."

She frowned. "You needn't feel guilty. If there is one thing I hate, it is another's pity. I would not be here if I did not want to be." She picked at her glove again.

Do not say anything to ruin this friendship, do not say anything to ruin this friendship . . . The phrase had repeated itself in his head so many times since that night when he'd involved her in the house party mess that he was convinced he recited it in his sleep. She was angry with him, though, and in a way he didn't fully understand, hurt. He took a deep breath and hoped he wasn't making a mistake.

"I feel many things for you, Eva, and pity is not one of them."

Her attention flew to his face, and he couldn't read her expression. He thought of several ways to walk his statement back but didn't know if she wanted him to. The silence stretched.

"I do not usually consider myself a cowardly man, but as it concerns you, I've been little more than a bumbling schoolboy. I value your friendship dearly, you see, and am unwilling to risk it. I would have you know, however, that—"

I love you, and I have for months.

The words flowed easily through his thoughts, and they were true. He could hardly tell her that right now. "I would have you know that looking forward to spending this time with you has been the brightest spot on the horizon I have had in ages. I know full well that you can accomplish anything to which you apply yourself, and also that this party is generosity on your part"—he waved aside her objection—"even though my mother has officially hired you to be here."

Still, she watched him, chewing lightly on the inside of her lip.

He waited. "I would dearly love some sort of response from you."

She finally spoke. "Perhaps you ought to consider putting your bachelorhood to rest. This house is full of suitable ladies who would love nothing more than to be Mrs. Nathaniel Winston." Her tone, while not hostile, subtly lacked her usual warmth.

He still couldn't read her expression. He felt as though he were walking carefully around a skittish kitten. Or perhaps a lioness. One wrong move might be the end of him. "I have been surrounded by what most consider to be suitable ladies for many years, and until recently, *quite* recently, the idea of wedded bliss has sounded anything but blissful."

He paused, mulling over her clipped comment and its rather terse delivery. The thought of him "ending his bachelorhood" with one of the ladies gathered at the party was not a notion that sat well with her. A slow glimmer of hope began to spread. Her careful reticence did not signal apathy. He was coming to realize it meant quite the opposite.

She'd once mentioned an affinity for games of strategy. She did not tip her hand, and as he thought back over time spent in her company, he saw a subtle pattern of guardedness in her interactions. She had been hurt before. How had he not seen it? And he called himself a detective.

"How would you define 'suitable'?" Nathan asked.

She lifted a shoulder. "Wealth. Status. Privilege. Someone raised in your social circles."

The corner of his mouth ticked upward. "I am afraid our definitions of 'suitable' do not match, Miss Caldwell."

She blinked.

"My definition includes elements of friendship, companionship, mutual interest, attraction, affection, love . . . nowhere do I list things like wealth, status, or privilege. I am far from blue-blooded, and even if I were, superfluous trappings would not signify. Not to me." He kept her gaze, held it.

"Oh." She swallowed. "I see." Her chest rose and fell with a deep breath.

"Have you been under the impression I feel otherwise?"

She frowned again. "Not until recently. You do not speak of your life outside of the Yard or our small social circle. I was unaware . . ." She looked around them and lifted her hands. "I thought I understood you better when I did not know you had . . . this."

"I daresay you *did* know me best when you did not know I have . . . this. That is my true self, and the one I would have you know. I certainly hope I've not behaved today in a way that alters your good opinion of me."

She took a breath and released it quietly. She rubbed her eyebrow with her fingertip. "I went to school with girls like Blanche Parker and Mathilda Dilworth."

He leaned closer to hear her hushed statement.

"I endured snide remarks about my parents' lack of prestige, and indeed attended the school only because Aunt Sally funded it and thought I wanted it. Truthfully, by the time I finished, I would rather have remained at home with my parents."

She shrugged. "I am afraid this afternoon's tea threw me backward in time for a moment. Old feelings returned, and I am more disappointed in myself than anyone else." She offered him a half smile. "My frustration with you is unwarranted. I suppose . . ." She frowned. "I suppose the thought of you fitting into that world was unnerving to me. It does not align with the . . . the *you* I have come to know and admire. You have not done anything to alter my good opinion of you." She smiled slightly, her reserve still clutched firmly in place. "I also value our friendship very highly, and I apologize for being short."

He watched her face closely. "What sort of man are you hoping to find, Eva?" he asked, matching her quiet tone.

Her eyes jumped to his and held them, as though hoping to read something there. He kept himself from smiling, but only just. He'd been probing for confirmation and had found it. Unless he was very much mistaken, and he didn't believe he was, Eva Caldwell was as tense as he was at the notion of pretending affection that was altogether too real.

She swallowed again, but rather than belabor the point and push her to answer, he smiled. "What do you know about tying cravats?"

She blinked again. "I'm sorry?"

"My valet is an old, old man who retires early these days, and my new valet's assistant is a young, young man who has other responsibilities at the moment. Do you suppose you might help me with this?"

She looked at his collar, at his open throat, at his sleeves that still lacked cuff links. She inhaled and quietly exhaled through her nose. Then she smiled and seemed to have found her footing. "I do believe I can be of assistance. My father was all thumbs at his cravats."

He turned toward her fully and watched her face as she caught her lip between her teeth, concentrating on the folds of the fabric. Her eyes flicked up to his, and she looked down quickly. She murmured something under her breath as she untied her work and started again.

"Am I making you nervous?"

"Certainly not," she scoffed. "I could do this in my sleep." With that, she muttered again and was forced to start over.

He chuckled, and she scowled; he lifted his chin higher when she nudged it.

"You are laughing now," she said, as her gloved fingers brushed his neck and adjusted his collar, "but you'd be better served to develop a plan that will help us escape the room unseen. While *your* reputation might not suffer unduly with the masses, I suspect your mother might have something to say about it."

He smiled. "This house bears a multitude of secret doors and staircases. I can get us out of anything."

Her mouth dropped open as she finished tying the cravat and smoothed the front of his waistcoat. "Please do not tell me there is such a thing in my room! I have a healthy fear of ghosts."

He wanted to say the only secret door in her room connected to his, but firstly, he was uncertain they'd reached that level of teasing, and secondly, it was untrue.

"Look, just over here." He led her through the bedroom to a panel on the far wall, near the balcony doors. He pushed on the right side, and the panel swung inward on silent hinges.

Eva gasped.

He pointed at the narrow passageway that had been revealed. "From what I understand, these were used in order to keep servants from being seen or heard by guests."

Eva shook her head in wonder. "I would never have guessed this was here."

"Rather snooty, to my way of thinking. Can you imagine balancing a full tea tray up or down these stairs? I would not wish to be a servant under those circumstances."

Eva smiled wryly as she looked at the staircase that continued upward to the third floor. "Under any circumstances, really." She paused, then pointed to the floor where the dust had been disturbed. "Someone has been in here recently."

He lifted a shoulder. "Perhaps the servants still occasionally use it as a shortcut." He closed the panel with a quiet click, hiding the darkened staircase away.

Nathan turned from the panel and offered his arm. He had found a new purpose for the house party. He was relatively certain Eva had known romantic disappointment somewhere in her past. If he could somehow overcome her reserve, convince her of his sincerity, perhaps after ten days had passed, Eva would admit she loved him—or at least was developing feelings for him.

"My lady," he said with a smile, "dinner awaits."

CHAPTER 9

Eva looked quickly under the hood of her camera at the guests who were seated at the long table, glasses raised and expressions fixed, and to her view, upside down. Sammy handed her the plate holder, which she slid into place.

"Please remember, the chemicals composing the flash powder will leave behind a cloud that is, regrettably, malodorous. It does allow for effective photography indoors, however, without the use of excessively warm gas lamps. We've opened the windows to air the room quickly. Now, hold please," she said with a smile. She removed the plate holder, leaving the plate in place.

Sammy ignited the flashlamp powder in its specialized trough, she removed the lens covering, the powder ignited and flashed, and she replaced the lens. The air was, as she promised, temporarily filled with white powder residue, and she waved it aside. "Thank you, everyone, well done."

Good-natured laughter and a few coughs filled the room, but as Eva had planned, the breeze dissipated the cloud quickly enough. The flash powder was a new invention, and because of the combustible nature of the chemicals—a mixture of antimony sulfide, magnesium, and potassium chlorate—dangerous.

She and Sammy had practiced repeatedly and, to date, had no mishaps.

Mrs. Winston signaled the first course to be brought in as Eva and Sammy secured the equipment. Sammy, for his part, was a perfectly behaved child—seen and not heard—and worked with Eva like a finely tuned machine. The butler, Jansen, surreptitiously watched the boy, and Eva noted his unspoken approval with a subtle nod here and there. It made her glad; the more adults Sammy had caring about his welfare, the better.

She moved the equipment and she and Sammy took the plate out to the portable darkroom carriage, which sat just to the side of the house. Nathan, oddly, had insisted guests be accompanied by at least one footman if venturing outside at night, so George Abernathy, an amiable young man in his early twenties stood guard outside the carriage.

The process of plate preparation, capturing an image using a camera, and then processing the plate, allowed for a window of only roughly fifteen minutes. Working area in the carriage was sparse, but given the tight timetable, she was obliged to manage it in her elaborate formal evening dress. Sammy, to his credit, was good-natured about vying for space with her bustle.

They went through the process of carefully pouring developing solution over the plate. They then rinsed the plate thoroughly in water and fixed the image with varnish by warming both the plate and the varnish before carefully pouring the varnish over the emulsion side of the plate. The negative was now fixed in place, and she would make prints on albumen-coated paper in the morning, along with the photo she'd taken of the group as they finished tea earlier that afternoon.

They secured the chemicals, wiped down each surface and bottle with clean water, and carefully laid aside their specially made gloves—Eva had secured multiple pairs—that protected their hands from the toxic materials. Checking twice and then three times that all was in order, Eva finally allowed herself to breathe the sigh of relief she always felt when the process was complete. The materials were so dangerously volatile—and she had told Sammy true horror stories to scare caution into him—that she was always on edge during the plate preparation process and subsequent development after the image had been exposed in the camera.

She locked the darkroom, and as they returned to the house, Sammy told her about George Abernathy's family history, his interest in rugby and cricket, and his aspirations to perhaps one day become a butler. The young footman blushed but smiled. They parted ways with him once reaching the front hall, and Eva put an arm about Sammy's shoulders. They paused at the stairs leading to the second floor. "Did the detective give you instructions as to turning in for the evening?"

"Yes, Miss Eva," he said quietly. "He made a place for me in his dressing room and said I'm to read one chapter in *Robinson Crusoe* before sleep." He scrunched up his nose. "Don' know why everyone always wants me reading."

She smiled. "*Robinson Crusoe* is the staple of every good student's education."

His face brightened. "He did say when I finish, we'll see it in a theatre. An actual play!"

She squeezed his shoulder. "That sounds splendid. Good work today, Sammy. Send word if you need me, yes?"

He nodded and hurried up the stairs.

Nathaniel Winston was proving to be a man of consistency, and she took comfort in it. The man who had taken special interest in Sammy's welfare after the abduction was now the same man looking after him and promising to take him to the theatre. She had been so at sea over the last several hours that she only now was finding her equilibrium again.

She was trying to reconcile Detective Winston with Mr. Nathaniel Winston, head of a family of consequence in financial and industrial circles. It wasn't as though he was ignoring her now that he was in a different social setting—if anything, he seemed more focused on her than ever. His intense regard earlier in her sitting room as he'd asked her carefully loaded questions had been unnerving in the extreme. She had the impression she'd tipped her hand and he'd seen every card. In the course of one day, she'd gone from comfortable admiration at a distance, to uncomfortable awe at his social status, to disappointment at Blanche Parker's cutting presence at the gathering, to realizing Nathan seemed to hold Eva in higher regard than she'd realized. She needed some quiet time to think, but it was not to be, yet.

As she returned to the dining table and took her seat between Grace Winston and Davis Jacobson, a quiet, well-mannered gentleman, she wondered why she still felt so untethered. Blanche Parker and Mathilda Dilworth sat several seats down across the table, laughing charmingly at something the Swedish guest, Jens Sorenson, was saying. Eva's stomach churned, and she realized she was afraid. She was a grown woman with a career she loved, money of her own to see to her needs, a family she adored, and the affection of true friends. Yet here she was, years beyond school, feeling every ounce the same as that young girl who had been humiliated and hurt.

She felt she knew the detective's character well—he'd certainly seemed to prove himself as a man of integrity in the months of their acquaintance—but she'd been burned once before by someone she trusted, and the scars remained. She murmured thanks to the servant who placed the first course before her. She couldn't help but glance at the head of the table where Nathan sat, chatting with his mother at his right. He looked at Eva now, and a smile turned the corner of his mouth. She felt the impact of it as butterflies seemed to take flight in her stomach.

"I look forward to seeing the developed photographs tomorrow," Grace said.

Eva turned her attention to Grace, flustered and distracted by Nathan. She managed a smile and mentally gave herself a good shake. In her mind, she heard Aunt Sally telling her to pull herself together.

"I do hope they'll be satisfactory," she said as she spread her napkin on her lap. "With so many subjects, one is never guaranteed success. Everyone seated for the picture might be spot-on except for one person who is little more than a blur because he moved too much."

Grace smiled, her green eyes seeming to warm. "What drew you to the field of photography?"

"My aunt. I saw an exhibition of photographs of London's working class, from fruit sellers to carriage drivers. The stories that can be told in a single image caught my imagination, and I was transfixed. She purchased equipment for me and tasked me with taking photographs for her newspaper, *The Marriage Gazette*. From there, I began booking private sittings, and now I find myself here."

"Fascinating! Your Aunt Sally was a guest here two years ago, and I was so intimidated I don't believe I uttered two words in her presence." She chuckled. "Sally Hampton is quite legendary in circles my mother and sisters and I move in. We support many academic and civic societies, and her successes are lauded—justly so." Grace smiled again as she picked up her silverware. "Your clear affection for her is a fitting tribute to her character. And yours."

Eva smiled. "That is a lovely compliment, thank you."

"True integrity derives itself from so much more than circumstances of birth, wouldn't you agree? I feel we are fortunate to live in an age where an individual's accomplishments are not predicated on ancestry."

"I do agree."

"My maternal grandfather, for instance," Grace said, glancing at her mother, "is just such an example. He was born in the alleys of Liverpool and grew to create a textile empire. And now, my mother sits at the head of it and continues to build it. Of course," she said, leaning closer and lowering her voice, "my brother's name still appears everywhere an official signature is required, but small steps forward and all that." She smiled a little and lifted her shoulder.

"Indeed." Eva returned the smile, appreciating the candor. "And with the new divorce laws and property enactments, women are allowed to keep that which is rightfully theirs."

"Exactly! Of course, that opinion is not always a popular one," Grace said with a light laugh.

"Oh, I quite understand," Davis Jacobson said, clearing his throat and interjecting himself into the quiet conversation with a subtle blush. Eva guessed him to be in his mid-twenties, and he was of medium height and build. His hair was a light brown, and while he might have been described as average by most, his cobalt blue eyes were stunning and compelling.

"Forgive me for eavesdropping," he continued, "but I fully appreciate the strides this country has made under the direction of the Queen and a mostly progressive parliament. My own mother was obliged to suffer in an unfortunate union with her second husband after my father passed." Mr. Jacobson's brow creased. "I would gladly have seen her free of it, given the choice."

"What's this?" The Honourable John Smythe, a young man to whom Nathan had introduced Eva, was the son of a baron. He was classically handsome, with dark hair and eyes. He carried himself as one who believed any woman would be grateful to be on his arm and any gentleman would be grateful to be considered a friend. He was seated across from Mr. Jacobson, and with a smirk on his face, waved his fork at the shy man. "Discussing something so reprehensible as divorce and property rights at the dining table?"

Mr. Jacobson flushed deeply as he searched for a reply. He was saved from having to respond as Grace said, "*Au contraire*, Mr. Smythe, we are discussing fair and equal treatment for women, which is the farthest thing from reprehensible I can imagine." Grace smiled at Mr. Smythe, softening her remark, and several within earshot chuckled. Whether the laughter was a result of genuine amusement or a collective desire to ease possible discomfort, Eva was uncertain.

Mr. Smythe rolled his eyes, but his handsome face sported a smile. "Upsetting the natural order of things, such is the situation with all that noise. Doesn't help a man's cause when one of our own parrots it, Jacobson."

Mr. Meyer, seated on Mr. Jacobson's other side, chuckled. "My mother had a saying, Mr. Smythe—loosely translated, it is this, 'A man who finds himself threatened by a woman is not truly a man.'" Meyer's light German accent touched his impeccable English. Eva was unable to see his expression, but despite the teasing tone, two spots of color appeared on Smythe's cheeks.

The other diners within earshot laughed, but Mr. Franklin Frampton, apparently seeing Smythe's discomfort, added, "I cannot speak for all Englishmen, Herr Meyer, but I confess to being frightened by a fair share of women in my life. I'd not cross my grandmother Frampton for all the tea in Christendom."

The laughter increased, and Eva noted an easing of tension in the air. Mr. Smythe had introduced it with his gauche comments, and while she appreciated Meyer's glib response, it had been subtly cutting.

By now, the rest at the table were attuned to the conversation underway.

"Perhaps matters between men and women are different in your country, Meyer," Smythe said, spearing his meal with a fork, "but here we do favor tradition."

"Oh, Mr. Smythe," Mrs. Winston laughed, "you'll not find yourself in a majority at this table, I'm afraid."

"Perhaps not," Blanche Parker interrupted, "but he is not alone in his opinions." She lifted her chin and nodded at the gentleman. "The closer we venture to the new century, the more we risk upsetting a system that has placed the British Empire at the head of the world."

Her pronouncement produced applause from Mr. Smythe and good-natured exclamations of dissent from others.

"Regrettably," Delilah Winston replied, "there was a day when we'd have not been allowed to dine with the men, Miss Parker, let alone speak our minds. Progress certainly has its merits; would you not agree?"

"Let's not be ridiculous, Alice. Behavior in the Stone Ages hardly relates now."

"I am not Alice." Delilah turned her tawny eyes to Blanche and smiled.

The guests laughed, and Mrs. Winston added, "The bane of their nannies year after year. The girls are always mistaken for one another, and heaven helped us *not* when they deceived on purpose!"

She had smoothly diverted the conversation, and small groupings resumed their discussions down the long table. Mathilda Dilworth was seated next to Mr. Smythe, and Blanche leaned around her to say something to him in an undertone. He laughed in response, and Eva wondered where Blanche's opinions truly lay—earlier at tea she'd claimed forward thinking for women's causes even as she'd insulted Eva's photography work.

Mathilda, seated across from Meyer, eyed him beneath her lashes as the meal continued. Eva was unable to read her expression and would have loved to know whether the young woman was impressed or repulsed. Jens Sorenson, seated on Blanche's other side, said something Eva did not hear, but which must have been witty, for the others at the end of the table laughed and raised their glasses in salute.

Eva looked at Nathan, who now raised his glass to *her* in salute with a smile. He glanced past her at John Smythe, and then back to her with an almost imperceptible shake of his head. Blanche Parker's lilting laugh carried up the table, and Nathan raised one brow at Eva.

She couldn't help but smile, and as she turned back to the meal, she felt more like her old self. She was among friends, especially Nathan's sisters, and others who were of a like mind with her, and she did not feel so alone.

"Now," Mrs. Winston said, clasping her hands together, "as music is a fundamental basis for entertainment, I have gathered you all here in the conservatory so that we might discover one another's talents. I have chosen this as the crowning activity of our first day together and call upon my own daughters to begin and warm the stage. You'll note, we have stringed instruments, as well as a newly delivered piano made at Erard's on Marlborough Street. We also possess a limited number of wind instruments, but I am certain I speak for all when I ask that you assault our ears with those in a limited capacity if your skills are not a credit to the instrument itself."

Eva chuckled with the rest of the guests, most of whom were still devoted to following their hostess's schedule to the letter. Eva, herself, was drooping. She'd not slept well the night before, anticipating everything she needed for travel to Seaside and concern that her darkroom carriage would arrive intact and unexploded.

She stood at the rear of the room, hovering near the doorway, preferring to see the group as a whole. Blanche and Mathilda still exuded an air of self-assuredness that bordered on queenly conceit as they situated themselves within a grouping of gentlemen and held court. A few other young ladies sat behind them, and Eva found the interplay among the groups particularly interesting. The younger ladies present seemed in awe of or were intimidated by Blanche Parker and Mathilda Dilworth. Ann Parker, especially, seemed completely overshadowed by her elder sister, both in appearance and temperament.

Eva tapped her finger against her folded arms, lost in thought. She had just made note of Nathan's absence—again—when a quiet voice sounded in her ear. "Do you play the piano, Miss Caldwell?"

She looked up over her shoulder to see Nathan and gave him a wry smile. "You have redeemed yourself, sir," she whispered. "Had you found reason to miss this event, work task or no, I'd have been quite piqued."

"I wouldn't miss this for the world." He motioned with his head. "Mr. Franklin Frampton wields the clarinet like a master, and after a few glasses of whiskey, can be prevailed upon to play Irish sea shanties with it."

Eva covered her mouth to stifle a laugh.

"It is true. I've been witness to it more than once."

Her lips twitching, she finally managed to ask, "Does your mother plan to serve whiskey soon? Because you gentlemen did not disappear after supper for drinks and cigars. Unless he carries a flask, I do not see how he'll manage it."

Nathan smiled at her. "I suppose we'll be disappointed. I shall have to orchestrate it another time. Now, *that* one there," he said, this time lifting his chin and gesturing toward the front of the room, "sings like an angel. Olivia."

"Your sister?"

He nodded. "Sings and plays, but Alice plays as well. She usually accompanies Olivia."

Eva's heart warmed. "You're proud of them."

"I am. Proud of all of them for different reasons." He nodded definitively, and if she didn't know better, Eva might have thought she noted a mistiness in his eyes. Must have been a trick of the low light.

A smattering of applause followed Mrs. Winston's remarks as Olivia stood before the group and Alice settled behind the piano. Alice opened a piece of music, and Delilah stood to her right to turn pages for her.

Alice lightly pressed one key and waited as Olivia heard the note and began singing, acapella, a haunting song of love and loss. From the first notes, she took Eva's breath away. To say she sang well was an understatement. She did have the voice of an angel. Alice took up the accompaniment after several measures, and the two proceeded to offer a performance Eva would have expected to see on a professional stage.

Olivia's tone was clear, the vibrato lovely, and her range covered several octaves. At one point, Eva turned to Nathan, her mouth open. His lips quirked in a half smile, and he nodded.

Eva was lost in the beauty of the music, and tears burned the back of her eyes. She put a hand to her stomach and sucked in a breath at the final measures of the song. Quiet filled the conservatory for a prolonged moment as the last strains of piano and voice finally melted away, and then the guests rose to their feet as one and applauded. A few whistles sounded through the room, and Olivia waved a hand in good-natured dismissal as she curtseyed.

"Thank you, everyone," she said. She held out a hand to Alice, who stood and offered a theatrical bow to renewed applause. Olivia smiled, and added, "And to Delilah, whose page-turning skills are second to none." She held a hand to her other sister and applauded.

The guests laughed, and Delilah put a hand on her heart. "I am certain we all agree that my task is extremely complicated and the most deserving of praise. Thank you, thank you all." She blew a light kiss to the crowd, eliciting continued laughter, and Eva joined in, still stunned in the aftermath of surprise.

"How can such a voice exist in such a young person?" Eva asked Nathan. "She is incredible!"

He shook his head. "Perhaps the most amazing part is that she has had that voice since she was a young teen. She always sang as a child and showed talent and an aptitude for music in her early years, but as she aged, it grew exponentially."

Mrs. Winston tried to cajole the rest of the guests to follow Olivia's performance, and finally two gentlemen agreed to play a stringed duet if Alice also would join them on the piano.

Eva turned again to Nathan. "Was she tutored?"

"Yes, and studied abroad in school, but seems reticent about doing anything professionally. Who can blame her—performers often garner poor reputations."

"Which is so unfair!" Eva looked at Olivia, who had resumed her seat and was chatting with Mr. Jacobson, who appeared to be complimenting her in an endearingly bumbling way. "If she bears a desire to share that voice with the world, she should do it."

Nathan raised a dubious eyebrow. "If you can convince her of it, I tip my hat to you. She is clearly comfortable performing but doesn't explain why she chooses to save her talents for small gatherings like this one. Perhaps because she is still young."

Eva pursed her lips, curious. She allowed her gaze to wander again over the gathered guests, the large room, along the bank of windows that composed the exterior wall, and at the beautifully large plants and greenery against it. A flash of something caught her eye and as she squinted, it came into faint focus.

A face.

She gasped and clutched Nathan's arm, catching the attention of a few of the guests seated close by.

"What is it?" Nathan cupped her elbow.

She looked again at the window but now saw nothing there. She laughed shakily and waved at those in earshot, embarrassed. "I am fatigued, certainly. I am jumping at shadows."

When the attention returned to the front of the room where the cello and violin were tuning, Nathan maneuvered Eva into the hallway just outside the door. "What did you see?" he asked.

"Nothing, I imagined—"

He shook her arm, tense. "What was it?"

She searched his eyes, confused by his urgency. "I thought I saw a face."

He muttered something under his breath and ran a hand through his hair.

"Nathan, what is it?"

He shook his head. "Go back in there and stay with the others." He nudged her toward the room and turned, jogging down the hallway until he was swallowed by shadows.

Eva slowly reentered the conservatory and took an empty seat near the rear. Two of the party's matrons, Polly Parkin and Betsy Larsen, were good friends of the hostess, and both had wandered the length of the room, presumably to stretch their legs. Mrs. Parkin was the rounder and shorter of the two, where Mrs. Larsen was tall. Both women had been genial and welcoming to Eva earlier, and now they approached her, gesturing to empty seats beside hers.

"Of course," Eva said, and smiled a little unsteadily.

"Are you well, dear? You look as though you've seen a ghost." Mrs. Parkin smiled at Eva, her tone light, but expression sincere.

"Oh, it is nothing. I am weary after a long day. I'll turn in for the evening soon so that I don't embarrass myself and fall asleep where I sit."

"I'd have been better served to avoid the second glass of

Madeira," Mrs. Larsen chuckled. "I am sleepy as a cat in the sun."

Eva smiled and tried to relax as the trio at the front of the room began their musical number. She looked at the windows repeatedly, uncertain if her mind had played tricks on her and hoping half-heartedly that she'd see the face again if only to prove she wasn't imagining things. As the musical performance continued, she kept scanning the windows, eventually noting the faint, narrow beam of a torch as it danced along the ground. It would be Nathan, of course, looking in an apparent panic for something she wasn't certain she'd seen.

Relatively few things bothered Eva, but being kept in the dark—literal or figurative—was one of them. She did not feel ignorance was bliss and would rather have the whole awful truth of a matter than live unknowingly alongside it.

When the musical number ended, she joined the others in applauding, and smiled at her two new friends who drew her into a conversation about her photography, their acquaintance with her aunt Sally, and their hopes for a good, bracing walk down to the beach early the next morning. All the while, she awaited Nathan's return. The evening was not over, not by a long shot. He had been unusually tense and alert the moment she had gasped. Something was afoot, and Eva had questions for the detective.

CHAPTER 10

Nathan massaged the back of his neck where tension was beginning to build. Stafford had men making rounds all over the property, and nobody had seen anyone outside the conservatory windows in the last thirty minutes. He might have thought Eva'd had the right of it when she said she was tired and perhaps seeing things in the shadows, if not for the footprints he found in the damp soil just outside the conservatory.

He made his way back into the house, frustrated. What good was a slew of security if someone was able to creep here and there with nobody the wiser? He'd asked Stafford and then Jansen, the butler, if either man had made note of anyone on staff he didn't recognize. As far as they were concerned, everything was fine and none of the staff were strangers to them.

He stood in the quiet front hall, debating his options. He could return to the conservatory and try to explain to Eva why he had reacted so strongly, or he could go upstairs, change into dark, comfortable clothing, and explore the grounds thoroughly. Was he being dramatic? Toole hadn't actually threatened his family but had just left a cryptic message in that cigar box at his flat. It could mean anything; perhaps Toole had access to legal help that would see his family somehow exonerated and released from prison. The clipped article about his sister's death didn't necessarily mean that Nathan's family was now in danger.

He felt it in the pit of his stomach—that was the problem. He *knew* the man had meant to directly rattle and threaten him, and Bernard Toole wasn't a man who made idle threats. The kidnapping plot that Nathan had foiled had been hatched, planned, and executed by Bernard, and the rest of his family had been accomplices. It was for that reason that none of them had seen the hangman's noose.

He frowned, wishing Michael Baker was in attendance at the party. He had come to rely on his partner's insight, and Nathan felt the weight of his responsibilities keenly. He'd placed one foot on the bottom stair when he spied movement down the hall leading to the conservatory.

He moved quickly into the corridor, deciding as he went to have Turner instruct the maids to leave the gas lamps turned brighter, even during late hours. He knew a moment of relief when he realized the person walking toward him was Eva.

"What are you doing?" he whispered as he closed the distance between them.

"What am *I* doing? What are *you* doing?" Her dark eyes were large, and the fringe of thick, black lashes added drama to her appearance. The low light and shadows seemed to wrap them in seclusion, but standing close together in a dark hallway left them very exposed.

He was coming to realize that though they were dancing around the notion of learning to know each other better, they had reached that point a long time ago. She was familiar with the side of him that thought and acted as a detective, and she was too perceptive for him to believe he might continue to keep her in the dark about Toole. Delaying taking her into his confidence was delaying the inevitable and wasting time. Still, he made a feeble attempt at it. He took a breath and rubbed the back of his neck again. "I was pursuing the intruder you spied outside."

"But I told you I might have imagined it, and you ran off as though it were Radcliffe at the window!" Her reference to the villain he and Michael had put behind bars the year before bore ironic similarities to Bernard Toole; they were both devious and vengeful and motivated by selfishness and greed. They played games with their victims and relished the macabre creativity of threatening messages. He winced involuntarily at the thought.

"Nathan." Eva looked over her shoulder as the laughter and clink of teacups emanated from the conservatory. "Your mother is serving a post–talent show tea. I've told her I'm turning in for the evening, and as you'd already disappeared, she told the others that work had likely called you away." Voices sounded louder and she grabbed his arm, propelling him back in the direction he'd walked. "Hurry, the parlor."

He rushed down the hallway with her and decided perhaps he was grateful the lamps were burning low. He heard the very distinctive laugh of his mother's friend, Mrs. Larsen, growing closer. He grabbed Eva's hand, breaking into a jog, and pulling her along with him. They ducked into the parlor, and he held his finger to his lips, ushering her to a corner untouched by moonlight that streamed through the wide windows.

They sat in two small chairs that were at right angles against a corner table. The only sound in the room was the rustle of her dress as she carefully maneuvered her bustle. She did it effortlessly, and he wasn't surprised. Everything about her was graceful. He'd watched his sisters through the years as they'd dealt with fashion difficulties, and he wondered if Eva had been obliged to go through the same hours of practice.

She took a breath, clearly a bit winded, and placed her hand on her stomach. Giving him a weak smile, she whispered, "This is why women are encouraged to eat very little at formal meals. There simply isn't room enough for food, drink, and one's internal organs."

He shook his head and leaned forward, elbows on knees, and looked at her. "Do you tire of it?"

"Of restrictive clothing? Absolutely. I imagine if all windows were thrown open at the same time of night, we would hear an immense, universal sigh of relief as women climbed out of their stays. Corsets provide structure, but they do make it difficult to draw a decent breath." She shook her head and lifted her gloved hands in a shrug. "Crude of me to mention such a thing to a gentleman."

"I would not have you ever censor your language with me, Eva." He meant it earnestly. "I would always have your open, honest opinion about everything from undergarments to the suffrage movement to the most mundane activity that occupies your time. You need not ever concern yourself with searching for 'more appropriate words' when conversing with me." He swallowed, torn between gratitude that it was so dark in the room and wishing he could see her better. Hushed, he added, "I would be the one person with whom you need never guard your words or your thoughts."

She was still and quietly breathed through her nose. She finally nodded. "Very well, let us begin our honesty in full. We shall start with you." She leaned closer to him. "*What* is happening? You were tense when I arrived earlier today, and I asked you about it then and you claimed it was work. Then, you were late to afternoon tea, also claiming it was work. Now, I believe I see a stranger looking in from outside, and you jump out of your skin."

He rubbed his eyes, suddenly very tired. The tension in his neck was traveling to his temples. He took a deep breath and began talking quietly. He told her about his undercover assignment with the Toole Family Carnival, saving the child, setting a trap to capture the culprits, and about the most important piece—who escaped. She never interrupted during the whole of his five-minute soliloquy, only scooted closer to the edge of her chair and leaned forward—as close as her corset probably allowed. When he stopped talking, she reached for his hand.

Giving a gentle squeeze, she quietly asked, "You believe Mr. Toole will come here and cause problems?"

"There is more." He told her about the cryptic delivery at his door before he'd left the city.

"Ah," she said, her eyes widening fractionally. "That is . . . worrisome. You've not told your family?"

"Just my mother, and only the barest details."

She sighed, still holding onto his hand. "When did this 'visit' occur?"

He smiled grimly and gently held her hand between his. He looked at it, rubbing the soft satin of her glove, feeling the slender fingers beneath the fabric. "The evening I left Hampton House after delivering my mother's invitation to you." He looked up at her face. "I ought to have told you then that what I was asking of you wasn't a ruse, not on my part. You have consumed my thoughts for a very long time, Evangeline. And now I have involved you in danger." He studied her hand again, tracing each finger softly.

"Nathan."

He looked at her eyes, large, shadowed, beautiful.

"I wouldn't be anywhere else but here right now. I . . . I also . . ." She swallowed and took a shallow breath. "It is difficult for me, you see . . ." She trailed off into silence.

He waited, patient, unwilling to disrupt her thoughts.

"I was betrothed once before. Well," she amended, "nearly betrothed. The night he was to speak with my father about his intentions, he was . . . distracted. Changed his mind."

He nodded. "I wondered," he said quietly.

She stiffened. It was subtle, but noticeable. He released her hand, and she placed it gently on her lap. Every movement was careful, controlled. He wondered now if it was her way to protect herself. If she was perfect, then everything else would be too.

"You wondered?" She paused, quiet. "Has my behavior implied the existence of former . . . scandal? Or worse, some sort of jilted, sad person?"

"No, Eva. Nothing of the sort. Your behavior is impeccable. I make a study of people, you know. I fancy myself a detective, after all, and I believe I've noted a . . . an interest from you. An interest in me. You're very careful about it, however, and I reasoned former hurt might be the cause."

She was quiet for a moment, and then shook her head with a rueful laugh. "We are facing possible danger and you are obliged to walk on eggshells for my feeling's sake. I shall be more balanced come morning; tonight, I am merely tired."

"My intention is not to pressure you to act any certain way, please know that." He paused and chuckled. "Allow me to rephrase. I would appreciate it very much if you would continue to pretend an interest in me so that I might avoid possible entrapment by the likes of Miss Parker or Miss Dilworth. You see, now, why I was so flummoxed when my mother asked me to be here."

Eva smiled, and he was relieved to see the upward tilt at the corner of her eyes. "Naturally, detective, I am willing to help you avoid any and all entrapment at the hands of such . . . people. And I thank you for your patience with . . . I want . . . I want very much to pursue a future that involves a family." She rubbed her forehead. "Charlotte has put a name to my reticence. She calls it 'matters of trust.' I do not have an easy time of it."

"Understandably."

"I would have you know, however, that I am not interested in any other man." She blew out a quiet breath. "I . . . mercy. I am making an absolute muddle of this. The correct words are stuck in my head."

"Eva." He held out his hand and brushed his knuckle against her knee. She placed her hand in his, and he drew her fingers to his lips, holding them there and placing a soft kiss against the cool satin. "I am not in a rush. Do I strike you as an impatient man?"

Her breath shuddered out on a quiet sigh. "You strike me as a lethal man."

He smiled against her gloved fingers. "I prefer 'patient.' Sounds much kinder."

"Oh, I did not say 'unkind.' There is a difference." He heard the humor in her voice.

"I am glad to know it." He winked at her and finally released her hand. His worries about Toole, although still present, had dimmed. He felt less frantic, as though a solution would present itself if he remained vigilant. Perhaps the subtle boost in confidence resulted from having confided the whole thing to someone he trusted to be solid in a crisis.

He straightened in his seat and stretched, rotating his head slowly.

"Are you in pain? I have headache powders, if you think that might help."

He shook his head. "Thank you, but I am ridiculously susceptible to medicines that make one drowsy. I need my wits about me." He then explained his security team's role and told Eva to be careful with both her welfare and Sammy's. "Be watchful," he finished. "The last thing that boy needs is another encounter with a frightening adult."

Eva shuddered. "I appreciate that you've taken him under your wing. It is far more than I ever expected. It is very good of you."

"There are many we cannot save, isn't that true? So, when there is one at hand for whom we can make a difference, what sort of people would we be if we didn't do just that?" He stood and again offered his hand, meeting her eyes as she rose.

A soft shaft of moonlight illuminated her face, and she looked at him as though in wonder. While her response quite did boost his male ego, he found himself feeling a bit bashful. Although she hadn't gone so far as to admit deepening feelings for him, he was hopeful. Now that he'd arrived at his own conclusions about his plans for the future, he was prepared to wait. He was a patient man, after all, and as it concerned games of strategy, he was very good at looking down the road. When she was ready, he would be there.

CHAPTER 11

Eva thanked the maid, Mary, for helping her undo the most difficult pieces of her evening gown, and some of the layers beneath it. She dismissed the girl, who looked as tired as Eva felt, and got herself ready for bed the rest of the way on her own. She'd not exaggerated her comments earlier to Nathan about disrobing at the end of the day. The relief she felt at taking in a huge breath after loosening the tight stays was immense. She availed herself of the Blue Room's dressing area and water closet, taking a quick bath and donning fresh nightclothes.

She nearly groaned in delight when she slipped into the soft bedding. It was like climbing into a cloud. She couldn't decide which was more exhausted, her body or her mind. The conversation she had been shoving aside since parting with Nathan now played itself repeatedly in her thoughts. She remembered every expression on his face—she'd leaned in close enough to see him even in the dark—and every touch of his fingers on her hand. He'd held it like it was something exquisite.

Tears she'd held at bay for a very long time now burned in her eyes and finally escaped. Nathan had been right, of course; she'd been young and in love and had been promised the moon by a young man of status and wealth who had masqueraded as a gentleman. Her heart had broken so completely at the time she didn't think she'd ever stop crying. Her mother had held her, her father had threatened to run the boy down with hunting hounds, and when Aunt Sally had heard, she had swooped in, given Eva the option to move to Town with her and cousin Amelie, and helped her mend wounded feelings and bruised pride.

Eva had decided then that she would take each of her strengths and raise them to a level of perfection that nobody could ever question. She would do everything well. Better than well. She would be graceful and elegant and very careful about any who would seek closeness with her. Amelie and Charlotte were easy—they were her best friends as well as her relations, and she knew she would never feel the pain of betrayal at their hands. Sally, her parents—they were also constants, and for that she was grateful. Anybody else, however, was an uncertainty.

Tears rolled down her cheeks and she turned on her side, reaching for the handkerchief she had stashed under the pillow. Gentlemen had approached her father, even her aunt Sally in the years since "the Betrayal," seeking to further an acquaintance, perhaps officially court her. Eva either was not interested or experienced panic so irrational that she questioned her own sanity. She had allowed opportunities to pass, with sadness, perhaps, but not regret.

She struggled now to understand the dam that seemed to have given way after so many years when she thought she was fine. She hadn't anticipated the potential resurgence of old feelings probable at a house party where certain personalities were likely to gather. Blanche Parker and John Smythe were like pieces of that painful past, and she'd walked blindly into their nonsense with her guard down. How odd that an adult could feel the same emotions she'd experienced as a younger person when in similar circumstances. She'd not thought it possible, or at least that it would happen to her.

She sniffled and wiped her nose, hearing her father's voice in her head. *Get to sleep, Eva-girl. Nighttime is not for thinking.* She smiled, wishing for a moment she could feel his warm embrace. He had always maintained that a sleepy mind was useless and that one's perspective was much clearer in the morning hours with the rising sun and a fresh day.

He was right, of course. She was always much more optimistic and clearheaded in the morning. For now, she decided, she would think about the man whose room was across the landing, about how her heart had raced when he had spoken to her in the parlor. Some of the reason for it had been because he told her a harrowing story, but also, his slow assault on her senses by doing nothing more than tracing his finger along her glove, by kissing her fingers—again through the glove—she wouldn't have imagined such a thing would be so thrilling.

A shadow crossed behind the curtains of the small balcony on the far wall. Behind the curtains, or in front? Now she wasn't sure. Frowning, she rose on her elbow, wondering if she was imagining things. She held her breath and watched the balcony doors, not daring to get out of bed and open them. Realizing she'd never go to sleep if she thought someone lurked outside her windows, she crept from under the covers and crossed to the hearth where she grabbed a poker.

She felt slightly foolish as she crept to the balcony, erstwhile weapon in hand, and stared at the curtains. There was nobody in the room; the shadow must have been outside. Slowly, she lifted the poker and used the end to move the curtains back. Spotty clouds allowed intermittent light from the moon, and to her relief, she realized the balcony was empty. She edged closer, looking on either side, just to be sure, and then sighed.

Her sense of relief was short-lived. The panel Nathan had opened earlier was to her immediate right, and as she slowly turned to look at it, her heart hammered painfully. The panel seam was just visible, so slight she mightn't have noticed it had she not already known about the passageway. Nathan had closed it completely, she was certain.

She ran her fingertip along the edge of the molding and contemplated her options. Not feeling nearly brave enough to open the panel wide and peer inside the dark interior, she instead placed her palm on it and slowly pressed, closing it completely. It now lay flush with the rest of the wall, invisible to the ignorant eye.

I am overtired, she thought, feeling ever more ridiculous. The panel must not have closed entirely under Nathan's hand, earlier. She closed the sheer curtains, followed by the heavier drapes. Wearily, she replaced the poker and climbed back into bed, wondering what her cousins would say when she confessed to them she'd been seeing things. Surely that's all it was.

The following morning during a late breakfast, Mrs. Winston announced that the activities for the day included games and tea on the lawn and later, a nighttime bonfire down on the beach. Eva did not have an opportunity to speak with Nathan alone for any length of time; while attempting to make good work on a full plate of food from the sidebar, he was obliged to share detective stories with some of the curious gentlemen who seemed to openly envy his occupation.

Upper-class opinion often dictated that one's desired "occupation" ought to be to have none at all, at least nothing that resembled trade work or earning a salary. The gentlemen hanging on Nathan's every word brought to mind an image of schoolboys sitting at an instructor's feet, and Eva couldn't help but smile.

She felt his attention on her several times, and she wasn't certain how she knew when he was watching her. Several times while becoming acquainted with the other ladies in the group, she glanced in Nathan's direction only to find his eyes on her. She reminded herself that they were playing a part for the others; it would be easy to forget that there was a simple purpose behind his attention. She also remembered, though, those few quiet moments the night before in the parlor, where they'd had no audience at all.

Her cheeks warmed now and again, and judging by the exchanged glances among the Winston sisters—to her relief they were accompanied by smiles—Eva reasoned she was executing her end of the performance well. The seating arrangement was less formal than it had been at supper the night before, and the gentlemen had plunked themselves down next to Nathan as soon as he sat. She didn't mind; she figured it gave them a good opportunity to "steal glances" at one another that supposedly nobody else noticed.

As she finished her breakfast, she spied young George Abernathy, the footman, approaching. When he reached her side, he leaned down and whispered, "Miss Caldwell, I am delivering a message from Master Samuel White. He would have you know he has finished his sweet rolls in the kitchen and is prepared to meet you at the darkroom carriage at your convenience. Do you have a message you wish me to convey in return?"

Eva looked at the young man, who had apparently tried to

deliver his statement in a dignified manner, but the smile playing at the corners of his mouth told the truth of the matter. She chuckled and whispered back, "Please tell Master Samuel, I shall meet him at the carriage in no more than ten minutes' time."

"Very good, miss." He bowed and quietly left the room.

Delilah Winston, seated next to Eva, laughed softly. "That must be the most entertaining exchange I have heard in ages. What a charming young assistant you have, Miss Caldwell."

"Please, call me Eva. And yes, Sammy is indeed charming. He is a very bright boy, and I am fortunate to have his help." She folded the napkin on her lap, capturing errant crumbs within it, and moved to stand.

Blanche Parker, seated across the table and a few seats down, now caught Eva's attention. "Miss Caldwell, I hope we shall be posing again for your camera this afternoon during the lawn games?"

"For some of them, yes, Miss Parker." She smiled, grateful that she had awoken that morning with a clear head and purposeful intent. She would not be rendered vulnerable again by the snide behavior of anyone at the party. She would be decent, of course, as she always was. She would be professional and courteous. She had once heard it said amongst tradesmen that the customer must always be the victor of any exchange, and she would view Miss Parker as a customer.

The customer now pouted very prettily; it was an expression Eva had quickly come to recognize as the young woman's signature affectation. "A pity you'll not appear in any of the photos yourself. I suppose such is the nature of your business."

Eva smiled brightly. "My assistant is knowledgeable about the photography process; he will manage a few of the photos so that I may be included in the fun with all of you."

"Your assistant? Ah, yes, the ragamuffin. You know, perhaps I ought to address you privately," she said, leaning forward and lowering her voice, "but I must insist you speak with the child concerning his early morning exercises with those dreadful dogs. The peace of my morning was interrupted rudely by shouting and barking."

Eva wanted to comment that it was fortunate Miss Parker had lowered her voice as she delivered her complaint; the others at the table surely overheard nothing as a result of her forethought. Instead, she nodded sagely. "Of course. I shall speak to him about it. I do not wish for any guest or staff to be disrupted by his behavior." That much was certainly true. She added, "I shall also ask Nathan—oh, excuse me, Mr. Winston—to admonish Sammy of the same. He does have quite a rapport with the child."

Blanche's pretty eyes widened, and she blinked. Mathilda exchanged glances with her, and then looked at the ladies around them with a smirk. "Oh, Miss Caldwell." Mathilda shook her head slightly. "Perhaps you are unaware, but in polite circles, it is not customary to address gentlemen, especially single gentlemen, by their given names."

"Hmm." Eva nodded. "You must forgive me. The detective and I move in the same vocational and social circles while in Town. We are the dearest of friends, and I suppose it slipped my mind entirely that not everyone here enjoys the same privilege with him that I do."

Eva felt the air around her shift, as though the women held their collective breath when she finished speaking. She then heard a stifled giggle and a few cleared throats. She held Blanche's and Mathilda's attention as she stood and carefully placed her napkin on her chair. She may as well have declared war on the women, and it went a long way to assuaging her privately wounded pride from the day before.

She smiled at Blanche, who seemed at a loss for words, which Eva was certain was a rarity. She knew she could expect subtle—and perhaps not so subtle—retaliation in the near future, but she welcomed it. Eva rarely lost her temper and nearly always maintained an upper hand with her calm. She did not doubt her ability to keep an advantageous position now that she was prepared for it. Blanche found her voice quickly enough, and she turned to Mathilda Dilworth and two other ladies near them, changing the subject entirely.

A quick glance at Delilah Winston, and Grace, who sat next to her sister, showed clear approval as they hid their smiles. Grace winked at her, and Eva tipped her head in acknowledgment. Alice did not bother trying to hide her smile, nor did her twin, Olivia. Directly next to them, Mrs. Polly Parkin lifted her teacup in salute.

Eva excused herself from their company and walked toward the door. Nathan looked at her with one brow raised as Mr. Handy asked him a question, and then repeated himself when Nathan didn't immediately answer. Eva smiled at him, wondering how long it would be before news reached the gentlemen's end of the table that Miss Caldwell was gauche and utterly a low-class sort of woman.

She left the room and made her way outside, turning her face up to a blue sky and sun. The weather was sublime—just warm enough for Mrs. Winston's planned activities—and she knew it would yield good results when she made prints from the photography plates she and Sammy had processed the night before. She used artificial light to develop pictures when the weather was uncooperative, which was admittedly often, but much preferred natural sunlight.

True to his word, Sammy stood waiting next to the darkroom carriage. "Miss Eva, this is Collins. 'E's our footman today."

"Hello, Collins." She smiled at the man.

He touched the brim of his uniform cap and shuffled his feet. "Madam," Collins said. His face was pale, and she wondered if he'd been recently ill. Domestic work was taxing—she knew how hard it was to be a maid or footman, or a housekeeper or cook, for that matter. Mrs. Winston was generous, but Eva knew the hours were long.

She unlocked the carriage and swung the door open, greeted by the familiar smell of chemicals that never failed to prompt a sense of excitement despite her ever-present worry about safety issues.

"May I offer you a hand?" Collins asked. He fidgeted nervously and glanced at the house several times.

Eva realized Nathan must have put the fear of God into the footmen regarding the seriousness of guarding the caravan. "No, thank you, I actually manage better this way." She smiled and gestured to the handles she'd had installed on the inside of the doorway. Climbing into and out of carriages was never a simple task—as a young schoolgirl she'd had lessons on gracefully managing complicated clothing while entering and exiting vehicles that rocked under movement—but her iron handgrips were a stroke of genius of which she was quite proud.

She grasped the handles and climbed inside. She'd dressed simply that morning in anticipation of working with Sammy in the tight quarters; her bustle from the night before had presented a bit of a challenge.

Sammy climbed up behind her and switched on the muted yellow light, closing the door behind him and blocking the daylight. They donned fresh gloves, beginning a routine that had become comfortable and familiar.

"Sammy," she said as they worked, "I was on the receiving end of a complaint about some noise outside this morning. Were you overly loud with the dogs?"

He nodded. "Weren't my fault, though. Jansen said the dogs is to stay out of the dahlias, an' they kept tearin' through."

"Suppose the next time they do that, you alert Jansen or one of the gardeners, perhaps. Then you aren't obliged to yell at the dogs." She smiled at him with a wink. "What do you suppose had them so excited about the dahlias?"

He shrugged. "Darned if I know."

"You didn't throw the ball into them?"

"Nay, miss. Too close to the 'ouse, and I don' want to break windows." He grimaced. "Burnette rapped my knuckles awful from that accident at 'ampton 'ouse."

Eva laughed. "That 'accident' occurred after she'd admonished you repeatedly to stop throwing the ball against the wall. That was a lesson you seemed determined to learn the hard way." She nudged him with her elbow, and he grinned ruefully. "It's fortunate for you that she held herself to knuckle-rapping. She was still fuming when I arrived home that evening."

"I musta looked awful sad." He gazed up at her with sorrowful blue eyes.

She tipped back her head, laughing. "Samuel White, you are incorrigible!"

"I *was* awful sad," he said, handing her the plates they'd developed after supper. "She rapped my knuckles and took the ball away. Wouldn't let me 'ave it for a week!"

"*Again*, count yourself fortunate, my young friend. Your punishment was not nearly what I would have imagined Mrs. Burnette to deliver after such a blatant infraction. You should have heard the tongue-lashing Miss Amelie used to receive from dripping her umbrella all over the front hall. And she is an adult!"

Sammy grinned. "Miss Amelie still drips 'er umbrella all over the 'all. Did it just last week when she visited."

"And did Mrs. Burnette take her to task over it?"

Sammy laughed and nodded.

"You see? You are a lucky young man."

"I am a lucky young man." He looked up at Eva with a smile, dimples showing in his cheeks.

For a moment, Eva's eyes stung with affection for the boy. She returned his smile but quickly busied herself with gathering the tray and chemical mix she required for imprinting the images on the specially treated paper. Clearing her throat, she said, "We'll print two of each image for Mrs. Winston's approval. We shall probably need to prepare more albumen-treated paper for the coming days. I asked Mrs. Snow for the extra eggs for the egg-white-wash mixture." She paused, brow wrinkled in thought. They had prepared a large amount of paper before leaving home. "I do not know yet how many of the guests will want copies for their own albums."

"All of 'em."

"You believe so?"

He nodded. "Ever body likes their pictures taken. Makes 'em feel special."

"You've the right of it, there," she said, reaching for clean cloths. "I have yet to meet a person who wasn't fascinated at his own image."

"Keeps us busy," he said, taking the tray from her and holding it as she stacked supplies inside.

"Yes," she agreed. "Even with Mr. Eastman's new Kodak 1. I worry they will put professional photographers out of business."

"*You push the button, we'll do the rest*," Sammy said, reciting the company's slogan. "'Cept New York is a long ways away to send a camera just to develop a few pictures."

She nodded. He was correct, but the benefit to Mr. Eastman's portable camera was that each camera held negative film containing one hundred images per roll. After developing, the company returned the pictures and the negatives to the owner, along with the camera, which was loaded with new film. It was an impressive system, and Eva imagined it wouldn't be long before people began taking advantage of it.

The concept gave her pause and, since learning of Mr. Eastman's ideas, had given her the occasional pang of uncertainty. She could only hope there would always be room for professionals, that at least people with means would continue to require a photographer's services. She couldn't imagine there would come a time when she wouldn't love the process; she had often thought that even as a wife and mother, she would still find space for it in her life.

Eva carefully descended from the carriage and held out her hands for the tray, which Sammy gave her before climbing down the steps and joining her outside.

Eva looked up at the sky, searching for the best vantage point to print the sample pictures for Mrs. Winston. She chose a spot just outside the carriage's shadow.

"Shall I get fresh water from the kitchen?" Sammy asked.

"Yes, but first, hand me the folding table, if you please."

Sammy retrieved a collapsible table that was secured to the

side of the carriage. They then arranged the tray, papers, and chemicals in preparation for printing.

"Two pitchers of water?" Sammy asked as he dusted off his hands.

"Yes, just to be certain we have enough."

He nodded and ran toward the back of the house, disappearing around the corner.

Eva realized she'd forgotten the plates and returned to climb back inside the carriage. "Oh, Collins," she said, realizing the man still stood sentry near the door. "You needn't remain here, truly. Sammy and I have things well in hand. We aren't carrying heavy equipment for at least three more hours."

"My instructions are very specific, miss, if you don't mind."

"Very well." She smiled. "Have you had breakfast? I'm happy to have Sammy fetch you some biscuits, or perhaps a sweet roll." She held up a hand to her mouth as though sharing a secret. "He has made good inroads with the cook."

He blinked in surprise. "Oh. No, thank you," he mumbled. "I ate."

She nodded and climbed back into the carriage, retrieving the processed plates. She returned to the other supplies she'd left on the folding table, examining one of the plates while she waited for Sammy. The image on the negative, silvery and an odd reflection of reality, always struck her with its unique, haunting appearance. The picture it produced on paper was, except lacking bright color, true life captured in time. The negative, however, was always a bit strange.

She spied Sammy rounding the corner of the house with Nathan, who carried one of the water pitchers. A few of the house guests followed behind, and she smiled, anticipating an impromptu demonstration. People had been sitting for photos for decades, but not everybody had seen the development process in action.

"Hello!" she called as the group neared.

Nathan smiled at her. "Are you prepared to showcase your talents?"

"Of course." She returned his smile. "Thank you for lending aid to my assistant."

"I *was* carrying bof pitchers," Sammy told her.

"He was," Nathan agreed readily. "Had the situation well in hand. I insisted I be allowed to help in order to make a positive impression on his employer."

"Consider her impressed." She forced herself not to smile at Nathan for too long. She didn't want to overdo her performance. She turned her attention to the handful of others—a smattering of both genders—who were now gathering around. "Are you here for a demonstration?"

"If it isn't an imposition," Mr. Burton Handy said with a polite nod.

"Hardly slept a wink all night in anticipation!" Franklin Frampton's grin split his face, and Eva couldn't help but laugh.

"This equipment is most impressive," Jens Sorenson said and elbowed Peter Meyer. "We posed for photographs only last week at the embassy, but did not see the development phase." He smiled, and the sun glinted off his blond hair. Eva wondered wryly how many hearts the young man had broken with that smile.

Mr. Meyer nodded. "I did see a photograph developed some time ago, but it was done at a studio, not outside a caravan." He smiled and tilted his hat against the sun. During an extended stay at a house party, many gentlemen dispensed with hat wearing. Eva wondered sympathetically if Meyer retained his because of the thinning nature of his own light brown hair when compared to his handsome younger companion.

"Thankfully," Eva said, "the portable nature of the caravan makes my work possible. I find it infinitely easier at home, of course, but although challenging, there's a charm to this that I quite enjoy."

Davis Jacobson cleared his throat. "Does the nature of the process pose a danger?"

"With the chemicals?" Eva asked, rolling back her sleeves from the cuffs.

The shy man nodded, and Jens nudged the man. "Never let Smythe know of your fears! You'll not hear the end of it."

The others chuckled, and Mr. Jacobson looked over his shoulder at the house as if Mr. Smythe lurked there.

Eva smiled. "I do worry about the equipment's volatility and potential for explosion. The chemicals are highly combustible, so my assistant and I follow strict protocols while we work." She turned to Sammy. "See if Collins would also like to join us, please. He might appreciate a peek at what he's been standing guard over."

Sammy walked back to the darkroom carriage as Eva began explaining what the onlookers would witness. When Sammy rejoined them, she was surprised he was alone. He shrugged. "Not there," he whispered.

Nathan shifted closer to the boy. "The footman left?"

Sammy nodded.

"I mentioned he needn't remain with us out here," Eva said, realizing he must have accepted her offer of relief of his duties and hoped she'd not created a problem for the servant.

Nathan shook his head and opened his mouth but stopped

just shy of responding. "Continue," he said to Eva. "I'll find him later."

Eva began by explaining the process she and Sammy had done the night before, and then showed them the negative of the dinner party. She hadn't gotten far into the process when she heard running footsteps from the front of the house and a breathless George Abernathy arrived.

"Apologies," he stammered to Nathan. "I—uh, apologies. Collins is ill." He clamped his lips together and faded back toward the carriage.

Nathan frowned. "A word later, when this is done."

George swallowed and nodded.

Even knowing everything Nathan had told her the night before, Eva wondered at the necessity of having a footman with them at the carriage in broad daylight. The darkroom was positioned close to the house, was visible from multiple vantage points, and she couldn't imagine anyone benefitting from any sort of interference. It wasn't as though the items within it were rare or unavailable to the general populace.

Perhaps she had overstated it to Nathan, however. She glanced at him as she continued with the demonstration, noting the tight set to his jaw. The man had concerns enough; she would put his mind at ease later and explain the dangers were few when the carriage was stationary and locked. She could say with near certainty they had nothing to fear.

CHAPTER 12

When Nathan arrived at the back lawn for his mother's first game of the afternoon, he spied a cluster of people bent over something, or someone. Hurrying over, he saw Eva in the process of righting her tripod with the aid of Jens Sorenson and Davis Jacobson. Jacobson was looking at Eva with trouble clearly reflected in his blue eyes, and Jens examined the camera as they settled it back into place, a frown on his handsome face.

"An accident?" Nathan asked Eva, moving closer to inspect the damage. She was the only one who would truly know the extent of it. Alice and Olivia also hovered close by, and Alice's fingers were pressed to her mouth in dismay.

Dahlia came running to join the group, followed by two other young women. "What has happened?" Dahlia breathed as she reached Nathan's side.

"I am not certain yet."

Eva ran her fingers over each inch of the camera, frowning when she came to the front corner. "Just splintered wood here," she said, "but no lasting damage to the camera, from what I see in the moment." She managed a smile and glanced up at the others who had helped. "Thank you so, everyone. I believe we've escaped disaster for the time. Perhaps a wind blew up from the water and tipped it over."

Each guest looked out over the property in the direction of the water. The air was relatively still and cloudless. What little breeze there was could best be considered pleasant.

"Yes," Jens Sorenson said slowly. "That must have been the cause."

Everyone nodded in dubious agreement, and as they began to move away, Nathan slipped close to Eva.

She looked up at him, trouble marring her expression. "I set up the camera, went around the corner to the darkroom for supplies, and when I returned, it was laying on the ground."

He looked at the box from different angles and saw a smear of grass and dirt on the side where Eva noted the chip in the wood. "We are probably fortunate the damage isn't worse," he told her quietly. "This seems to have hit the ground with some force." He looked around at the milling crowd and staff who were preparing for the activity. "Who was out here at the time? Nobody saw anything?"

Eva shrugged.

Delilah put a hand on her shoulder and asked, "Is there anything I can get for you? A cup of tea?"

Eva put her hand over Delilah's with a smile. "Oh, thank you, but no, Delilah."

Delilah smiled. "You've already mastered the skill of telling us apart."

"You have tawny eyes, as does Alice." Eva laughed. "I might be confused to see you both holding very still, but Alice is quite animated."

Delilah's smile lit up her face. "So very true!" She chuckled and patted Eva's shoulder before stepping away. "I shall be close by helping Mama if you need anything."

"Thank you," Eva called after her, and then her smile dimmed a bit. She looked at Nathan, clearly concerned. "Someone knocked this over," she muttered.

"Who was around when you set it up? Do you remember?"

"Nearly as many as you see here now. It happened no more than three minutes ago. I was prepared to show it to several of the guests who have asked about its mechanics, but I hadn't even begun talking to anyone." She closed her eyes. "When I steadied it and made certain it was on even ground, I left it here." She opened her eyes and added, "Alone. I didn't see anyone near it in that moment. When I returned, the gentlemen appeared to have just noticed it and reached it before I did."

Nathan frowned, scanning the crowd. "Perhaps someone bumped into it and is too embarrassed to claim responsibility."

She nodded. "That may be. Certainly not the first time a tripod has been upended." She huffed out a breath as if shaking free of suspicions. "Accidents happen all the time."

Nathan tried not to grimace as his mother tied his right ankle to Franklin Frampton's left with some strips of cloth. He did not enjoy lawn games aside from, perhaps, croquet. Three-legged races were so far down on the list of things he liked to do as to be barely a footnote. He spied Eva, who was standing with a group of ladies around her camera tripod and reasoned he might not hate three-legged races if he could just be paired with her. The images brought to mind were those he'd rather not be pondering while tied to Franklin Frampton, so he resolved to put the notion out of his head.

The camera appeared to be in working order, and he had questioned a few of the people he knew had been close by at the time of the mishap. Alice, whom he suspected might have knocked it over accidentally, judging by her horrified reaction, swore on "a stack of bibles and *Mrs. Beeton's Book of Household Management*" that she was across the lawn when it happened. She ran up on the crowd as Eva was setting it to rights.

For the most part, Eva seemed to have regained her equilibrium from the night before. He had reflected late into the night about the things he'd confessed to her in the parlor. He knew that if nothing else, he'd been honest. Perhaps she might come to share the depth of his feelings, and perhaps she might not. He would have to find a way to live with the negative, should that occur, because the longer he thought about it and the more he considered his life and what he wanted his future to be, the more determined he was that Eva Caldwell be a central part of it.

"There," his mother said as she secured another strip of cloth, this one at his and Franklin's knees. "I paired the two of you because the length of your legs is similar, and I hope to provide every advantage to each guest."

"Thank you, Mother," Nathan said drily. "I do not suppose you'll honor my earlier request to bypass this contest altogether?"

Franklin laughed. "Good one, old boy. What's done is done. What say we make a concerted effort to win this thing!" He threw his arm around Nathan's shoulder, and Nathan put his around the man's torso.

"If we do manage a win," Nathan said to his partner, whose face was uncomfortably close, "I request you honor us at some point with your repertoire of sea chanties as rendered on the clarinet."

"Oh, that is a loaded request, my friend. I can only manage those after a bottle of whiskey."

Nathan's brows lifted. "An entire bottle?"

"Preferably."

Nathan's lips twitched. "I shall procure a bottle. Having witnessed your performance last year at the club, I believe it well worth my time to facilitate an encore."

They hobbled together over to the starting line, where others had already positioned themselves. Peter Meyer was paired with Jens Sorenson. Davis Jacobson was tied to Burton Handy, a quiet man who was hopelessly enamored of Blanche Parker, who would never deign to dance with him, let alone entertain the idea of courtship.

John Smythe was the final gentleman in the lineup and, as the party had run short of gentlemen guests, was obliged to be paired with George Abernathy, the footman, whom Nathan had questioned about the earlier confusion at the portable darkroom. As John was the snootiest and most class conscious of all the gentlemen, Nathan smugly relished that his mother had paired him with a footman. John was insufferably arrogant and horrifically rude. The downside of the pairing, of course, was that he couldn't help but pity Abernathy.

The lawn had been cleared for the activity, and Nathan glanced at his mother, who was happily in her element. Staff were busily conveying food and supplies to the shaded gardens near the pond in preparation for the afternoon picnic tea, the weather was cooperating beautifully, and excitement in the air signaled her success as a hostess. He smiled to himself. As if there had ever been a doubt that Christine Winston was the reigning house party queen.

Alice stood at the far end of the lawn with a white handkerchief to begin the race. She rang a bell to signal everyone's attention. Once the runners were set, she shouted, "Ready, steady, go!" and waved the handkerchief.

Nathan gritted his teeth as Franklin's leg shot out and did his best to keep pace with his partner, who seemed extraordinarily intent on leading them to victory. They quickly found their rhythm, and Nathan glanced at the others to monitor their progress. To his surprised satisfaction, they were leading the pack. Regrettably, John and George were quickly closing the gap.

"Go, Franklin," Nathan grunted, "faster!"

"I am going . . . as fast . . . as I can . . . old chap!" Franklin's breath came in quick gasps as they hobbled their way closer to the finishing line, where the ladies had gathered and were cheering as though at a cricket match.

Eva had aligned herself with Nathan and Franklin and shouted at him to hurry. She jumped in place and clapped, glancing down the row at the others and shouting louder. "Come on," she yelled, laughing as she urged them forward.

Out of the corner of his eye, he saw that they were neck and neck with John and George, and as the finish came into sight, he stretched with all his might, taking himself and Franklin to the ground in the process.

"Huzzah!" Eva and the others were doubled over laughing, his sisters chief among them. Several maids and footmen had paused and joined in the laughter and applause.

The other contenders crossed the line, with Jens Sorenson and Peter Meyer bringing up the rear by several lengths. Jens was apparently berating his friend in rapid Swedish, while Peter

Meyer shrugged. Jens switched belatedly to English, prompting more laughter, and scolded Peter for becoming distracted and slowing their race.

Nathan was gratified to see John Smythe and George Abernathy had also fallen to the ground. Alice waved the handkerchief over Nathan and Franklin, declaring them the race's winner by "just a hair!"

"You slowed my pace!" John Smythe accused his partner.

"Keep it together, Smythe," Nathan called to him. "Without Mr. Abernathy, you'd not have been nearly so close!"

George Abernathy turned his head from his angry partner, grinning as they managed to make it to their feet. The other four gentlemen laughed and shared good-natured insults with each other, and Nathan was forced to admit, it was an effective strategy for building rapport among the guests.

"No, no! Do not untie yourselves yet!" Eva spoke quickly as the men began attempting to loosen the knots, which Mrs. Winston had tied with impressive strength. "Apologies, but I must ask you to hobble over to the camera. I've set it up there to take best advantage of the light."

Faux groans of complaint filled the air, even as the pairs began making their way back across the lawn. As they stood in a group at Eva's direction, many of them beaming at her praise for their heroic racing efforts, Nathan noticed Sammy, who stood at the tripod, touching the camera with a confused expression.

Eva finished posing the gentlemen and made her way back to the camera, where she exchanged a few hushed words with Sammy, who seemed near tears. He gestured toward the far end of the house where the portable darkroom was situated just out of sight. Eva frowned and pulled the plate holder from the camera.

He watched her lips as she whispered, "Are you certain?"

The boy nodded miserably, and she put her hand on his shoulder, turning him away from the adults as she leaned close and spoke in his ear. He nodded again, and she gave his shoulder a squeeze. He ran toward the servants' entrance and disappeared inside.

Eva returned to the adults. "I apologize, everyone, we have a problem with the camera equipment, but it will be functioning again soon. We just need to prepare new plates. Please," she smiled at the gentlemen, "forgive me for insisting you trip over here still tied together, all for naught."

"These things happen on occasion," Nathan said. "No apology necessary."

"Certainly, Miss Caldwell," a few of the gentlemen echoed.

John Smythe huffed, but refrained from comment, and Nathan's mother and sisters hurried to remove the ties binding the various legs together.

Nathan looked at Eva, who had removed the plate holder from the camera and flipped it open to reveal a notable absence of a prepared collodion plate. He knew from watching her work on more than one occasion that Sammy would have prepared the plate in a solution of silver nitrate in the darkroom for fifteen minutes before sliding it into the plate holder. Once the holder was inserted into the proper camera compartment, the plate was released, and the holder could be withdrawn. That she now flipped open the holder was a clear sign she'd known something was wrong; if the plate had still been inside, exposure to the light would have ruined it.

Nathan's mother's friends, Mrs. Larsen and Mrs. Parkin, joined Eva at the camera, as well as several of the other young ladies. He couldn't hear what was said, especially as Franklin Frampton, who was still attached to Nathan's leg, guffawed at a comment from one of the others. Blanche Parker had subtly woven her way through the group of ladies and now stood next to Eva.

Eva looked sharply at Blanche, and her response was delivered through a tight smile. Nathan felt a heaviness in the pit of his stomach. Would Miss Parker be so petty as to sabotage Eva's equipment? He impatiently answered his own question; of course, she would. She had tried to entrap him once in a compromising position and he knew of her conniving firsthand.

If she had tampered with Eva's belongings and he found proof of it, he would insist Miss Parker be escorted home immediately.

He was finally free of his partner and shook Franklin's hand amiably before making his way to Eva.

A tall young woman named Inez Shelton, with a head of thick, curly hair and friendly eyes, now stood next to Eva since Blanche and Mathilda had moved away to speak with Nathan's mother. As he neared the camera, he heard Miss Shelton say to Eva, " . . . cannot be certain, there were so many people about, but I do not remember seeing them with us at the finishing line." Inez touched Eva's arm. "I am sorry; I hope you will tell us if there is anything we can do to help."

Miss Shelton glanced at Blanche and Mathilda, and then back again. "Louisa might remember—I believe she was standing on this side of the lawn."

Another young lady, blonde and petite, joined the conversation, her voice quiet. "I cannot say who may have been over here by the camera, but I do know *certain ladies* did not pass by me to watch the race at the finishing line." Her lips thinned. "The blame may fall on your young assistant, Miss Caldwell, and I should hate to see that happen. He was most careful in bringing the equipment from the carriage to the camera. Just here, he set down a carrying tray bearing two of those." She pointed at the empty plate holder Eva had rested atop the camera.

Eva nodded. "Thank you, Miss Wilhite. I appreciate your vote of confidence in Sammy." She shrugged and managed a small smile. "I shall get to the bottom of the matter."

Nathan cast an eye about the people gathered on the lawn. Blanche and Mathilda chatted with John Smythe now, sharing something apparently humorous. Mathilda glanced over at the camera and Eva twice, but the other two did not. George Abernathy, having been freed from his temporary imprisonment with John, was taking instructions from Nathan's mother.

After Eva's demonstration for some of the guests earlier, she had spoken with Nathan and explained to him that when she and Sammy were not utilizing the darkroom carriage, the vehicle was locked and secure. He had relented, dismissing George Abernathy from his post at the darkroom and sending word to the staff that he wanted the carriage watched only if he or Eva requested it. Now, however, someone had apparently tampered with the equipment, although it didn't seem to have happened at the carriage.

"If you please, ladies and gentlemen!" Nathan's mother clapped her hands for attention. "Let us enjoy a game of croquet before our afternoon picnic. I have each of your names placed in this basket, and Grace will be my assistant in drawing random pairings for teams."

Nathan circled around to Grace and the basket, and whispered, "If you draw my name or Eva's, set it aside. We shall miss this activity."

She nodded and looked over at the camera. "Did someone intentionally cause mischief?"

"I do not know yet. I must speak with Eva and Sammy alone."

As he passed the mixture of guests who now gathered around his mother and Grace, he heard a feminine voice murmur, "What does one expect when allowing a street urchin near valuable equipment? Did you know her *cousin* brought that boy home from *Whitechapel* last year? To live in their house!" The group shifted and moved as Grace began drawing names, but Nathan could guess who the speaker had been.

Eva was securing the camera and equipment, her brow creased in a frown, when Nathan returned to her side.

"Tell me what you are thinking," he said quietly.

She shook her head, pursing her lips. "Sammy didn't lose the plates." She closed the camera's protective box and fastened the straps. "He had just finished the silver nitrate bath and secured them in the holders."

"Where did you send Sammy?"

"To the kitchen. He's understandably distraught." Eva looked around. "I must speak with him, but I do not want to leave the camera."

"I can carry everything to the carriage where it would be securely locked," he offered.

She shook her head. "I'll be photographing the picnic."

He looked at the staff still working outside and spied George Abernathy. He signaled to the young man and, when he jogged over, told him to stand watch over the equipment and not leave it unattended.

The footman nodded. "Yes, sir."

Nathan took Eva's elbow. "Let's speak with your assistant. My guess is he's found a sweet roll."

CHAPTER 13

Eva's heart beat quickly as she and Nathan sat at a large table in the kitchen with Sammy, who stared glumly at the tea cake Mrs. Snow had placed on a plate in front of him. Mrs. Snow seemed torn between shock that the boy wasn't wolfing down the treat and shock that Mr. Winston was sitting in the kitchen.

"Tell me exactly what happened, from the beginning," Eva said to Sammy.

He sighed. "I prepared the plates in the carriage, watched the timepiece for fifteen minutes, put the plates in the plate holders. Two of 'em. Carried everything outside an' set it down next to the tripod." He swallowed, but bravely met first her eyes and then Nathan's. "Stepped away to see who would win the race. Left the things alone, an' someone took the plates. It's my fault." He paused. "I fink it was the ghost."

"Ghost?" Eva looked at Nathan, who raised his brows in clear surprise.

"I wasn't aware we had a ghost here," Nathan said. "Mrs. Snow, are you acquainted with a ghost?"

"No, sir." To the woman's credit, she kept a straight face.

"Sammy," Eva began, "I understand—"

He shook his head. "Nay, Miss Eva. There's a ghost. I saw it in the picture."

"Sammy, you know sometimes images blur; we've seen it happen before."

"I am tellin' ya, it's not the same fing. It's in the picture we printed today."

Eva frowned. "Which one?"

"The supper one."

"You see a ghost in the supper picture?" Nathan asked. "In the room?"

He shook his head. "In the window."

Nathan slowly straightened in his seat and looked at Eva. "Where is the picture?"

"I printed three today during the demonstration. Two of them are in the carriage and one I gave to your mother. I believe she left it on the mantel in the parlor."

The three of them stood as one and left the kitchen in single file. Eva followed Nathan's long stride down the corridor and around to the parlor. She heard Sammy trotting behind her, but it was the only sound in the hall. Her heart thudded as she remembered the blur of a person she'd seen in the conservatory window the night before and the footprints outside Nathan had discovered.

They entered the parlor and found the picture sitting where Mrs. Winston had left it on the mantelpiece. Nathan grabbed it and Eva looked over his shoulder. Sammy hurried to Nathan's other side and pointed to one of the dining room windows in the far right of the photograph.

"There! See? That's a face."

Eva squinted at the spot, and she grabbed Nathan's sleeve.

"That does look like a face," she murmured. "Have you a magnifying glass?"

He quickly found one in a side table and crossed the room to the windows for better light. The laughter and bustle outside in the garden beyond seemed far away. Eva waited for Nathan to examine the photograph before finally losing patience and holding out her hand for the items.

He gave her the picture and magnifying glass, and as she angled for a good view of the corner of the photograph, she asked Nathan, "Do you recognize him?" To her frustration, there clearly seemed to be a person looking into the room from the outside, but he was illuminated only by the light from within the room, and most of his face was in the shadows.

Nathan shook his head. "I believe you are correct, Sammy, that someone was outside. I do not think it's a ghost, however." He smiled slightly and ruffled the boy's hair. "You may put your mind at ease about that."

"Don' know if that's better," the boy admitted dubiously. "Who's lookin' in the windows at night?"

"Who, indeed?" Eva kept looking through the glass as though expecting the face to come into focus, to step into better light. She handed the items back to Nathan, who studied them again.

"Can the image be enlarged, Eva?"

She shook her head. "I could make a bigger image, but I do not believe it would be of benefit. The face will still be blurred and shadowed. My ability to focus happens only through the camera itself, at the moment the subjects are posed for the picture."

Nathan patted the window seat, and Eva sat down, her mind spinning. He took a seat next to her and motioned to Sammy, who moved to stand beside him.

"Now that we've determined there is no ghost, I still wonder who might have taken the plates during the three-legged race. Do you remember anyone hovering nearby?"

"Lots of people, but nobody I know."

"So, maids, footmen? Party guests?"

"Yes, all of those."

"When did you notice the plates were gone?"

He scrunched his nose. "When I went back to the camera after the race an' picked up the holder. Wasn't heavy enough. I thought maybe I forgot and already loaded the plate in place, but it wasn't in the camera. Picked up the other holder, an' that was too light, too."

Nathan nodded, lost in thought.

Eva knew he had worked with her enough to remember that the plate holder couldn't be directly opened anywhere but the darkroom. Only after the picture had been taken and the plate inserted back into the holder, returned to the darkroom, and processed with chemicals could the plate safely see outdoor light. Sammy didn't have the option of opening the holders to see if the plates were still inside. Eva had drilled that into him from the beginning of his tenure as her assistant, and, true to form, he hadn't disobeyed her directive. She had been the one to open the holders herself after the three-legged race when Sammy had told her the plates were missing.

She sighed. "The plates are definitely gone."

"I did everything right," Sammy said, scuffing his shoe against the rug.

"I believe you, Sammy. I know you did." She smiled at him and took his hand, giving it a squeeze. "Someone took the plates as a joke. To be funny."

"'S not funny." He scowled. "Takes lots of work and wasted collodion."

"I know, dear. It wasn't a very good joke. From now on, we shall make certain we have a third set of eyes working with us at all times, even in the house. Perhaps Detective Winston can spare one of the footmen. George, or Collins, perhaps. That will help us feel more secure as we are working."

Sammy nodded. "Sorry, Miss Eva. I shouldn't have left the 'quipment, even to watch a race."

Eva shook her head. "This is not your fault. You have nothing to be sorry for. We have never had someone steal from us, and so we were surprised by it."

"More importantly, did you see me win the race?" Nathan asked Sammy.

He nodded, allowing a small grin and one dimple to show. "Good show, sir."

"Thank you, Master Samuel. Unless Miss Eva requires your help immediately, I suggest you return to the kitchen and eat that delectable pastry before Mrs. Snow offers it to someone else."

Sammy nodded, and his thin shoulders relaxed. "Thank you, sir." He turned to Eva and asked, "May I?"

"You may. I shall send for you when the time comes to photograph the tea."

He offered her a quick head bow and ran from the room. The sound of his footsteps gradually faded and then the room was silent, save the activity still happening outside.

Eva turned to Nathan, who was studying the bustle beyond the windows. His lips were pursed in thought, and she recognized the state he often entered when working on a case.

"Do you believe the 'ghost' is Mr. Toole?" she asked.

He frowned, still observing the activity out on the lawn. He rose and put his hands in his pockets, and looking at his profile, Eva was struck for the hundredth time at how handsome she found him. He kept his dark blond hair short, and his eyes, reflecting the light from outside, were gold. He had a strong jaw, was tall, and had a broad set to his shoulders.

He and Michael Baker were quite the pair when on assignment; they were formidable and professional, and their personalities played off one another effectively. The two of them together usually elicited responses from people they questioned, and while Eva doubted the house party would be the scene of a full-blown investigation, she knew Nathan felt an extra boost of confidence when Michael was with him. If matters escalated, she wouldn't be surprised to see Nathan request a visit from Michael.

"The man in the photo could be Toole," he said, rubbing a hand along his jaw, "but I've only ever known him with heavy facial hair, and that was at a distance. If he shaved, I'd have a much harder time of it." He looked at Eva and smiled. "An odd twist to a Seaside house party, is it not?"

"What fun would it be otherwise?" She smiled back at him. "We might become bored, and that would never do."

"I am sorry about your camera being knocked over, and the missing plates. My initial supposition was that Miss Parker and Miss Dilworth had taken them. Would they know how to do that, though?"

Eva shrugged and rose from the window seat, scanning the activity outside. "I believe Miss Dilworth was among the group earlier when I demonstrated the mechanics of the whole process. She might remember."

The croquet game had been set up, and the guests laughed and chatted as they took turns hitting their ball with a mallet. Blanche Parker appeared to be paired with Burton Handy, and

Eva winced for the gentleman. She'd learned through gossip at breakfast that Mr. Handy harbored a *tendre* for Blanche Parker, and Eva figured the sooner he could set aside his adoration, the better he would be. Blanche was highly unlikely to entertain any sort of attention from him beyond the minimum required for social niceties. Even that much wasn't a guarantee, as she was learning firsthand.

"He may have money, though," she mused aloud.

"Who?"

"Oh." She glanced at Nathan with a laugh. "Mr. Handy. Did you know he secretly admires the elder Miss Parker?"

He nodded, his lips in a half smile. "I believe everyone here is aware of that, which makes me pity the man all the more. He is a decent fellow and deserving of a woman who would appreciate him." He nodded. "And yes, he does have money. Third son of a baronet with an inheritance from his recently passed maternal grandmother. I presume you are thinking that might induce her to consider him in a more serious light?"

"I suggest that is the *only* thing that would induce her to consider him in a more serious light. He is much too nice and unassuming for her."

He eyed her askance, and, after locking eyes with Eva, stated, "I understand you set her quite effectively in her place this morning."

"I did. Must maintain our pretense, mustn't we?" She raised a brow at him.

His half smile was back. "Of course, of course. I am glad you honor our charade so thoroughly."

"Do I detect a note of cynicism, Detective?"

"Oh, never! No, indeed. You are a very good and loyal friend to remember the most crucial element of this entire gathering is to keep me safe from the wolves. Your acting abilities are to be commended."

"As are yours, good sir."

"I am not acting." He held her gaze, maintained his pleasant expression.

With his hands in his pockets and her arms folded, she imagined they resembled fighters at a standoff. She opened her mouth to retort back that she was not acting either, but the words wouldn't come out. They were true, but she did not dare utter them. As soon as she did, there would be no taking them back. She wasn't ready.

"Is that so?" she said instead.

"Just so." He turned his attention back to the window. "If I did not believe you would have an attack of the vapors, I would pen a letter to your father this very day."

"I do *not* have attacks of the vapors!" She faced him fully. "What a ridiculous thing to say to me. I am the least fainting sort of woman of your acquaintance, corset notwithstanding! I photograph murdered people!"

"You do," he agreed, turning to face her as well. "And I posit that you would rather photograph murdered people than voice the truth of the matter."

Her eyes widened, and she felt herself edging toward genuine indignation. "What is the 'truth of the matter,' then, Detective?"

He stepped closer to her, and she fought to stand her ground. "The truth of the matter, my dear Evangeline, is that your affection for me grows daily, and if ever there was a man you might consider as a suitor, it is I."

She felt herself sway toward him, just the tiniest of fractions closer, as though he were a magnet pulling her in. His eyes searched hers, traveled over her face, her hair, and she wished he would take his hands from his pockets and touch her cheek. He would slowly pull her into his arms and kiss her, helping her forget fully every unpleasant thing she had ever known. Unbidden, her eyelids drifted down to his neck, the skin she had brushed against when she tied his cravat, the hollow of his throat she knew lay just behind the fabric covering it.

"It appears as though the croquet game is finishing," he said quietly, and he turned his attention back to the window. He didn't step away from her, though, and if she took a deep enough breath, she would brush up against him. He looked back down at her with a smile. "We had best prepare for the tea. I'll assist you with the photography process this time—suppose we allow Sammy to enjoy his pastries for the afternoon."

Sammy? She blinked. Who was Sammy?

"I'll tell him and then meet you at the portable darkroom." He smiled, and confound it if he didn't look smug! He moved away from her, breaking the intimate spell, and headed for the door. "Ten minutes." He glanced back and her and then disappeared, his footsteps echoing down the corridor, along with a softly whistled tune. As it carried back to her in the parlor, she realized it was the melody to a popular love song, "Come and Meet Me, Rosa Darling."

She gasped a quiet laugh and put her hand over her mouth. He was, she realized, stealthy. He was launching a slow assault on her senses, breaking down her reserve, and trying to pull from her the things she was too afraid to admit. He would be patient, and dogged, just as he was in every aspect of his life. He was a determined man, and he did not quit.

Her heart beat a steady thrum in her chest, and the last of the whistled tune faded away. She hoped she was right. She hoped he wouldn't give up on her. His intentions now, if they hadn't been before, were clear. She just was not certain she could be brave enough to take the leap.

Nathan went outside, making a pretense of checking on the croquet game. He approached the dining room window and studied the ground, stepping between two plants. He exhaled quietly at the sight of definite impressions in the soft soil— shoes, clearly belonging to a man. Whoever it had been had walked along the length of the window and then stopped.

Thoughtful, he straddled the prints' final position and peered inside the window, wondering what the watcher had hoped to see. He squinted against the glare of the sun and cupped his eyes for a better view. The object of the "ghost's" attention could have been anyone, but it was with sinking clarity that Nathan recognized the spot where Eva had sat. Another glance at the ground had his heart beating in his throat. With the toe of his shoe, he nudged a single black feather sitting ominously against the dark earth.

"Winston! Looking to steal the silver later on?"

Nathan turned at Franklin Frampton's teasing, forcing himself to chuckle as he made his way out of the bushes. He left the feather untouched. "You've caught me in the act," he said, smiling and hoping it made him look carefree. He'd a sneaking suspicion it did not. Someone was playing games with him, and he felt the truth of it sink like a stone in his gut.

CHAPTER 14

The guests arrived at the beach later that evening to enjoy a bonfire and sit by the water. Camp chairs and tables were situated in groupings, and a few sturdy blankets had been spread on the ground for those who preferred to stretch out.

As Nathan was strung tighter than a bow, he dearly wished he could take a quick swim to work away his tension. He had talked with the staff directly following the picnic earlier in the day, but nobody seemed to know anything about Eva's missing photography plates. Additionally, he tasked Stafford with doubling perimeter security around the house when night fell; that someone was able to sneak around unnoticed did not sit well with him.

Sammy had been ill, furthering Nathan's delay to the beach. The boy must have eaten his weight in sweet rolls; Nathan could think of no other reason for him to have become so violently ill. Nathan had cared for Sammy himself, not wanting to add another burden to Eva's stressful day. After drinking the water Nathan had plied him with and losing the contents of a day's worth of food in his stomach, Sammy had finally settled down to an early evening's sleep.

Perhaps causing most of his tension, however, was Eva. He

had assisted her with the photography process at the picnic and working alongside her had been both sublime and frustrating. More times than he could count, he'd wanted to run with her behind a tree and kiss her senseless. The web he'd impulsively woven around her in the parlor had snared him as well, and he'd known then he could have kissed her. He wouldn't rush the matter, though, couldn't risk it. She couldn't even admit aloud that her affection for him was growing; he could only imagine the progress they would lose if he kissed her too soon.

He made himself busy, adding wood to the small fire. The stretch of beach fell within their family property and wound back into an alcove where Nathan had often retreated as a convenient and quiet thinking spot. All things considered, the Seaside property was beautiful, and he was glad to have it in his life. He had to admit, the break from Town was something he'd needed. He breathed in the refreshing sea air and closed his eyes.

"Tired, Nathaniel?"

He smiled and opened his eyes to see his mother standing beside him. She was the only one who ever used his full name. His sisters had even shortened "Nathan" to "Nate," but Christine Winston remained steadfast.

"Perhaps a bit," he said and put an arm around her shoulders. "You, however, ought to be exhausted. These parties have you running from sunup to sundown and beyond."

She looked up at him with a smile. "I enjoy it. And the fundraising benefits each year are life-changing for many." She put an arm around his waist and hugged.

"I like her," she whispered.

He didn't need to ask who she referenced. "I am glad," he answered honestly. "But I do not know the extent to which her affections for me match mine for her."

Christine chuckled, and she looked up at him. "Oh, son. You clearly do not see how she looks at you. Her heart is on her sleeve. And her face, and in her hair . . ."

He laughed quietly. "I fear much of that is for show." He paused, debating whether to say his next piece. He sighed, resigned. "She agreed to pretend an affection for me in hopes that others would keep a distance."

"I know."

His eyes widened. "You *know*?"

"I knew that day at home when you told me about this supposed 'interest' you had in someone else."

He was flabbergasted. "How did you know?"

"I know you better than anyone, silly. I knew you would either admit your prevarication to me or somehow contrive events to support your claim. It did not take long to realize that the attraction between you is very much real."

He sighed. "She has been hurt, Mother, and I am not certain how best to proceed."

"Cautiously. Honestly. Patiently." She smiled. "It was not so different for your father and me."

Nathan looked at her in surprise. "I did not know."

"I was left at the altar. Rather, nearly at the altar. The day before the wedding."

"What on *earth*?"

She nodded. "My heart was broken, my pride was in tatters, and if not for your grandfather's influence, my reputation would have been ruined forever. Then I met your father, and slowly, everything changed. Became so much better than it might have been. In the end, I was grateful the first cad had left."

Nathan took a moment to absorb the stunning admission. When he found his voice, he asked, "Were you afraid?"

"When your father came into my life?"

He nodded.

"Terrified. I had decided to embrace spinsterhood and continue working with my father. Much safer for my heart if nothing else. Eventually, I grew to trust your father, and because he was patient, it worked." A shadow briefly crossed her face. "I miss him fiercely."

"I am sorry." He kissed her temple. "There are days I don't think of him except in the periphery, and somehow that's worse than missing him. I would rather miss him than forget him."

"He would be so proud of you. He *is* so proud of you." She smiled mistily. "Incidentally, all four of your sisters approve." She nodded toward the circle where Eva sat with the Winston girls. "That is a feat I never imagined possible."

"Do you have hopes for any of them with this smattering of gentlemen?" He cast a dubious eye toward the men who were tossing rocks into the water. "Handy and Jacobson are good sorts, would provide well, but I don't see them keeping pace with any of my sisters."

Christine laughed. "I had hopes for Mr. Jens Sorenson, but he has some living to do before settling down." She pursed her lips in consideration. "I am undecided. Now, Mr. Smythe is a noncontender. If one of the girls showed an interest there, I would check for high temperatures or signs of delirium."

Nathan nodded. "Naturally."

"He would not have been included on the invitation list but for his deep pockets and desire to appear generous. He donated twice the usual amount. I believe he has designs on Miss Blanche Parker, of course."

"They do seem a match made in . . . well, perhaps not

heaven, but they are a match. I wonder why they have yet to become official."

"Rumor has it," Christine said, lowering her voice further, "that Mrs. Parker is determined her daughters rise to the level of countess. Perhaps marchioness. Poor Ann does her best to distance herself from both her sister and her mother. I do feel bad for her." She indicated her head farther down the beach. "The remainder of the ladies here are lovely—I believe they are rallying around young Ann."

Christine gave him a squeeze. "I must mingle. I propose you take a stroll down the beach to the alcove with a certain photographer."

"Mother, surely you jest. A walk alone, unchaperoned?" He grinned.

"Only if you intend to marry her. Otherwise, please leave her untarnished. On second thought, best to stay in clear view. Some of our guests would delight in sullying her good name. You would be branded a cad, but *she* would lose everything."

"The scales do not quite balance."

She patted his chest. "Why do you suppose I support so many suffragette causes?"

He thoughtfully watched his mother make her way among her guests, chatting, offering refreshment, putting them at ease. He was fortunate, and well aware of it. He had a smart mother.

Darkness eventually fell, rendering the ocean a black expanse and the firelight the brightest spot on the beach. Christine had small lanterns placed on the camp tables near the chairs, and many of the guests lingered as the night continued. Blanche,

Mathilda, and John Smythe pleaded fatigue early and returned to the house with the intention of taking tea in the parlor where the seating was "more conducive to comfortable lounging." Mrs. Parkin and Mrs. Larsen, both a few years Christine's senior, exchanged glances and made comments regarding the irony of their remaining behind with the "young folk" despite their advanced age.

Following the others' departure, the immediate change in the air amongst the guests was palpable. It was as though the entire group relaxed as one. It wasn't long before songs broke out, and at Nathan's direction, the clarinet from the conservatory was delivered to Franklin Frampton. For his part, Frampton was a good sport and shared a variety of songs—surprisingly well played—even without the promised bottle of whiskey as an aperitif.

Nathan watched Eva as she conversed with the others, easily drawing in the shyer female guests and handling the flirtatious Swede with humored ease. Nathan joined in conversation with others sporadically but realized more than once he preferred the pastime of staring at Eva Caldwell like a lovesick fool. He found himself apologizing for the third time to Davis Jacobson, who was sharing details of the most recent professional journal issue of the Society of Avid Amateur Arborists. ("Treble-A, we like to call it!")

"Frampton," Nathan now called across the circle, "do you know the American tune, 'Come and Meet Me, Rosa Darling'?"

"Of course! I do not know it well enough to play on the clarinet, however."

"We shall sing it then," Nathan's sister Olivia said, her eyes twinkling at him. "It was all the rage five years ago, but hopefully we will remember the lyrics." She began the first verse, and most of the guests joined in.

Franklin fumbled his way through the melody line, eventually doing a passable job accompanying by picking out harmonies that worked well enough. The group mostly laughed their way through the first verse, and Nathan, while not a soloist by any means, joined in on the chorus.

Come and meet me, Rosa darling, when the evening
*   shadows fall,*
I'll be waiting near the arbor by the lonely garden wall.

He caught Eva's eye, and to her credit, she held his gaze until they began the second verse and she broke the contact.

There I'll tell you, Rosa darling, while the merry crickets
*   sing,*
How I fondly love you dearest, and the joy your glances
*   bring;*
There I'll offer tender kisses to those lips of rosy hue,
While the purest love-light sparkles in your hazel eyes
*   so true.*

Excepting the "hazel eyes" part, everything else fit. Eva sang along with the others, finally looking at him again as they repeated the chorus, and the song ended with laughter and applause.

"Why, Nate, you romantic!" Delilah, sitting next to Nathan, elbowed him. "Next you'll tell us that you've seen *The Pirates of Penzance* more than the one obligatory time we compelled you to take us to the Opera Comique."

He nodded once. "As it happens, I have returned to the theatre since and have watched that very play twice more." He glanced over at Eva with a grin. "Once was when my partner,

Detective Baker, and Amelie—Eva's cousin—were engaged. Amelie twisted Michael's arm, so we all went."

"And the other?" Delilah pressed.

He cleared his throat. "I went . . ." He trailed off.

"You went?"

"I went by myself." He held up a hand at the eruption of laughter that rang into the night. "I wanted to be certain it had indeed been suitable for my sisters to attend."

"*After* we had attended it? *With you?*" Delilah doubled over, and he scowled at the group, mostly his sisters, who laughed so much they wiped away tears.

He was unable to maintain the faux irritation for long and smiled ruefully at Eva, who wiped away tears of her own. She shook her head at him, still laughing, and he decided he'd watch the silly play a dozen times over if it made her happy.

Miss Shelton suggested a song from the play, and Franklin happily took up the cause. His mother, Mrs. Larsen, and Mrs. Parkin rose, making quiet apologies about finally turning in. Nathan stood and moved away from the warmth of the fire, meeting his mother at the base of the stairs leading up to the house.

"Shall I have the gentlemen help tear down camp when this thing dies down?" He glanced over his shoulder with a smile. "I've a feeling some of our guests are feeling lively enough to last for hours."

"Three footmen have been instructed to bring up anything that would blow away in a stiff wind, and the rest will be cleared in the morning."

"What a good boy you are," Mrs. Parkin said. "Always was a responsible one."

"That is very true." Christine reached up, and he bent down

so she could kiss his cheek. "I need not worry with this one around."

Nathan rolled his eyes but winked at Christine's two friends, who had been by her side for decades, through thick and thin. As they departed, however, Christine's last comment rang in his ears, and he hoped his mother wouldn't have reason to worry.

He strolled back to the group and caught Eva's eye. He gestured with his head toward the stretch of beach behind him and was glad when she quietly excused herself to join him. The singing continued, laughter rang in the air, and despite present dangers, he was actually glad to be at the party.

"My goodness," Eva said, pulling a shawl around her shoulders, "I've not enjoyed songs around a bonfire for some time."

He held his elbow out and she took it as they began strolling along the water's edge. "When was the last time you did so?"

"Oh, mercy. I would say at least three years; I attended the autumn fete at home with my parents and became reacquainted with friends I'd not seen for some time. It was altogether lovely, except for one moment when a boy I'd known since childhood lured me behind one of the vendor carts and attempted to kiss me." She looked at him, smiling, and a soft breeze blew curls away from her face. The moonlight bathed her in a glow that made her face shine and her hair gleam blue-black. "I might not have been so angry with him had he not tried to push matters further. He was quite a bit larger than I, and he tried to pull me down a side street."

Nathan frowned. "Rather makes me want to plant my fist in his face."

"Oh, but you see, I was able to handle the matter without having to scream for help. Aunt Sally taught my cousins and me when we were quite young about what to do in such situations."

"And what did you do?"

"I kicked him squarely between the legs." She nodded once, fiercely.

He barked out a laugh, nodding his approval. "Excellent! I am assuming he then doubled over and you ran back to the crowd of festival goers."

"Precisely." She sighed. "I might have understood his motivation had I been the least bit encouraging of his attention. It didn't seem to matter to him."

"Some are rather thickheaded that way. I certainly hope I never make that mistake."

She looked surprised. "With me?"

He nodded.

She laughed. "You needn't concern yourself on that score. Your attention is never unwelcomed." She glanced at him as she said the words, and were it not for the low light, he wondered if he'd see a blush.

He felt a sense of relief settle into his chest. "I am glad to hear it."

She laughed through her nose and shook her head. "As though you didn't know."

"We have agreed to pretend an affection for one another, and I am leery of mistaking the act for truth."

She looked at him again, so beautiful she took his breath away. "I believe, Detective, that in some things, you know me better than I know myself."

He forced himself to keep walking. "It really is only fair that I tell you in advance; I will kiss you at some point."

Her lips twisted in a coy smile. "Will you, now?"

"I sincerely hope the moment will be right, and I'll not be a recipient of Aunt Sally's defensive maneuvers."

She laughed softly, looking at him and then away again. Her fingers had tightened on his arm, and he wondered if she realized it. As they walked, she swayed closer to his side until the fabric of her skirt blew against his leg. Had they not been walking so slowly, he realized, he probably would have tripped and taken her to the ground like he had Franklin Frampton.

She smelled divine, a subtle mixture of roses and something that was uniquely her. The urge to take her into his arms and pull her close was overwhelming, and he miraculously kept placing one foot in front of the other. The others' campfire singing grew softer in the distance as they neared the bend in the beach that led around the corner and to the alcove.

"We should stop here," he said, his voice husky, "or we'll be truly out of sight of the others."

"A pity," she whispered. "I should very much like to see what lies around the corner."

"And I would very much like to show you." He raised her ungloved hand in both of his and pressed his lips to it. "Regrettably, not tonight."

She nodded, standing close, and the gentle breeze blew an errant curl across her face. He tucked it behind her ear, his fingers lingering, barely brushing her neck, the line of her jaw.

"We should return to the others." The curl he'd tucked behind her ear drifted against her throat. He took it between two fingers and rubbed the glossy strands. "So soft," he murmured. "I don't know that I've ever seen it down."

"Likely not." Her voice was hushed and unsteady.

"Inappropriate of me to say such a thing."

She nodded. "Entirely."

"Apologies."

"Unnecessary. We are enamored of one another, are we not?"

He looked from the lock of hair, which he still held, into her eyes. "We are, are we not?"

She nodded again. "Very much so." She put her hand against his chest, and he wondered if she meant to put distance between them. She slowly curled her fingers into the fabric of his waistcoat and held it tightly. She inhaled and released the breath on a quiet, shuddering sigh.

He placed his hand over hers, and she relaxed her fist, flattening her palm against his heart.

"Nathan," she whispered, "I—"

Someone at the campfire must have shared a joke because laughter rang loudly and she blinked, pausing. He inwardly cursed the wretched timing, but the moment had passed. He closed his eyes and tipped his forehead against hers.

She sighed again and finally pulled her hand away from his chest. It slipped out from under his, and he immediately felt the loss. He wanted to grab it and place it again over his heart.

She stepped back with a shaky smile. "You're right. We should return."

He eyed her evenly for a long moment. "This is a conversation we will continue."

"I certainly hope so."

Another song from the play started, accompanied by the full-throated enthusiasm of Mr. Frampton's clarinet. Her lips turned up and she gave a small laugh. Taking his arm again, she began walking them back to the group, and he figured it was probably a good thing she had taken the lead. He'd have stood there all night if she'd let him.

She whispered something to herself, and he wasn't certain, but it sounded like the word *lethal*.

He smiled.

CHAPTER 15

The village of Seaside doubled in size during the summer months. What began as a small fishing community and a sometime getaway for the very wealthy had become more accessible to the masses with the addition of train lines and adjusted work hours. Hotels lined the tidy streets, along with shops, cafés, and a few pubs. A lending library had been established and was stocked full of a wide variety of literature, ranging from naturalist guides—complete with hand-drawn illustrations detailing local flora and fauna—to penny dreadfuls.

Vendor carts were situated along the boardwalk, as well as colorful bathing huts, and a pier extended far over the water, bearing still more shops and restaurants. Traveling bands, most consisting of six or fewer members, made their way along the beach and boardwalk, entertaining the crowds with demonstrations of the most popular tunes of the day. At the far end of the beach, a grand theatre reminiscent of something from the streets of Cairo sat majestically, ruling over her smaller neighbors with a superior eye.

Mrs. Winston's house party guests roamed in and out of shops, searching for specific items listed on a sheet of paper handed to them on their departure to the center of town. The end of the exercise was to be announced later, but Mrs. Winston was insistent that each guest find as many of the items as possible.

As they shopped, they split along familiar lines—the elder Miss Parker and Miss Dilworth strolled along with Mr. Smythe and occasionally Jens Sorenson and Peter Meyer, making little attempt at conversation with anyone else. Blanche Parker had already irritated most members of the group by her insistence that a maid redo her hair before they headed into town. She had delayed their departure by thirty minutes, leaving them to mill about either in the parlor or gardens while they waited. It was Jens Sorenson who finally suggested to Mathilda Dilworth that she hurry her friend along, and only then, when Mathilda had dragged down a disgruntled Blanche, were they able to proceed.

Eva consulted her list as she strolled along with the others. She walked three abreast with Inez Shelton and Louisa Wilhite as she read aloud, "Three lengths of ribbon, one yard each, and differing in color."

Inez pointed to the next shop on their right. "Haberdashery. They will certainly carry ribbons."

Eva looked behind them at some of the other party guests and called out, "Ribbon," pointing to the store. To the amusement of the women present, the gentlemen's lists were identical to theirs, and many of the items requested were of a decidedly feminine nature. She spied Nathan, who brought up the rear of the group, chatting frequently but continually and subtly scanning the surroundings. She knew he thought constantly of Bernard Toole and the danger he presented to the guests and family.

Eva could think of little else aside from the potential danger Nathan Winston presented to her sanity. She'd tossed and turned throughout the night, reliving those moments on the beach when they'd nearly kissed, when she'd nearly confessed her affection for him. If not interrupted by noise from the other guests—despite their distance and relative seclusion on the beach—she might have laid bare all her feelings.

His assault on her senses was relentless, and most of the time, she admitted to herself, he probably wasn't even doing it deliberately. Walking near him today, she detected subtle hints of his shaving soap. When she heard his voice, even when speaking to another about something innocuous, the timbre vibrated through her chest. He was handsome without his hat, but with it, and dressed for a day on the town—even a casual holiday town—he struck such a figure he quite took her breath away.

More often than not, when she looked for him, he was already looking at her. He would give her his half smile, even while carrying on a conversation with someone else. While walking along the boardwalk, pausing to look out at the crowd on the beach and beyond, she felt him behind her before she even turned around.

She entered the crowded haberdashery with Inez and Louisa, and they spied spools of ribbon on a counter against the wall. Before long, others in their group also entered the store, and the small space was filled with people. She drifted to the end of the counter and found herself separated from Inez and Louisa. The crush of people was becoming untenable, and she thought to make her way back out until the crowd cleared. She was trapped in the corner near the front display window where several hats for both men and women were situated to showcase their best advantage.

"*Oof*," she grunted as an elbow found its way to her midsection, and she mumbled, "Pardon me." She had resigned herself to being stuck in place until the masses shifted, when a hand grabbed her wrist and squeezed uncomfortably. She frowned and uttered a small gasp as the pressure increased. She couldn't see who was holding her, only the flash of a black sleeve and glove. Someone shoved something into her hand and closed her fingers around it firmly, and then released her.

She tried to see past one very round woman and another very tall gentleman as she lifted her hand, which still clutched what now proved to be a reticule with something inside. It clinked as she lifted it. Someone bumped against her, another someone gasped in surprise, and a gentleman uttered a disgruntled, "I say!" The bell above the shop's door rang, and Eva strained to see who exited, but her view was blocked.

The bell rang again as a few more people left, and the crush eased. She still held the strange reticule and, with no idea what was inside, was anxious to get out of the store. She threaded her way through the remaining customers, nodding absently to three Winston sisters and Ann Parker, before spying Nathan across the room. He must have seen the confusion on her face, because after she made her way outside, he soon joined her.

"What is it?" He touched her arm and leaned close.

Baffled, she looked up and down the street, not certain who she thought to see. "Someone gave me this." She lifted her hand. "Insisted I take it, actually. I couldn't see who it was, and then I think he left the store."

He put his hand on her back and they walked next door to a café offering alfresco dining. She spied a free table in the shade and back a distance from the street and indicated it to Nathan. They reached it and sat, and by now he had joined her perusal of the people strolling down the walkway.

She set the reticule on the table, afraid to open it. Nathan looked at her, and finally pulled it closer and untied the strings.

He looked inside, and a muscle in his jaw flexed. Spreading the fabric wider, he showed her two broken photography plates that had been treated and prepared for exposure. A single black feather sat atop the shards. Eva looked closely at Nathan's face; he was ghostly pale.

"Someone approached you and handed this to you?" he asked.

"No, someone shoved it into my hand." She absently rubbed her wrist, which was a bit sore. "It wasn't someone standing next to me; an arm reached through the crowd and grabbed me." She paused. "Remind me of the significance of the black feather."

His jaw tightened, and he looked down at the reticule. In a low voice, he told her, "A black feather is the signature symbol of the Toole Family Carnival. Part of the logo seen on the caravans, their merchandise."

She drew in a breath, a sense of dread settling upon her. "So perhaps it wasn't an angry guest who did this. I'd assumed it was one of those who've taken a dislike to me."

"If it were someone other than Toole, someone whose help he might have enlisted," he said quietly, "a guest or other staff, he may not have had the foresight to avoid leaving evidence of the crime. It was done in a rush, and sometimes people make mistakes. I'll take a closer look at this when we return to the house."

She looked absently at the crowd passing by and noted several of their party who had finished their purchases in the haberdashery.

Ann Parker passed by, unaware Eva was watching. She laughed together with Inez and Louisa, and then Franklin Frampton and Davis Jacobson added to the conversation as they trailed along behind the women.

Across the street, she noted the Mean Ladies (so dubbed by Alice) themselves, exiting a flower shop. Both women were carrying a small bundle of flowers, and both looked back with smiles at John Smythe as he exited the shop behind them. Jens Sorenson and Peter Meyer, who had also been in the haberdashery, now called to the threesome and jogged across the street to join them, with Burton Handy on their heels.

"Sammy didn't eat breakfast this morning," she said, chewing on her lip. "After his illness through the night, I'm growing concerned." Eva felt her eyes burning with unshed tears. She swallowed and cleared her throat.

"He was much improved this morning," Nathan said quietly. "If he hadn't been, I was prepared to send for the doctor. I still will, if you wish it."

Eva managed a smile. "You're an angel to have cared for him so. I wish you'd have told me and saved yourself the trouble."

"It was no trouble. I quite like my new valet assistant." He smiled as he said it, but Eva wondered if the lines around his eyes were due to fatigue or worry.

"The others will wonder where we are." Nathan tied the reticule and gestured to a shopping bag carrying a few of the items Eva had purchased from the list. "Suppose we put this in your bag with the rest of your things?"

"Where are *your* things, incidentally? Have you not been shopping?"

"Of course, I have," he hedged. "My purchases are with Franklin's."

"Mr. Frampton is carrying your bag?"

"He very politely offered, and I very politely accepted."

She narrowed her eyes. "Has he also been making the

purchases for you? We were all given specific instructions, Mr. Winston."

"I was with him at every purchase."

"What color ribbons did you purchase?"

He chewed on the inside of his lip. "Blue."

"Pshaw. You do not even know. I am going to tell your mother that you let your friends do all the work for you."

She shook her head as they stood. He was entirely unrepentant. She looked down at the table and saw the black reticule, and every bit of levity she'd tried to throw into the conversation fell back flat. She reluctantly opened the shopping bag, and Nathan carefully placed the reticule inside. She sighed and looked at him, feeling like the world was spinning out of control.

"What sort of gentleman would I be if I did not offer to carry this for you?" He smiled at her, but it was strained.

She sucked in a breath and stood, smiling and hoping hers was more convincing than his had been. "But, Detective, what sort of message would that send to curious onlookers?"

This time, he grinned. "Exactly the sort of message I hope to send. A gentleman carrying his lady's purchases."

His words sent a thrill through her. "To facilitate our charade, of course," she murmured.

He eyed her askance as he held out his hand for her to precede him away from the café. He then rested his hand comfortably on her back, leaned close to her ear, and whispered, "What do you think?"

CHAPTER 16

The guests finally finished their shopping and returned to the house. The rest of the day consisted of afternoon tea, a later supper, and games in the drawing room for those seeking to extend the day. Deciding to spend some time writing a letter for her cousins that could be sent with the morning post, Eva retired to her room earlier than the others, keeping Sammy close. To her relief, the color had returned to his cheeks, and he'd even managed to eat some bread and cheese for supper.

When morning dawned, Eva did not feel refreshed in the least. Memories of the odd occurrence at the haberdashery the day before dogged her thoughts. Energy buzzed through her like a swarm of bees; she jumped at her own shadow, wondering who might grab her, unseen.

Who on earth had returned the plates to her in such an odd fashion? If Toole had actually been there, in the shop, wouldn't Nathan have noticed him? Perhaps not, as the store had been packed full of people, and he'd admitted not knowing what the man looked like clean-shaven and with neatly trimmed hair. Was the intent to frighten her? She readily admitted it had worked. When Sammy and then Amelie had been abducted the year before, it had shattered her sense of peace and belief that she and her loved ones lived a relatively charmed existence that was untouched by the harsher realities of life. The truth proved to be far more complicated. Nobody was ever immune from misfortune.

In the sitting room, she found a note from the maid, Mary, that she would be along shortly. Eva rolled her eyes—not at Mary, but at the reason Mary had been obliged to leave the note. Yesterday morning, Mary had confided to Eva that Miss Blanche and Miss Mathilda, despite bringing their own maids along, kept her and two other maids busy helping them instead of seeing to other guests. Apparently, they needed an entire entourage of help. Eva decided not to tell Mary that Alice had dubbed the two women the "Mean Ladies," because she was determined to remain professional. She was sorely tempted, though, as she knew the young woman would appreciate it. Irritation took root, the sort that Eva usually kept at bay. She had a very long fuse, the patience of Job, but *sometimes* . . .

Eva's morning routine was uncomplicated, and she managed it well enough on her own. She designed a simple coiffure, pinning braids into place, and spritzed a light mist of rose water in the air around her head. As she still had a few minutes remaining, she sat at the vanity in the beautifully decorated Blue Room and trimmed her nails and cuticles.

While she worked, she tried to reason why the plates had been thrust upon her in the haberdashery. At first, she'd figured that whoever had given her the plates yesterday was someone associated with the house party—that narrowed the field somewhat. But the black feather was, according to Nathan, Bernard Toole's signature symbol.

She sighed and looked at her reflection in the vanity mirror. Her brow was tight in a frown, and dark circles under her eyes were proof of a restless night's sleep. She opened some cosmetic powder Aunt Sally had given the girls at Christmas ("I found it in Vienna; the benefit, my dears, is that it's formulated to provide the lightest of touches; nobody will mistake you for a theatre harlot . . .") and dabbed it on her skin, smoothing and concealing the discoloration. Eva was impressed; she'd had rare occasion to use the cosmetic but saw the appeal. It worked like a charm.

She pinched her cheeks to provide a bit of healthy color and made an earnest effort to smooth away her frown. The furrow between her brows disappeared and she offered herself a smile. There. Perfectly normal. Just another day at a house party where anyone might be guilty of crimes large or small.

She frowned at a small drawer in the vanity, where one of her hair ribbons trailed out. She opened the drawer, and her breath quickened at the sight of her small jewelry pouch--it was open, contents scattered.

She pulled the drawer out completely and rifled through it, putting things back into the pouch. She breathed a sigh of relief when she realized nothing was missing.

"Losing my mind," she muttered. She must have been in a hurry earlier in searching for the right accessories. "Absolutely losing my mind." She replaced the drawer and tidied the vanity's surface.

With a final glance in the mirror, she stood and fluffed her skirt, arranging the folds until everything fell just so. She was edgy, her mood still unruffled, and didn't know if it was a result of the reticule strangeness, irritation over the Mean Ladies and their obnoxious Mr. Smythe, or a mad desire to shove Detective Nathaniel Winston into a pantry and kiss him senseless herself rather than wait in anticipation for him to do it. She felt everything gathering inside like a summer storm.

Truly, she groused as she grabbed her reticule—one containing a handkerchief, not smashed photography equipment—and the bag containing the purchases from the day before, and left the bedchamber, crossing the sitting room and then exiting into the hallway. *The anticipation is driving me mad. What is he waiting for? An engraved invitation?* A tiny stream of logic tried to thread its way into her thoughts, but she immediately snapped it in half.

The restless bees she'd had buzzing through her when she awoke now became bees in her bonnet. Her irritation grew until she fairly marched the distance to the landing at the top of the stairs. She stopped short when she saw Nathan, who leaned against the railing, hands in his pockets, looking altogether too handsome.

She scowled. "Hello."

He straightened in surprise. "Is something wrong?"

Yes, everything is off-kilter, and I am annoyed. I prefer my life well ordered. "Nothing beyond the usual. Nothing new." She waved her hand and continued toward the stairs. "I am well; everything is fine. God's in His heaven and all is as it should be."

"*What?* Eva, what is the matter?" He scrambled to keep pace with her as she descended the stairs, one hand gripping the railing as she went.

She glanced at him sideways. "Why do you suppose something is the matter? Am I not allowed to occasionally awaken out of sorts? Little, perfectly calm Eva has her moments of irritation, just like the rest of the world, Detective."

"Eva, wait!" He stopped one step below her and touched her arm. She glared at the spot where his fingers rested on her sleeve. He withdrew his hand and took an audible breath. "When we parted last night, you were not angry. I am concerned about why you seem to be now. Is Sammy ill again?"

"Sammy is fine." She met his beautiful golden eyes, which were now at her level because she stood one step up. She managed to think objectively, for future reference, that such was not bad placement. She could throw her arms around his neck and be on equal footing. What she intended to do after that, she did not know.

"The confluence of events over recent days has left me feeling a bit out of sorts. I did not intend for you to bear the brunt of my frustration." As he was part of the frustration, that was only marginally true.

"How can I help alleviate it?"

She looked at him evenly, her lips firming. "You cannot."

"If you need to leave the party, Eva, I will make arrangements for it immediately—"

Her nostrils flared. "I do not wish to leave the party, Nathan."

"Then tell me what I can do to fix this!"

"You cannot fix everything!"

Voices sounded from the hallway behind them.

His eyes widened and he leaned closer. "What do you want?"

She mimicked his action, leaning in. "I do not know!" She was winded, as though from running. That was the problem, she supposed. She didn't know exactly what she wanted from him. She knew he was not the same as the foolish young man who had jilted her years ago. She did not worry that he would be faithless. She wanted definition, though—a clear path forward. The only way she could maintain her unruffled sense of calm was to know exactly where she was headed. Now, with a madman from Nathan's past possibly lurking outside the windows, the timing seemed extraordinarily bad to be obsessing over her possible romantic future.

Nathan pulled back first, clearing his throat and offering her his arm, glancing pointedly at some of the other guests who were rounding the corner to descend. She sucked in a breath as deep as her corset would allow and took his arm. They walked down the stairs at a much more sedate pace, and Eva put her smile back on.

"I agree," she now said with some volume. "I am also curious about your mother's plans! I cannot begin to imagine what they might be. She *is* your mother. Surely you must have an idea?"

He shook his head. "She moves in mysterious ways, my mother. I've not a clue." He shrugged and smiled at her as they reached the hall, his eyes still bewildered.

Eva was certain she would feel badly for her outburst, but that would come later. She was working her way toward brutal honesty in her head, and she needed the clarity of it. She was in love with Nathaniel Winston. They had danced around the attraction to each other for nearly a year, but beyond that, she liked who he was as a person. Their interests were similar, she valued his insights, and she was content conversing with him for hours. That had happened on a few occasions, and she'd left each encounter with him exhilarated and thoughtful. Had their acquaintance moved any more quickly, had they been nothing more than friends in the beginning, she would have run far and fast from it.

Now, however, her patience seemed to have snapped. As they continued their way to the parlor, she realized that as long as she was on her journey for truth, she must admit that her loss of patience was aimed at herself, not Nathan. She had required time to get to know him, and whether he had been aware of that or not, he'd given it to her. Now that she had made a decision, had come to the realization that she didn't panic with him, she trusted him, she *wanted* him, she was tired of waiting. She knew a sense of urgency; she didn't want to waste another moment.

"There you all are!" Grace stood at the parlor door, smiling. "Mother has the most . . . interesting day planned. Please, enjoy your breakfast and then we shall get right to it."

"What is it?" Nathan muttered under his breath to his sister as they passed her.

Grace spoke through her smile. "Something you will love." She spied Eva's shopping bag. "Oh! Are those your purchases? I am to gather everything and deposit them in the ballroom. Nathan, where are yours?"

He looked for someone. "With Frampton's."

Grace wrinkled her brow at him. Eva handed her the bag and watched in amusement as Grace took the shopping bags from each guest and then disappeared down the hallway. Inside the parlor, Mrs. Winston was directing staff in preparation for the day. Delilah, Alice, and Olivia were also already in the parlor, helping their mother.

"Seems they are preparing something quite elaborate," Eva murmured, noting Nathan's uneasy nod. They made their way to the dining room where the others were gathering for breakfast, and Eva couldn't deny the curiosity that had her eating quickly to see what Mrs. Winston had planned.

The guests eventually trickled into the parlor, and Nathan and Eva took a seat on a settee. Alice approached them, and Nathan quietly demanded, "What are we going to be doing, Alice?"

She grinned, tawny eyes dancing, and placed a kiss on her brother's cheek. "No need to be nervous, Nate. It will all be great fun."

"I bought three yards of ribbon, feathers, and buttons yesterday. I cannot begin to imagine what sort of fun we are in for."

"Silly man. And you, a big, strong detective inspector. You've nothing to fear."

Eva's lips quirked at Nathan's clear discomfort, and at Alice's warmth, felt some of her tension ease.

"Eva, that dress is the loveliest shade of spring green! I must know the name of your favored shop or seamstress." Alice sat adjacent to Eva, all smiles. "I am ever on the hunt for just the right sort of green." She turned at a noise near the parlor door and her smile slipped at the sight of the Mean Ladies. "I'd rather hoped a magical fairy would hear my wishes last night," she murmured under her breath.

Eva laughed softly. "Is your belief in magical things now crushed?"

Alice sighed. "Perhaps momentarily." Her eyes lit up, and Eva noted Jens Sorenson, who entered with John Smythe and Franklin Frampton.

Eva leaned closer. "Do you fancy the Swede?" she whispered.

"Ah, if only." She sighed again and turned to Eva. "Nobody is as handsome as Mr. Sorenson. Even Mr. Sorenson."

Eva laughed and nodded at the astute observation. "I do believe his sort occupy most of the space when in any sort of companionship."

"Indeed," Alice agreed readily. "There was a time when a younger version of myself was quite heartbroken at his lack of ability to see beyond his own looking glass. Lesson well learned; wouldn't you agree?"

Eva smiled at her. "I would agree, Alice. You're absolutely right. Gratitude for bullets dodged is much healthier than self-pity or regret." She didn't add that such was a lesson she had only just realized herself.

"Even so," Alice continued, her gaze following Jens across

the room as he sat with two of her sisters and the other gentle-men, "a work of art ought to be appreciated, don't you think?"

"Well, then." Nathan stood abruptly and Eva squashed a grin. "I'll see if Mother needs assistance."

Alice blinked up at him, all innocence. "You needn't bother—she has everything quite under control."

He shot a dark look at her before crossing the room to his mother, who was now conversing with Mrs. Parkin.

Alice laughed softly as she watched him walk away and leaned over to Eva. "Wretched of me to tease, of course, but you should see his face every time Mr. Sorenson pays attention to you."

Eva gaped. "No!"

Alice nodded. "Yes. I would never have considered my brother a jealous sort of man, but I've also never seen him in love before." She smiled and reached for Eva's hand. "He has spent obligatory amounts of time at balls, soirees, dinner par-ties, and the like. He feels responsible for us." She looked over at him, her expression fond. "I have seen him dance, converse, play cards, and fend off zealous debutantes with patience. I have never, however, seen him look the way he does with you."

Eva's eyes suddenly felt hot, and she inwardly winced. She couldn't allow such a genuine person to believe that some-thing she had been witnessing was not entirely as it seemed. Reluctantly, she admitted, "We have agreed to be 'interested' in one another to keep the likes of the Mean Ladies at bay. We cer-tainly enjoy one another's company and are good friends, but—"

Alice shook her head with a gentle smile. "Nate is not the sort to playact or engage in any sort of . . . well, nonsense. The only reason he would ever agree to such a thing would be if the emotion behind it were genuine. Besides," she finished, patting Eva's hand, "I know my brother. He is a wretched actor."

Eva raised a dubious brow. "He has gone effectively under-cover on investigative assignments."

Alice waved her hand in dismissal. "Pretending to be some-one else is entirely different than pretending emotion you don't feel while *being* yourself. He is not that sort of man." She smiled again, suddenly seeming very much like a wise, old soul. "Nathan doesn't pretend anything. My guess is that this was an excuse for him to pull you in close."

Eva was saved from responding when Nathan returned, clearly not having found the diversion he hoped to with his mother. Alice gave Eva's hand a squeeze before releasing it and hopping back to her feet. "Lovely to speak with you both." She smiled and blew a kiss to her brother as he resumed his seat next to Eva.

The settee was small, and his leg pressed against hers. He glanced at her as though uncertain whether or not she was still irritated for reasons he didn't understand. She managed a smile for him, Alice's words tumbling around in her head. He'd told Eva blankly in that very parlor that his attention to her was not an act.

" . . . *I've never seen him in love before* . . ."

The phrase wrapped gently around her heart like a cocoon, and he must have seen something in her eyes that manifested it. He traced her ear as though tucking a stray curl and gave her his half smile. He didn't say anything, but he didn't need to.

"Very well," Mrs. Winston called out and clapped her hands. "I shall explain our activities for today!"

Nathan tensed, and Eva grinned. "Surely your mother wouldn't devise an activity you would hate."

"My mother is a consummate hostess and entertainer. I do not trust her one whit."

CHAPTER 17

Nathan stood at the ballroom threshold, torn between annoyance and relief. His mother had set up two large tables, which held the piles of items each guest had purchased the day before in town. She had also just announced to the laughing crowd gathered around the tables that they would be competing in a hat-making contest. The trick was, however, that the gentlemen were to make the hats, and the ladies would then choose their favorite one. Whoever made the hat would be paired in a few hands of whist with the woman who chose it.

It wasn't as bad as it might have been, so for that, he felt relief. He wouldn't have to wear the hat himself. The annoyance, he realized, was not so much that he'd be forced to make a woman's hat, but that while the men were hat making, the women would be in the library so as to avoid cheating. He didn't want Eva in the library, and he didn't want to be in the ballroom. He wanted very much to snag a few moments of private conversation and convince her to tell him what in blazes had happened before breakfast.

He had never seen her so irritated, and when he'd realized at least part of it seemed to be directed at him, he'd known a moment of panic. He couldn't think for wanting to right whatever wrong he'd committed, and she had refused to tell him what was on her mind. She might have gotten there eventually had they not been interrupted on the stairs. He'd been close enough to her at that point to surprise her with a kiss—and it had crossed his mind to do so—but he'd have likely pulled back a bloody stump.

She'd softened toward him, though, and it was after speaking to Alice. Should he corner his sister and demand she tell him what they'd discussed? He hated courtship rules with a passion, and the indirect manner with which most people maneuvered the finer points of romance was frustrating.

He didn't want to write her a letter, or speak with her friend, or with his sister, for that matter, to discover the nature of her feelings. Eva was a grown woman, and he was a grown man, and he wanted a direct conversation with her that didn't involve innuendo—pleasant as that was—or prevarication with details. He'd already broken with convention concerning her in the past few days as it was, so he didn't imagine the societal rule monitors could castigate him any worse.

He straightened his shoulders. It was his house. He was head of the family. The lord of his castle. He wanted one simple conversation with a woman and saw no reason not to insist upon it immediately.

"Gather round!" his mother called, herding the gentlemen into seats. "Nathaniel!"

With a sigh, he obediently took a seat at the table and glared at Alice and Eva, who left the room, laughing with the rest of the women, who were off to more civilized climes.

"A gentleman holding a sewing needle is disgraceful," John Smythe grumbled, and for once, Nathan almost agreed with the man. He had been obliged to mend his own clothing while on investigative assignment, however, and so could not with integrity endorse the statement.

"Now, gentlemen," Christine said, "you needn't fear a little exercise in hat making. Quite honestly, the humor of this game is that the hats usually look ridiculous when the gentlemen are finished making them. The ladies will be delighted."

They all looked at her in silence, before Franklin finally broke it by saying, "Excellent! Very well, gentlemen, are we cowards or are we valiant?"

"That's the spirit!" Christine smiled broadly. "I've enlisted the help of my daughters, Grace, Delilah, and Olivia, who are obliged to sit out this activity in order that the numbers are equal. Also helping are Mrs. Parkin and Mrs. Larsen. You see, I've not left you out in the cold."

Grace pulled up a chair between Franklin Frampton and Davis Jacobson. "Not to fret, gentlemen, the needle is your friend."

Nathan snorted, remembering times when he'd drawn copious amounts of his own blood in an attempt to affix a button to a shirt or a pair of trousers. Mrs. Parkin took the seat next to him and patted his arm. "I'll find a thimble for you, dear. We've gathered several in a bowl here somewhere."

"Yes," his mother added. "You'll notice we've placed everything you purchased yesterday into separate piles. Mrs. Larsen is now going to give you each a straw bonnet you'll decorate using these elements."

Mrs. Larsen very dramatically presented each gentleman with a bonnet, and with that, the haberdashery-ment commenced. Nathan remembered Eva's penchant for choosing blue, so he reached for a wide blue-velvet ribbon that then slipped through his fingers. Jens Sorenson had the other end of it and smiled as he draped it over his bonnet. "Sorry, old man. Advantage goes to youth."

Nathan eyed him evenly for a moment, turning over several insults in his mind before deciding to take the higher road. It was true, Jens was younger than Nathan, and as he looked around the table, he realized that he was the eldest male at the party.

To his dismay, all shades of blue ribbon quickly disappeared from the pile. The men began chattering good-naturedly, even snooty Mr. Smythe. Nathan gritted his teeth and reached for a green ribbon. Mrs. Parkin handed him a threaded needle and a thimble, which was too small for his fingers.

He smiled tightly and wrapped the ribbon around the bonnet, then began stitching it in place. While he worked, he listened idly to the conversations flowing around the table. Jens flirted outrageously with every female present, despite the fact that half were old enough to be his mother. Davis Jacobson told Mrs. Larsen about his menagerie, and Franklin Frampton was answering Christine's polite questions about his years as a clarinet student.

Mrs. Parkin, seated next to him and across the table from Grace, said to her, "Mary told me this morning that two more maids arrive tomorrow from town—I imagine that will ease some of the pressure on the staff."

Grace nodded. "Turner interviewed yesterday while we were out. A pity the work won't last longer than the length of this gathering. Mother mentioned the girls were grateful for the opportunity, even if temporary."

John Smythe added, "Miss Parker, Miss *Blanche* Parker, believes her bedroom was disturbed in her absence. I certainly hope the staff are indeed well referenced."

Nathan's mother looked up sharply. "I hope Miss Parker would come to me or Turner with any concerns about violation of her suite."

Smythe lifted his chin. "She will, I am certain, if she has not already. I would imagine she didn't want to bother you with the matter right now in the midst of the activities."

"Did she say anything had gone missing?" Grace asked him.

"No, she did not. Only that some of her belongings had been disturbed. Moved."

Mrs. Parkin looked at Nathan's mother. "She brought her own maid, did she not?"

Christine nodded. "With so many wardrobe changes and differing activities, however, she has required extra assistance from Mary." She delivered the statement without the sarcasm Nathan knew lurked behind it. Christine was a firm believer in as much self-sufficiency as one could muster, having little use for helplessness in either women or men.

He finished sewing the green ribbon to the bonnet, pleased with his relatively neat stitches. He wondered about getting a message to Eva about which bonnet was his, and contemplated bribing one of his sisters. He grabbed a few buttons from a dish and prepared to sew them onto the green ribbon.

"Dear," Mrs. Parkin said, "have you looked at the colors you're combining?"

He looked down at the button he was holding against the green ribbon. "Pink and green are unacceptable?"

Franklin nodded at the bowl. "I should think yellow a better choice."

"Just what I was thinking," Jens said, and picked the three yellow buttons out from the rest.

Nathan looked at the young man, blinking. "You do not need those three yellow buttons, my friend."

"But I do! Blue and yellow are the colors of the Swedish flag, of course. Perhaps you should search for red, white, and blue. Ah, but then *nearly all* of you would be obliged to use those colors, and nothing would set you apart from the others." His face was split by a handsome grin that Nathan was finding more irritating by the hour.

He turned to his mother. "All the more reason he should not be allowed to use those buttons. He might as well attach a sign bearing his name!"

"Nathaniel, did he take the yellow buttons from your hand?"

"No, but he knew I wanted them."

"No," Jens scoffed. "Frampton suggested the yellow. You did not say you wanted it."

"I didn't have time to say it!"

Grace's mouth twitched. "Nate, I quite like pink and green together. I am sure many of the women would agree."

"If only in pity," Jens added, nodding.

Nathan clenched his teeth together to keep from snapping something he'd regret, or worse, something that would have his mother banishing him to his bedroom. On second thought, he mused, that was an option worth considering. Then, unbidden, he imagined Eva choosing the Swedish flag hat amidst his eviction from the festivities.

Exhaling loudly through his nose, he bent to the task of sewing pink buttons onto the bonnet, swearing under his breath only once when he stabbed his finger and bled on the ribbon.

CHAPTER 18

"Ten more minutes, ladies!" Jansen, the butler, announced from the library doorway.

Eva nodded, glad she'd been monitoring the time. She'd sent word to Sammy, who was out in the portable darkroom, to begin the silver nitrate process with the plates. By the time the ladies and men reunited, the plates would be ready for the camera. George Abernathy, the footman, was standing guard for the boy. He would accompany Sammy and the plates personally to Eva.

The contest was charming, and one that Mrs. Winston specifically wanted memorialized in photograph. Eva was willing to wager that each member of the party would desire a copy, so she and Sammy would be busy.

She'd spent the time in the library chatting with Louisa Wilhite and Inez Shelton, learning they had been friends from childhood. Ann Parker was subtly delightful. She was shy, initially, but opened with natural and lovely animation after a time. She lived in her elder sister's shadow, but with a bit of luck, Blanche would find a gentleman to marry and allow Ann some room to breathe.

Eva rose from a comfortable seat near an open window overlooking the back gardens from the second floor. The late morning sun shone brightly, and a gentle breeze caressed the room. She wandered to the lower tier of bookshelves, perusing the titles and admiring the fine leather-bound tomes. In her periphery, she saw someone walking toward her. She turned to see Blanche Parker approach, looking resplendent in her signature soft pink. Her blue eyes looked troubled, and she stopped near Eva, asking, "Miss Caldwell, may I have a word in private?"

Eva nodded, bemused. She looked around them, wondering what kind of "private" Blanche required. A door to the left of the hearth stood ajar, and Eva peered inside. It was a sparsely furnished study, hosting a bare desk and two leather club chairs. She entered and switched on a light, and after Blanche entered, closed the door partially.

"What is it?" Eva asked, growing concerned.

"I—that is—oh goodness. This is more awkward than I expected. Perhaps we should take a seat."

Eva took one of the chairs, her heart beginning to beat faster, and Blanche took the other. The lamplight picked up tones in her brilliantly blonde hair, lending her an ethereal look. She imagined Ann living in Blanche's shadow and felt sad for the girl. Such physical beauty in a world that valued it highly would be difficult to compete with.

"What is on your mind, Miss Parker?" Eva asked.

"I shall come directly to it. I have noticed your clear affection for Mr. Winston, Miss Caldwell, and I certainly understand, because he is quite handsome. He is wealthy, of course, and an attractive prospect despite his penchant for working-class pursuits; I imagine, however, that this is not a tick in the 'negative' column for you."

Eva raised one brow.

"My aim in seeking you out is this: I would be remiss if I

did not tell you of an incident last year at the Kingsworths' ball." She paused, taking a small breath, and looked at Eva as though in compassion and pity. "Mr. Winston had a note delivered, inviting me to meet him in the gardens at a certain hour. As his reputation is stellar and his mother's name respected, I saw no reason to deny the request. I met him, but to my surprise, he was quite alone. There wasn't even a footman or maid in sight."

She looked down at her hands. "I do not know what he intended, but I can only imagine. My family, you see, is descended of nobility, whereas the Winstons are new money, just two generations old. I can only presume he attempted to orchestrate a scenario where I would be found in a compromising position with him so that we would be obliged to marry, thus tying his family name to landed gentry." She offered a light shrug, her blue eyes bright with unshed tears. "If not for the timely arrival of one of my friends who was searching for me, Mr. Winston might not have run off the way he did, inadvertently saving my reputation."

Eva watched her as silence fell in the room. It lengthened, as Eva slowly inhaled and exhaled. "Miss Parker," she finally said, "if his intention was to compromise you by being discovered alone with you, why did he 'run off' when your friend arrived? That would seem a perfect scenario, would it not?"

Blanche's lips parted fractionally. "I . . . well, I am certain I do not know the nature of his thoughts at the time."

"Are you certain that, if such an event actually occurred, it was not *you* who orchestrated the scenario?" Blood pounded in her ears as history, in a twisted frame, repeated itself.

Blanche's mouth dropped open, and two spots of color appeared on her cheeks. "I am . . . I am shocked and *insulted* that you would suggest such a thing to me! How dare you, Miss

Caldwell? How dare you besmirch my good name? You clearly have no notion whatsoever of the power my father wields!"

Eva leaned forward slightly in her seat, proud of herself for keeping her hands folded in her lap. "I know *this*, Miss Parker: my aunt has associates in every level of government extending to the prime minister himself. She owns a widely circulated, respected daily paper that members of the ton await eagerly each morning to read over their tea. If you *ever* again repeat such slanderous nonsense about Mr. Winston, there is no height I cannot reach in exposing you for the lying, spoiled girl you are."

Splotches of color spread across Blanche's face and down onto her pale neck.

"Furthermore," Eva continued, "I am well acquainted with Director Ellis, who heads the Criminal Investigation Division at the Yard. Are you aware that slander is a crime? Are you prepared to repeat that story to authorities, to swear to its truth under oath if *sued* for slander?"

Blanche remained frozen, and Eva registered somewhere in the back of her blazingly furious brain that it was the perfect pose for an excellent photograph.

"Are you aware of the consequences of lying under oath? A beautiful woman like you would not fare well in Newgate." Eva hoped the girl would not verify the truthfulness of that last claim—she had no idea whether or not someone would find himself in Newgate for slander.

Blanche eventually closed her mouth. Her eyes narrowed, and she lifted a trembling hand to her temple to brush away a curl. When she found her tongue, she utilized it like a whip. "You are a crass, *hideous* girl who works for a living like a common dockside trollop!"

"I am *not* a dockside trollop, Miss Parker; however, yes I do earn my own money. See that you stay out of my way for the duration of this gathering, or I shall be tempted to show you crime scene photographs guaranteed to instigate nightmares for months." She rose and brushed past the young woman who was still glued to her seat. As an afterthought and hoping to see guilt or innocence in the reaction, she added, "And stay away from my camera equipment!"

"Oh!" Blanche now rose, her fists clenched at her side. "Why would I break your ridiculous *money-earning* camera equipment?"

Eva stared daggers at the girl, taking a breath. "I never said anything was broken."

Blanche paled. "I didn't do it." She sank into the seat. "I didn't do it. I . . . I only found the plates—"

"Found them where? Were they intact or broken? You certainly managed well to scoop up lots of tiny shards and put them into the reticule."

She shook her head, her lips colorless. "I found the two glass plates intact."

"What of the black feather? Do you know Mr. Toole?"

Her expression was caught somewhere between wary and bewildered. "What feather? I do not know someone named Toole!"

"What did you do with the plates after you found them?"

Her eyes darted away from Eva's. "I didn't . . . Nothing. I just left them."

"You left them?" It was more accusation than question. Eva watched Blanche closely, eyes narrowed and waiting for her to give something away.

"I already told you! I found them and then left them."

Eva slowly moved closer, hands on her hips. Her anger congealed into a cold pit in her stomach. "You found them *where*?"

Blanche swallowed. "In the bushes beside the labyrinth. They were there yesterday morning when I was walking with . . . Mathilda."

Eva slowly shook her head. "Mathilda is not a morning walker, Miss Parker. I heard her saying so at breakfast when she was aghast at the early morning hours you keep." Eva paused. "Interestingly, Miss Dilworth also mentioned Mr. Smythe's penchant for early walks."

Blanche remained silent, but the color rushed back into her face.

"Surely you wouldn't make the mistake of meeting yet another gentleman alone."

The only sound in the room was the ticking of the clock.

Eva lifted a finger and spoke through clenched teeth. "Not one more word about Mr. Winston. Not. One."

Blanche nodded shakily, barely, but it was acknowledgment enough. She remained frozen in place, and Eva gave her a last, long look before leaving the room and pulling the door closed with more force than was strictly necessary.

She stopped short at the sight of Grace Winston, who stood just outside the door with her hand over her mouth. Before Eva could respond, Grace put her finger to her lips and pulled her across the library, under the spiral staircase, and to a door in the corner that she quickly opened. She ushered Eva inside and clicked the door quietly behind them, switching on a lamp. She stared at Eva, breathing heavily, and then launched herself, wrapping Eva in a tight embrace that squeezed the air from her lungs.

Grace put her hand at the back of Eva's head and held her cheek close. Eva felt the trickle of moisture on her face, but the tears weren't hers. "A moment," Grace whispered, and Eva gently rubbed her shoulder.

Grace finally pulled back and clasped Eva's hand while wiping at her eyes with her other. "Miss Caldwell, Eva," she began, fumbling in her pocket for a handkerchief.

Eva noted a mirror arrangement of the office she'd just inhabited with Blanche. She sat in one of the chairs and tugged Grace's hand to the other.

Grace sniffled and shook her head with a small laugh. "Apologies for the theatrics. I had come to the library to fetch the two of you, and I heard that girl spewing her lies. I nearly interrupted but then heard your response. You have the exact right of it, you know. Blanche did arrange to have Nathan caught in a compromising position with her—I later bullied her friend for the truth—but he realized right away what she was about and quickly extricated himself."

She wiped her nose and eyes, clutching the handkerchief. "He is mindful of what can happen to a woman if her name is besmirched, so he wasn't about to spread her machinations far and wide. He figured she was young and foolish but might have been rattled enough by his scathing dismissal of her to avoid trying it again in the future. He did tell me, however, so that I might keep watch if she expressed any sort of interest in him again."

She sighed. "He didn't want to say anything to Mama, figured the fewer people who knew, the better. By the time I realized Mama had accepted the Parkers' petition for their daughters to join the party, it was too late to gracefully rescind. Her parents had already pledged large donations for both Blanche and Ann, and Mama had formally accepted."

Eva inhaled slowly and blew out the breath. She closed her eyes for a moment, and then unburdened her heart. "When I was seventeen, a young man I'd fallen quite in love with was set to ask my father for permission to court me. The day before, I received a note to meet him by the walking path near the pond on the outskirts of town. When I arrived, I found him in an extremely intimate tableau with a girl I had known at school. A nemesis very much like Miss Parker. She had sent the note, of course, and later admitted to a mutual friend that she couldn't stomach the thought of my marrying so far above my station."

"Oh, Eva. She was jealous and spiteful." Grace's vibrant green eyes clouded again.

"I confess, there is such a striking similarity between her demeanor and Miss Parker's that upon first meeting her here, I was momentarily bamboozled. I felt like my seventeen-year-old self all over again."

"Yet you defended Nathan just now without hesitation." Grace paused and sniffled. "How were you so sure she lied?"

"I know him." Eva nodded, realizing it was true. She'd not believed Blanche for a moment, even while her heart had raced, and the scene had felt eerily familiar.

Grace sighed and smiled. "I believe you do."

"Have you told your mother, even against Nathan's wishes? She really should be informed."

Grace nodded. "I informed her the very day he came to visit her in London—the day he told her he was interested in someone else and therefore any matrimonial hopes for this holiday were wasted on him. My mother had been extremely upset at the news about Blanche, upset that we'd not told her. She wanted him to be here, and she wanted to find a way to 'uninvite' Blanche.

"When he blurted out his 'interest' in someone else, she saw a way to avoid embarrassment for the Parkers and still insist Nate attend. Knowing you would be here, and with Nate making it clear that his heart is spoken for, she hoped it would be enough to force Blanche's decency." Grace shook her head. "Mama has worried about him, as I suppose a mother does. Worries about the heaviness of his work and the lonely flat he goes home to at the end of the day."

"He loves his family very much," Eva said. "Adores each of you. He seems especially close to you, however; am I imagining it?"

Grace smiled. "You are not imaging it; we are similar in temperament. We have always shared a bond. He has borne a heavy sense of responsibility from a young age, and as I grew older, I didn't want him to feel so alone. I have tried to be reliable for him, to be someone on whom he can count without question."

Eva smiled. "So, when he swore you to secrecy about a scheming girl he could easily ruin, you agreed."

Grace nodded. "I've told Delilah since taking my mother into confidence regarding it, but not the younger girls." She chuckled and sniffled again. "I think Alice would take her apart, limb from limb."

Eva laughed. "I do not know her well, but I suspect you would be correct."

Grace exhaled slowly and straightened. "We must return to the ballroom. By now, Mrs. Larsen or Mrs. Parkin will have been obliged to stand in for you. Possibly Blanche, as well. I wonder if she has joined the others or gone to her room." She raised a brow at Eva. "You quite eviscerated her, and deservedly so. If I were she, I would be headed for home at the first opportunity."

"Oh dear." Eva rose. "Sammy will have brought in the plates by now, and I fear too much time has passed to use them."

"It is my fault," Grace said, moving quickly to the door. "I was ridiculously overwrought."

"It is *her* fault," Eva said. "I am comfortable laying the blame at her feet."

They rushed from the room, through the library, and down the hall to the ballroom. Eva halted abruptly at the entrance to see Sammy finishing a photograph of smiling people wearing funny hats. He hadn't mixed the chemicals for the flash powder, which she would never have allowed him to do on his own, but he had situated the subjects facing the big windows to take advantage of the bright morning light. Now, as he replaced the lens covering, he said, "Perfect! Thank you all."

He was greeted with a round of applause, and Eva stared at the boy in wonder. She didn't know why she was surprised; he had mastered every step of the process as well as she had.

She and Grace entered the ballroom, and she quickly enveloped a surprised Sammy in a hug. "Well done, you!"

He beamed, dimples showing in his cheeks. "Thank you, Miss Eva. Figured since you weren't here, best be quick 'bout it."

"I am so proud of you. You have absolutely saved the day. Let's get the plates processed, shall we?"

He nodded, and she inserted the plate holder, capturing the plate and pulling it back out. Mrs. Winston directed the crowd back to the library, where several hands of whist were about to commence. Eva looked up to see Grace speaking with Nathan. They both looked at her, Grace smiled, and Nathan crossed the room to join Eva.

"I hear you had a chat with someone," he murmured.

She nodded, suddenly feeling the emotion settle on her shoulders. She smiled, though, and blinked quickly. "I am fine, truly," she told him, continuing to busy herself with the camera.

"We can talk later—you go play whist while Sammy and I get these plates processed."

"You'll take—"

She nodded. "We'll take George Abernathy with us." The footman stood at the door, waiting.

"Eva, I—"

"Go," she whispered. She did not want to cry in a crowd of people, and she didn't know why she suddenly felt teary. She'd lambasted Blanche quite effectively without becoming weepy, had spoken with Grace about a painful part of her past, and had managed without incident. Suddenly seeing Nathan, however, with his tall form and broad shoulders and the way he seemed to envelop her, wrapping her in something deliciously warm . . . She shook her head and shoved at his arm with a light laugh. "Later."

He looked at her closely for another moment before finally turning away and offering his arm to Mrs. Larsen, who had indeed stood in for her and had apparently chosen his bonnet—a lopsided confection with green ribbon, pink buttons, and a few bright feathers stuck to the side for good measure.

Jens Sorenson sauntered by proudly with Miss Shelton, who wore a bonnet with beautiful blue ribbon, tied in a lovely bow, and accented with yellow buttons. Eva's smile broadened as she caught sight of the couples who laughed and made their way out of the room. It was a clever activity that encouraged people to broaden their horizons and form acquaintances with people they might otherwise never choose to know. Miss Blanche Parker, interestingly, was absent, obliging Mrs. Parkin to take her place.

"Ready?" Eva smiled at Sammy, who gathered the tray and other supplies he'd carried in. They met George Abernathy at the door, and he saluted smartly. Sammy laughed, and the trio made their way through the corridor, down the stairs to the front hall, and outside to the awaiting darkroom.

When they finished processing the plates and cleaning the darkroom for the day, it was well after the noon hour. Eva stepped out of the carriage and stretched, feeling restless. "You go inside," she told Sammy and George. "I must stretch my legs for a bit and then I'll be right behind you."

George frowned. "I am not to leave you alone outside, miss. Please do not ask it of me. Mr. Winston is most insistent."

Eva smiled. "Very well. Sammy, you go in and ask Mrs. Snow for a snack—I can hear your stomach grumbling."

The boy grinned, and she watched as he ran around the back of the house to the servants' entrance. She looked at the labyrinth, which was situated a short distance from the side of the house. "George, I am going to wander into the labyrinth only to the first turn. If you like, you may stand guard right here at the entrance." She smiled at him. "I only need a few moments of quiet to clear my head."

"Very well, miss." As they neared the labyrinth, he reached into a box on the ground and retrieved a bundle of bamboo rods. "These connect like so," he demonstrated, fitting one atop the other until they formed a long pole. "If you are lost in the labyrinth, you raise this high. Someone standing on the balcony will shout directions." He grinned. "Primitive, but effective."

She laughed. "Thank you, Mr. Abernathy." She took the bundle of rods and ventured into the groomed maze, which was well above her head. She took a deep breath and wandered past the first turn, but kept walking—just a bit, she told herself—until she found a spot to sit.

Something sharp poked her leg as she walked. Frowning, she put her hand into her skirt's interior pocket. Her heart thumped as her fingers brushed against something faintly smooth. She paused and pulled it out, opening her fingers to reveal a small black feather.

She closed her eyes tightly and exhaled, torn between fear and exhaustion. She would give it to Nathan later, but for now, she couldn't bear to look at it. She put it back in her pocket and straightened her spine. She wanted two minutes alone in the labyrinth, and she was determined to have them.

On shaking legs, she wandered closer to the center until she sank down on the thick grass, pulled her knees to her chest, and let the tears finally fall.

CHAPTER 19

By the time several rounds of whist were finished, Nathan had assumed Eva would have returned from the darkroom. He checked the parlor, then the kitchen where he found Sammy, regaling Mrs. Snow and the kitchen staff with tales from London.

"Miss Eva?" he asked Sammy.

"Outside," he pointed. "Wiff Mr. Abernafee."

He felt a sense of relief she'd allowed the footman to remain with her when she could have easily sent him inside. He'd not fully relaxed since the day before when she'd been given the broken photography plates and black feather.

He grew concerned that he didn't see them anywhere near the house or darkroom and wandered toward the lawn before turning to the labyrinth. George waved at him, but he was alone.

Nathan quickly reached him and asked, "Where is Miss Caldwell? Has she wandered off alone?"

"No, no, sir. She wanted to go into the labyrinth to clear her head. I gave her a safety pole, and she promised she wouldn't go farther than the first turn."

Nathan nodded. "Good man." He patted George's shoulder, his mouth lifting in a smile. "Hand me a pole, would you?"

"Yes, sir." He retrieved a bundle of rods and handed them over, adding, "shall I await you here?"

"Please. If you hear me shout, you'll know we are lost."

"Very good, sir."

Nathan smiled and ventured into the maze. He passed the first corner and did not see Eva, nor was he surprised. He kept walking, imagining which way she would turn if entering for the first time. He paused, and, from the other side of the hedge wall, heard something. He rounded the corner, cursed at the dead end, and circled back. He tried a different turn, and at another dead end, saw Eva. The angle of the sun cast the corner in shadow. She was seated on the ground, arms wrapped around her knees, and crying.

"Eva." Her name was like an ache in his throat.

She whipped her head up and quickly stood, wiping her eyes. "Nathan! What are you doing out here? How did you find me?"

"George told me you promised to stop after the first turn." He approached her slowly.

She nodded, clutching her bamboo rods. "I memorized the number and direction of the turns. If nothing else, I have these." She waved the rods and smiled, but it was wobbly.

"I thought maybe you were upset because you were lost," he teased.

"No. I am—I am fine, truly." She shook her head and looked away, tears gathering again and rolling down her face.

"Yes, you seem fine." He reached her and stretched out his hand, and to his relief, she took it. He took her bamboo rods and dropped them to the ground with his. Slowly, he reached for her, and she melted into him with a single sob that broke his heart.

He cupped her head, rubbing slow circles on her back as she

cried into his chest. She held her handkerchief to her nose, her shoulders shaking, and wrapped her other arm around his back, holding tightly. He couldn't say how long they stood there, but eventually, her sobbing slowed and her shoulders relaxed.

She lifted her head and exhaled a wobbly breath. "I'm so sorry. I am simply a mess, and I am never a mess."

He smiled and thumbed away traces of tears on her cheeks. "No, you are not, Evangeline. You are never a mess, and you hold the mess at bay quite well. Perhaps sometimes it just needs to come out."

She laughed a little and wiped her eyes. "The last time I let it out, I didn't think it would ever stop." She still held her arm around his waist, and he wasn't about to move. He did manage, however, to reach inside his pocket to offer a fresh handkerchief. She mumbled her thanks and dried her face and nose.

"Better?"

She nodded. "I believe so." She looked up at him. "I am sorry."

"You've nothing to apologize for." He traced her brow with his thumb.

"I've been ridiculously emotional all over your person."

"I welcome it. You need to release it, and I am glad to be the one to hold you while you do it."

She smiled, sheepish. "You're a very good friend, Detective."

He chuckled. "Oh, certainly. I am a very good friend." He rocked slowly, side to side, as though they danced while standing in place. "You should know I do not do this with Michael, and I consider him a very good friend."

She tipped her head back and laughed. "I'll consider myself special, then, that this is not the sort of support you offer to all of your friends."

"I would never offer this to anyone else." He traced her jaw, her chin, her cheek. "Not like this." He followed the lines of her face to her ear, slowly inching the tips of his fingers into the wealth of her hair, massaging in slow circles. "Will you tell me why you were so upset this morning when we went down to breakfast?"

She sighed, and her eyes drifted closed. "Lethal. Very well, I was afraid and concerned about that business in the shop where the stranger thrust the broken plates into my hand, I was irritated about Blanche Parker and the fact that she commands the attention of everyone around her and runs the staff ragged, and I was especially irritated—"

He waited for her to continue, finally prompting, "Yes?"

"Irritated with you."

"I thought so. I even asked what I could do to fix it. You said I could do nothing. That doesn't sit well with me, because I'm certain I can do something to make things right."

"It wasn't entirely a falsehood—you couldn't have done anything in that moment to fix it."

He smiled, recalling his earlier frustration with the lack of plain speaking. They were taking a roundabout approach to the matter now, and he quite enjoyed it. "Is it something I can do now?"

She smiled. "I believe so."

"Allow me to ask again: Eva, why were you irritated with me?" he whispered.

She shivered in response. "Because you have not kissed me yet."

"I wasn't certain that was your wish."

She eyed him flatly. "You seem to know everything else."

His lips twitched. "What is it I seem to know?"

"That I love you."

Her whispered confession halted his movement. She'd caught him by surprise and beat him at his own game.

"*Eva.*"

He lowered his head, meeting her lips with his as he pushed his hand farther into the thick locks of her hair. It was a soft, silky mass, and a perfect match in sensation as he explored the softness of her full mouth. He kissed her until they were both winded, and he finally broke the contact, resting his forehead against hers and trying to slow his racing heart.

"Eva, I love you. I have loved you for a very long time." He lifted his head and looked into the dark depths of her eyes. "There is nobody else here, I am not putting on an act, and I would not have there be any misunderstandings between us." He searched her gaze, willing her to understand. "*I love you.* I adore you. You are witty and charming and so beautiful, I ache. You are brilliant and compassionate. You put everyone around you at ease, you *care* about people, regardless of status or creed." He softly kissed her eyelids, tasting the salty remnants of her tears. "I will catch you each time the mess threatens to erupt. I will hold you and keep you safe and love you with everything I have and am."

She reached up to touch his cheek. "Do you know how long I have wanted this? Because I do not. I feel as if I have wanted this from the first moment I saw you standing at the Misses Van Horne's entryway last year. Do you remember?"

"Do I remember?" He smiled. "I remember the time of day, Eva. It was 6:04 p.m. I stood there with Michael and Radcliffe, and the three Hampton cousins arrived. I saw you." He paused, his eyes trailing over her hair, which he had loosened impressively from its pins. He tucked a long curl behind her ear.

"Will you marry me? This is hardly the time and place I had planned. Apologies for that." His heart thudded in his chest.

She smiled. "Where had you planned?"

He paused, sheepish. "I hadn't actually created a good plan yet."

"I like this spot, right here and now. It is perfect." Her eyes filled again. "Yes, Detective Inspector Nathaniel Winston, I will marry you."

He released an anxious breath. "Good. I will talk to your father as soon as we finish this infernal party."

She smiled at him, and for a moment he was stunned that she was in his arms, that she had actually agreed to marry him.

"What are you thinking?"

"That I am the luckiest man in the world." He shook his head. "I hardly dared dream of it."

"You should kiss me again. Often. So I don't become irritated."

He lowered his head, teasing, smiling against her lips. "But if you're irritated, then I can enjoy the process of fixing it."

With an impatient huff, she put her hand at the back of his neck, searing his lips with a kiss that stole his breath. She wound her arms around his neck, and he held her tight, thinking they should return to the house but shoving the thought aside. Supper wasn't for another few hours.

She smiled, pulling back slightly, and looking in his eyes. "You've compromised me now, Mr. Winston. Ironic that I just spent a significant amount of energy insisting you are not the sort to do so."

He waggled his eyebrows. "Part of my evil design. Spend a year admiring you without admitting it, trick you into pretending to carry a *tendre* for me as an act for a house full of people, and then compromise you in the labyrinth."

"Hmm." She placed her hands on either side of his neck, her thumbs softly touching his face. "There is a flaw in your plan, however."

"Which is?"

"There is nobody here to discover my debauched, compromised state."

"I suppose we could call for George Abernathy. He still waits at the entrance."

She frowned. "How are we to keep this secret?"

"Should we?"

"Shouldn't we? You've not spoken to my father yet."

She made a good point. "True. Well, we shall be circumspect."

"I am quite accomplished at being circumspect."

He nodded, kissing her again. "I will be thinking of this moment out here with you every moment of every day until we are officially wed. I daresay my logic will be absent and good judgment totally lacking. I am glad you are strong of will and accomplished at circumspection."

"I am weary of it. Perhaps I wish for you to be strong of will and circumspect for both of us."

"Oh, Eva. We are doomed."

CHAPTER 20

That Eva was able to sneak back into her room unnoticed was a miracle. She took one look at herself in the dressing room mirror and laughed. Her hair was hanging, pins dangling, and her eyes were puffy from crying. Her lips looked very red and thoroughly kissed. Provided others in the house could spare Mary, she would make good use of her talents.

The black feather in her pocket poked her leg again, and she pulled it out, shutting it away in the small vanity drawer. She would tell Nathan about it before dinner.

She paused, then crossed the room and checked the panel to the passageway, reassuring herself it was tightly closed. For good measure, she pulled a chair in front of it. Now she would know if it were opened.

Still feeling the high emotions she'd carried with her into the room, she returned to the vanity and cleaned her face. She pulled all of the pins from her hair with a wince and rubbed her scalp. She then stripped down to her shift and fell back onto her bed, arms outstretched. She looked at the plaster medallion that circled the gasolier suspended in the center of the room, at the lovely molding and coffered angles of the ceiling.

She closed her eyes and tried to remember every moment of

the labyrinth from the time Nathan had found her, emotionally spent. His kiss had been everything she'd ever dreamed of, and more. She couldn't have imagined the intensity of it, and she laughed, remembering Amelie's comment about avoiding chaperones had Eva known what she'd been missing.

She wrapped her arms tightly around herself, sighing, realizing she seemed very dramatic, and not caring one whit. It was her moment, it had been magical, and she wanted to enjoy the luxury of holding it close in the peace and quiet of the lovely Blue Room.

She eventually pushed herself upright, tired, but happy. For all that the world around the house party grew more bizarre by the hour, at the center, it was divine. She wandered into the dressing room and chose an ensemble for supper. Midnight blue, this time, that shimmered almost black when hit by light at just the right angle.

She laid out the dress, and then the layers of petticoats. She pulled on her stockings and began donning the undergarments that would give shape to the dress. When she had put on as much as she could without help, she finally tugged the bellpull, which would ring in the kitchen signaling the need for a maid. She almost hated to do it—it was late in the day, and she imagined being the staff who had to answer it.

One of the new maids, hired that morning from town, answered Eva's call. She was a bright girl named Jane, and her smile was infectious. She helped Eva finish dressing and created a stunning work of art with her hair. When she finished, Eva looked at herself critically in the mirror, astounded. "Jane, you could make a living doing nothing but ladies' hair."

She nodded. "Always did like doin' my mum's hair. She said I have a gift."

"She's absolutely correct." Eva donned her matching gloves and prepared to leave the room. "Will you be available tomorrow?"

"Yes, miss." Jane beamed. "My first time as a lady's maid."

Smiling, Eva followed the girl out of the sitting room and closed the door. Mary had stuck her head out of one of the rooms further down the hall and now beckoned to Jane. Turning in the opposite direction, Eva spied Nathan on the landing.

Looking at him, all she could think of was where they had been a short time before and wishing they were there again. The warm expression on his face when he saw her suggested his train of thought was similar to hers. He looked resplendent in formal black evening attire, complete with a snowy white shirt and black neckwear.

"Miss Caldwell." His voice was like warm honey, and as she made her way across the landing to him on legs that felt wobbly, she hoped she wouldn't disgrace herself by falling to the floor at his feet.

She distracted herself by commenting on his new neckwear. "That is new, and very fashionable."

"Do you like it?" He straightened his collar. "My ancient valet has learned about the newest in neckwear from some of the other gentlemen's valets, apparently. It's a four-in-one knot. I do believe I prefer this to a complicated cravat, although finding help tying a cravat has definite advantages."

He smiled, and took her hands and kissed first one, and then the other. He didn't release them, but pulled them close against his chest, tugging her forward in the process.

She laughed and then cut herself off when the sound echoed through the landing and out into the cavernous front hall. She looked quickly down the guest corridor and then down the family wing, grateful to see both hallways empty.

"Nobody's here," he whispered, and captured her lips in a kiss that truly did have her knees threatening to buckle. He caught her with an arm around her waist and spanned the side of her neck with his other hand.

She broke off with a breathless laugh and caught his wrist, holding it tight. "Do not shove your hands into my hair again," she whispered. "The new maid is a genius and will soon be in high demand if she isn't already. We don't have time for her to fix it."

He smiled and tipped her head for one more kiss before reluctantly releasing her. "Perhaps I should learn to be a lady's maid. Then I'll finally see your hair down."

She tapped his chest, wishing for the sake of dramatic effect that it was a fan instead of her finger. "Good things come to he who waits." She smiled. "Patience is a virtue."

"How many more platitudes apply here?"

"Several, I am sure."

"Here is one: 'Hope deferred maketh the heart sick.' Surely you do not wish to see me sick at heart."

"Ah, you must maintain your hope, then." She lowered her voice and lightly grasped his lapels. "Hope for the quick passage of time for the remainder of this gathering so you can formally speak with my father."

"And then there is a wedding to plan, and more time that will probably crawl at a snail's pace. My hope is definitely going to be deferred." He paused and placed his hands over hers, enveloping them in warmth the gloves couldn't provide. "There is always elopement, you know. We could leave now by rail and head for Gretna Green. We'd be back in no time."

She widened her eyes and laughed. "I almost believe you are sincere in that suggestion!"

He nodded, his face grim. "I think I might be."

She smiled and leaned into him, turning up her face, which he met with a soft kiss. "Do you know how very sad our families would be if we robbed them of a wedding?"

He kissed her again, as if unable to stop himself. "I suppose so."

She wiggled her hands and laughed breathlessly. "Someone will see us here!"

He smiled. "Good. Etches our fate in stone."

"We're already engaged! There's nothing more to be gained than abject embarrassment."

"Speak for yourself."

She arched one brow. "You are incorrigible. One more." She stretched up again for one more kiss that she knew would never last long enough.

A gasp from the family wing echoed through the hall, and Eva pulled away so abruptly she stumbled over her dress. Nathan lunged forward and caught her around the waist, his other hand splayed across the stiff bone corset. She winced and coughed as it dug into her ribs. He tried to help her straighten, but it was a challenge to do so without stepping on her hem. The ensuing scramble was probably humorous to witness but was mortifying to live through.

"Oh, mercy," Eva breathed when she finally stood solidly on her own. Nathan still had a hand wrapped around her arm as though afraid to let go. She was uncertain from a distance which sister stood in the hallway, frozen, but it was soon a moot point, because she was joined by the other three, who looked at their sister quizzically, followed the direction of her gaze, and then froze identically.

The first began laughing, her hand on her stomach.

"Grace," Nathan growled.

She turned to the other three, and in a stage whisper, said, "I caught them kissing!"

All four looked at them again, and Eva was sure she would later see the humor in it.

"Huzzah!" One sister put her fist high into the air and then ran toward them.

"Alice," Eva murmured.

"Yes." Nathan sighed.

"I told you we would be caught."

"You also said 'one more.'"

Eva gasped, looking at him, wide-eyed. "You cannot blame this on me!"

His lips twitched and he winked at her. "I would stand here all night with you, my darling, and not care one whit who walked by. I gladly accept blame for anything."

Alice hugged Eva. "Apologies, of course, for the effusive display, but I am so happy. I must know what kind of kissing Grace witnessed. Simple kisses between friends, or the kind that mean we are embarking into territory that is significantly more friendly?"

"Alice," Nathan interrupted with a frown, "how many 'simple kisses between friends,' are in your repertoire?"

"Silly. Like this." She kissed the air on either side of Eva's face.

"That is *not* what I witnessed." Grace joined them, followed by Delilah and Olivia. "While I will not accost you like this one," she gestured to Alice, "I must say that knowing you both to be great persons of integrity and dignity, this sudden display of affection might be an announcement of sorts."

Eva managed a weak smile. "I . . . not so much officially . . ."

"It is absolutely official," Nathan said. "I will speak with Mr. Caldwell in a week, and then the wedding date will be set."

Eva finally nodded. "We had decided to keep that secret to ourselves—I should hate for my family to learn of this news through gossip."

Nathan had the grace to look contrite. "There is that," he admitted. He straightened his jacket and his fashionably knotted necktie. "Very well. Not a word to anyone." He held up a finger, admonishing his sisters, and Eva bit the inside of her cheeks to keep from laughing.

Delilah raised one single brow at her brother. "*We* do not have a problem keeping secrets safe. *You*, however," she said, waving her hand at Eva and Nathan, "are likely to be your own worst enemies."

Eva nodded, willing to admit to the truth of the statement. Nathan pursed his lips, as though considering a counter argument.

"Perhaps," Alice said, "you should take a train tomorrow to visit with Eva's father. Then we can all celebrate together in proper fashion." She smiled, having solved the conundrum to her apparent satisfaction.

Eva opened her mouth to respond but was cut off by Olivia. "They would both need to leave, and mother would suffer apoplexy."

Eva closed her mouth. Olivia's comment was similar to what she'd been thinking. "For goodness' sake," she said, "I am certain we can manage a bit of propriety for a few days." She looked at Nathan for confirmation, took in his breathtakingly handsome dinner ensemble, the way the jacket fit like a glove over his broad shoulders, and quite forgot what she'd said.

Nathan offered his signature half smile, which had become by far her favorite. His eyes traveled over her hair, her simple pearl necklace, seeming to appreciate for the first time the cut of her dark blue supper dress.

"This is a disaster," Grace muttered. She moved between them and took each by the arm. As though speaking to very young children, she said, "The two of you are not official yet, and unless you wish to cause hurt feelings, you had best behave like priests. I shudder to think what could have happened had someone else come upon you first. Word would be reaching London by now that Detective Inspector Winston and Miss Eva Caldwell have been behaving very badly while on Seaside holiday."

Eva tried not to look as guilty as she felt as Grace walked between them all the way down the stairs. They stopped when they reached the front hall, and Eva looked at Grace, working exceptionally hard to keep from smiling.

Grace's expression softened and she leaned over, kissing Eva's cheek. "I am so glad," she whispered.

Eva's eyes burned as she gave Grace's hand a gentle squeeze. "Thank you," she whispered.

One of the sisters following behind them sighed.

Jansen entered the hall, not missing a step at the impromptu gathering at the base of the stairs and nodded a bow as he passed. A footman followed quickly on his heels and handed him a piece of paper with a quick whisper.

Jansen nodded and approached Nathan, stating, "Fortuitous to find you here, sir. This has just arrived from London."

"Thank you, Jansen." Nathan scanned the paper, and all traces of lightness fled.

Eva's heart sank, and Grace asked, "What is it?" She looked down at the paper as Nathan folded and tucked it away in his inner coat pocket.

"Work," he said, and managed a smile that clearly took effort. "To the dining room, shall we?" He held out his hand.

Grace nodded, stepping out from between him and Eva. She turned to her sisters and motioned with her head. "Shall we check with Mrs. Snow on supper's progress?"

"We should check with Turner first," Olivia said as the three joined Grace and they made their way across the hall. "Mrs. Snow does not appreciate being circumvented." They glanced back at their brother with uncertain smiles, and he blew them all a kiss.

"We shall meet you in the parlor for an aperitif," he told them, and he and Eva watched in silence as the women made their way out of the hall.

Nathan looked at Eva, and he must have known she would ask. Without prompting, he said, "Toole's mother has just passed from the same illness that took his sister."

CHAPTER 21

Nathan sat at the head of the dining table and made a valiant attempt to focus on the conversation around him. His mother and sisters were seated closest to him, with Eva next to them. Between his blinding attraction to Eva—especially now that he'd known the bliss of holding her in his arms—and the news in the telegram that sat like a stone in his pocket, he figured he was fortunate he remembered how to eat.

Toole was in Seaside; he knew it in his bones. He was likely the one who had been lurking around the house, and the feather in the reticule along with the missing photography plates was as much an announcement of his presence as knocking on the front door and introducing himself to Jansen.

His sisters eyed him now and again with concern, and he did his best to smile and alleviate their worry. Eva occasionally caught his eye, and he managed a wink for her, and the small smile she gave him in return told him she understood his anxiety.

The guests chatted with one another, and as his mother had often observed a few days into a house party, he saw that a noticeable shift had occurred. As people grew more comfortable together and spent time getting to know one another better, conversation flowed easily, more naturally. The clink of silverware, laughter, warm dialogue, and friendly debates over mundane issues were all hallmarks of a successful gathering, and he was glad for the sense of normalcy it provided.

Even Blanche Parker had ventured from her bedchamber. Why she remained was a mystery to Nathan. Eva had provided Nathan with a word-by-word account of the discussion she'd had with Blanche. He readily admitted, if he were the other young woman, he'd have left the party. Her immediate come-uppance—at the hands of a woman who wielded a sword so subtly one wouldn't realize she'd been cut—had been complete and swift. He was happier than he could say about Eva's valiant defense of him, and of her succinct and efficient method of en-suring Blanche refrain from future meddling in his life.

And yet, she remained at the party. He looked at her, seated farther down the table next to John Smythe. Perhaps pride kept Blanche from retreating to the safety of London. Perhaps she stayed on her sister's behalf. Her smile was brittle, her face un-naturally pale, and she didn't so much as glance in his or Eva's direction.

Mathilda Dilworth conversed with Peter Meyer, a light blush staining her cheeks. For all that she appeared to be devel-oping a *tendre* for the German, she didn't seem conventionally happy. From what Nathan had observed, however, Mathilda never seemed conventionally happy. Perhaps she grew weary of being forever in her bosom friend's shadow, or perhaps she found Blanche grating and was merely using the association for her own ends.

He wondered if the other guests noted her sullenness. The dynamic among the guests had subtly shifted. Rather than the prior intimidation clearly felt, especially by the female guests, they seemed to come into their own. Blanche and Mathilda did not hold the same sway over them, and whether that was the reason for their subdued moods or there was something else, it gave Nathan pause.

He knew Blanche had had a hand in the smashed photography plates, and he wouldn't have been surprised to learn she had been the one to knock over the camera. She'd admitted to Eva that she'd "found" the plates, and that they'd been intact at the time. Presumably she'd broken them—must have taken a mallet to them after placing them in the reticule—but how on earth had the feather made its way into the small bag? Why had she kept them instead of simply throwing them away? She'd insisted she did not know anyone named Toole, and Eva's recollection of the exchange was that Blanche had seemed baffled by the question. How else to explain the presence of the feather? If she were somehow connected to Toole, the prospects were grim. She now had an axe to grind with Eva, with him, and with his family, who made no secret of their ambivalence toward her.

He would speak with her immediately following supper but wasn't sure how effective the interview would be. Self-preservation was a strong motivator, and Blanche Parker was one who possessed it in spades.

As dinner wound down, Nathan's mother announced that they would be gathering in the ballroom for dancing and dessert. An excuse to hold Eva close would have been welcome news before he'd known about the Toole family matriarch's death. Now, as he looked at his own mother, his concern climbed. Should he call a stop to the gathering altogether? Send everyone home for their safety as well as his family's? And would his family truly be any safer? Sending them away would likely send Toole after them; at least Nathan had a reasonable expectation that the man would remain in the vicinity if the Winstons did also. He would need help from the Yard.

Christine gave instructions for the guests to reassemble in the ballroom in twenty minutes. As they cleared the room, Nathan watched Blanche Parker. Mathilda tapped her from behind, surprising her, and Blanche jumped in fright. He heard John Smythe say, "What gives, Blanche? You've seen a ghost?"

Blanche tried to laugh off her reaction, but several people around her had seen it. Others offered platitudes to assuage her embarrassment, but the fact remained clear: Blanche Parker was afraid of something.

Most of the women quickly returned to their chambers to freshen up before meeting in the ballroom. Nathan had decided to catch his mother and sisters at the library to give them a barebones version of his history with Bernard Toole, but he saved the details for later. He caught sight of Eva and Olivia first, but rather than smiles, both women looked troubled. Alice, Grace, and Delilah followed, and each expression showed the same concern. His heart thumped, and he braced himself. Something was wrong.

His anxiety increased as the women drew closer and he spied something Olivia held against the folds of her dress. It was a cigar box, just like the one he'd received in London, and now he felt his heart beating in his ears. He motioned to all of them and they entered the library as the other guests found their way, laughing and chatting, to the ballroom next door.

He quickly closed the door as Olivia held up the box. Eva

took it from her and handed it to Nathan. "Where did you get this, Olivia?" His voice was hoarse.

"It was on my bed."

"We all received one," Delilah added. "Eva told us briefly about your history with this man. Mr. . . . ?"

"Toole?" Grace said.

Nathan's jaw tightened as he lifted the lid and saw the black feather laying atop the cheap cigars. "Were there notes? Anything else?"

They all shook their heads. "What does it mean?" Alice looked baffled.

Nathan rubbed his forehead. He explained his assignment with the traveling carnival and Toole's justification for his anger at Nathan.

"You believe he is here?" Delilah asked.

"Or he has somebody here doing his will," he said.

"How well do you all truly know the guests?" Eva asked them, her gaze coming to rest on Nathan. "Could any of them have an association with the Toole family?"

Nathan was at a loss, as were his sisters, given their confusion.

"We've been loosely acquainted with each of them for some time," Grace said, frowning, "but some more than others."

"Jens Sorenson and Peter Meyer are newly arrived in society this season," Olivia added, "and I confess I do not know the origins of the older gentlemen."

Nathan cast a mental glance over the guest list. He would request a file from London on the families of all attending, but it would take time. From what he'd wrangled out of his mother regarding the rest of their schedule, they still had a day at the beach, a night at the theatre on the promenade, a trip to the new lighthouse, complete with a ride on the newfangled elevator that lifted guests high above the ground, and a faux fox hunt in the forest, whatever that entailed. There were several days still to spend in the company of the others, but it may not be enough time to do background research on each of them. If Toole was now increasing his efforts at intimidation by giving his sisters the gifts only Nathan would know were threatening, he had to assume the escalation would continue.

"For now," he finally said, "be vigilant. Do not behave any differently than you have to this point, and alert me at once to anything concerning. Before you retire for the evening, each of you take your 'gifts'"—he lifted Olivia's—"to my bedchamber."

Eva caught his sleeve as his sisters continued on to the ball-room. "I also found a feather today," she told him quietly. "I was distracted earlier and forgot."

He swallowed a rising surge of fear. How could he possibly keep her safe? "Was it in your room?"

She shook her head. "In my skirt pocket."

He grasped her arm, pulling her back into the library. "In your *skirt*?"

She nodded. "Someone has been in my room. I don't know how else they'd have managed it. The pocket is hidden within the fabric folds."

"Eva." He put a hand on the back of her neck and pulled her gently to him. He kissed her forehead softly, his gentle and deliberate actions belying the fear and anger that were growing in equal proportions. "I am so sorry."

Chatter and laughter sounded from the corridor. Tugging her farther into the shadows, Nathan placed a hard kiss on Eva's lips. "Try to never be alone," he whispered. "Perhaps one of the maids can sleep in your sitting room."

She put her hand on his cheek. "I'll be fine, and very vigilant."

"And you'll tell me *immediately* if you receive any more of those blasted feathers!"

"Of course. Go now, take that box to your room, and I'll join the others in the ballroom."

He kissed her again, wishing he could chain her arm to his the way he would a criminal. At least then he would know she was safe.

Nathan returned the cigar box to his room while Eva and his sisters continued on to the ballroom. He quickly checked his mother's chambers but found only her maid, who told him Mrs. Winston was already in the ballroom and no, she'd not received any gifts or packages. During the informal ball, Nathan made a point of surreptitiously wandering among the guests, who danced to the music playing on the Victrola or ventured out onto the balcony through the double doors that were thrown wide to invite in the pleasant, summer's night breeze.

He noted a subtle happiness about Ann Parker and hoped she was finding her way apart from her sister's shadow. She conversed more easily with the gentlemen, danced with Davis Jacobson and Franklin Frampton, and a pretty blush touched her cheeks.

Burton Handy seemed glum; his attention veered unerringly back to Blanche time and again, and he, also, seemed aware of her changed mood. *Put that dream to rest, old boy,* he wanted to tell him. *It's a ship destined to sink.*

Franklin Frampton and Inez Shelton danced together twice, and at one point, Nathan overheard a lively debate about the aural merits of woodwinds versus brass instruments. Louisa Wilhite listened patiently to, and may have been genuinely interested in, Davis Jacobson's tales of his taxidermied menagerie.

His description of the Mice at Tea vignette sounded especially unique.

Olivia and Alice wandered arm-in-arm in an attempt, Alice had told him, to overhear any discussion among the Mean Ladies and John Smythe. Jens Sorenson seemed determined to dance every number and even cajoled Mrs. Parkin onto the floor at one point.

Nathan paused at the refreshment table and procured a drink. He saw Eva chatting with Mrs. Larsen, but noted her attention seemed specifically focused on someone stepping onto the balcony. He watched her excuse herself from Mrs. Larsen and follow Burton Handy outside. Grace appeared at his elbow and murmured, "What is that about?"

He looked at her and then followed her gaze; she'd also watched Eva exit behind Mr. Handy. "She is intuitive," Nathan said. "Perhaps she saw something."

"In Mr. Handy? He is as meek as a sparrow."

Nathan tipped his head, thoughtfully observing the conversation on the balcony. "He is also desperately enamored of Blanche Parker. I ought to have considered that more fully."

"Ah. Of course." Grace nodded and retrieved a glass of punch for herself. "Eva will likely coax more from him than you would, however."

"True enough. He does seem rattled, though. He stepped back."

"She's incredibly beautiful, and he is shy. Perhaps that accounts for it."

Nathan smiled, remembering a time when Michael had described what he knew of the three cousins at the beginning of his association with them. He had said that Eva would have rendered him tongue-tied as a youth.

He knew since taking up photography that she had made a study of appearance, demeanor, and the sort of messages one sends without even uttering a word. She now perched on the edge of a small chair, positioning herself below Mr. Handy's diminutive height. Her shoulders were relaxed, her hands folded loosely in her lap. It was a subtle maneuver, but effective. Mr. Handy stopped retreating, and leaned in slightly, probably because she'd lowered her voice. Before long, he was speaking.

Nathan smiled. "She's good," he murmured. "If there is anything to be learned from the gentleman, I wager she will find it."

Grace nodded, impressed. "I am not surprised. You've chosen very well, brother." She smiled and hugged his arm.

Mr. Handy now spoke earnestly to Eva, glancing inside the ballroom. She nodded and held out a placating hand, and while he seemed for a moment to consider speaking again, he abruptly turned and left the balcony, crossing through the ballroom without stopping and then leaving the room altogether.

"She must have shaken something loose," Grace observed.

Nathan nodded.

"Is there anything I can do to help?"

"I've been meaning to ask Turner and Jansen about any new domestic help."

"How new?"

"Within the last two weeks."

Grace looked at the wide double doors leading out to the hall. Two footmen stood sentry, and she tapped her fingertip against her arm. "We've employed Thompson and Bentley for years. I wonder . . ." She trailed off and then handed her glass of punch to Nathan. "They would know every bit as much as Jansen, possibly better."

She left him and crossed the ballroom to the footmen. He

raised his brows, looking at the two glasses he now held. Setting them toward the back of the table, he selected a fresh glass and headed for the balcony. Eva's back was to the ballroom, and he took in the graceful lines of her neck and shoulders. Wishing very much he could surprise her by placing a kiss just beneath her ear, he instead cleared his throat to avoid startling her, and when she turned, handed her the drink.

"You seem thirsty."

She laughed and took a sip. "Do I? How odd. I was just now wishing on a star that a handsome prince would join me on this very balcony."

"You'll settle for me, I hope." He smiled, keeping his hands very intentionally in his pockets. "Our friend, Mr. Handy, did not qualify as such either?"

She sighed and spoke quietly. "He was the one who handed me the reticule in the shop yesterday."

Nathan nodded. "How did you know?"

"Because he would fly to the moon and back for Miss Parker." She smiled, but it seemed sad.

Nathan faced her, leaning a hip against the railing to better keep an eye on who was in earshot. "Did he admit as much? That it was at her bidding?"

She shook her head. "He would only say he was doing a favor for a friend, whose confidence he would not betray. He did not know what was contained inside the reticule, and he apologized profusely for the abrupt manner in which he managed the task."

Nathan frowned. "Why would he not have done the deed here? Why fight through the crowds in town?"

"Because there were crowds in town." She smiled. "He was to deliver it as soon and as anonymously as possible, taking care to remain unnoticed and avoid questions. He tried several times throughout the morning to slip it into my bag, but I was apparently always too quick to move away. His friend grew more 'urgent,' apparently, and so he took advantage of the masses in the haberdashery."

"I should talk with him."

"What will you do? Interrogate?" She shook her head. "We know full well whose bidding he followed. I do not believe it necessary." She smiled at him. "I am not a detective, however."

He leaned closer, unable to help himself. "Amelie insists Michael deputized her. I could do the same for you if you wish it."

"What would that entail, I wonder?" she whispered. "Working together, long hours . . ."

He took a breath and shook his head with a rueful smile. "I would find myself entirely too distracted to be effective, I fear. I do not know how Michael manages it."

Eva laughed softly. "My supposition—and mind, I cannot say for certain—is that they do not get much work done. Of course, her deputy status is only ceremonial, so when at work, her tasks are different." She smiled. "How does she fare in the office?"

"She's brilliant," he admitted. "She graciously offers help to me as well. Notes typed and filed, detailed to the last item. I imagine she's missed at *The Marriage Gazette*."

Eva nodded. "Very much. But Charlotte and I manage without her. Michael's sister, Clarissa, has been filling in, but I see wedding bells in her future, and she may not be able to devote as much time as before. Sally mentioned looking for a replacement, and I wonder about Inez Shelton. She is well read, exceptionally bright, and seems just the sort who would take to the work with success."

"I love you," he whispered.

Her eyes flew to his face, and she slowly smiled. "I wonder if I shall ever tire of hearing that."

"I hope not."

"I cannot imagine a world where I would. I love *you*, Detective." She turned toward him, and her dress rustled. The balcony lanterns caught the shimmering patterns in the fabric, surrounding her in a dark symphony of color. He wanted to bury his hands in her hair, pull her close for a kiss.

"You are exquisite," he murmured. "Please, come with me to Gretna Green."

She tipped back her head and laughed, and the sound warmed him through.

"Or we could use my necktie and handfast. Perfectly legal." He grinned.

Her laughter continued. "Only in Scotland! And only civilly. The church certainly doesn't recognize it."

"Am I to assume that is a refusal?"

"Yes," she nodded definitively, her smile wide, "you are to assume that is a refusal. But only temporarily." She leaned closer. "We shall be wed before you know it, and you'll grow tired of your nagging, shrewish wife."

"Never." He used every ounce of willpower to refrain from closing the scant distance between them and capturing her lips in a kiss. Voices intruded from the ballroom, and he stepped back. This time, they were in full view of an audience. Regretfully, he straightened. "Miss Caldwell, you drive me to distraction."

"Excellent. I hope I always do." She smiled and turned, deliberately, he was certain, brushing along his arm as she lifted her skirts and returned to the ballroom.

"Minx," he murmured under his breath, his smile wry.

She cast a glance at him over her shoulder, and he wished

very much he had been able to convince her of the merits of handfasting.

As he turned to follow her back inside, a sound from the library balcony to his right caught his attention. He peered into the darkness but saw nothing. The night outside was calm and quiet, and he wondered what had alerted him. The sound was a familiar one, perhaps the rustle of fabric?

As a child he had jumped from the balcony where he now stood to the library balcony several feet away. He had slipped, of course, and smashed hard against it, breaking his nose and left wrist. He had hung onto the railing by sheer dint of will, finally slinging one leg around a wrought iron pole. He hung there, screaming, until first Jansen and then his father had come running. Had he not been so traumatized, he believed now his father would have been tempted to thrash him within an inch of his life.

The memory flashed through his mind like an old, forgotten relic. He thought of the affection he'd felt for the boy he'd rescued from the Toole carnival two years earlier and how, in the past few days, he'd grown accustomed to the innocent presence of Sammy White. The thought of these two boys made him appreciate what his father must have felt all those years ago. As he looked at the distance between the balconies now, it didn't seem so far. He could probably reach it easily with one leap.

Deciding to take the practical route and walk around through the house instead, he left the balcony and made his way to the library. He opened the double doors, unsurprised that the room was dark, but very surprised to feel a breeze and realize the balcony doors were open. He crossed the room and stepped outside, looking across at the ballroom balcony. There was nobody here, and after a cursory check in the library, there appeared to be nobody inside either.

Hearing things, then. He wasn't surprised. He was tired. He closed the balcony doors, and at the last moment caught the scent of cheap cologne. He whipped the door open again and stepped outside, looking around at the grounds, beneath the balcony itself, and inhaling deeply.

There was nothing out there, and he wondered if he was finally losing his mind. He noted several of his security men making their rounds, covering the property in an organized grid. At any rate, the smell was gone—if it had even been there in the first place.

He reentered the library, took one last look outside, and quietly closed the balcony doors. As he frowned into the dim hallway light, Grace appeared from the ballroom. She saw him and quickened her step. Breathless, she pulled him farther away from any potential eavesdroppers and whispered, "Something odd has happened. According to Thompson and Bentley, the footmen, one of the new hires has gone missing. It's left them shorthanded, and they've been forced to cover for each other."

"Who is missing?"

"His name is Collins."

In a flash, Nathan remembered when Eva had demonstrated her development process outside at the caravan and Collins had left his post. What had Abernathy said? The man had taken ill? He mentioned it to Grace, who nodded.

"That must be the last he was seen. According to Thompson and Bentley, nobody remembers speaking to him after the first morning's activities."

Noises at the ballroom doorway halted further conversation, and they returned to the others. Nathan's sense of apprehension rose with each step. The time had arrived to send for reinforcements.

CHAPTER 22

"Cave exploration!" Mrs. Winston stood in the ballroom next to an odd assortment of objects. Eva suddenly realized why the instructions for the morning had included simple, light-weight clothing. ("Regency era would be ideal.")

As Eva was not in possession of Regency-era clothing, she'd made do with a simple blue skirt sans bustle, white shirtwaist, and a fashionable tie that matched the fabric in the skirt. It was an ensemble she preferred to utilize when working in the close quarters of the darkroom carriage or on assignment for a sitting. She hoped it would be equally functional in exploring caves.

Apparently, nobody else in the group possessed Regency-era clothing either; as she surveyed her fellow party sisters, she wondered at the wisdom of such an adventure.

"Not to fret," Mrs. Winston said, "you'll not be hanging from ropes or scaling the sides of anything. It is little more than a stroll through a park. A dark park. Ladies, you may choose to carry along a light pelisse, as it has been known to be chilly inside."

Eva caught Nathan's eye, and he shook his head impercepti-bly with a little eye roll; she tamped down a smile. Miss Wilhite, dressed in a lovely gown of admittedly lightweight but pink satin, looked down dubiously at herself.

"Perhaps you have something in a linen?" Eva whispered.

She shook her head, her eyes troubled.

"Not to worry," Eva said. "We are nearly the same size and I have another skirt and shirtwaist, if you'd like."

"Ooh, yes, please." Louisa smiled and bounced a bit in place. "Have you also another of those neckties? I should love to try one!"

"Absolutely! I am so glad you like it. They are all the rage in Montreal, I hear, and—"

Eva noted the silence in the room and stopped abruptly to see several pairs of eyes on her and Louisa.

Mrs. Winston smiled patiently. "I am giving instructions that must be carefully followed."

"Yes, of course." Eva nodded, chastised.

Nathan eyed her sternly, his lips pursed to prevent a smile. Had she not been aware of others' lingering eyes, she'd have stuck out her tongue at him.

She glanced side-eyed at Louisa, who eyed her likewise. Louisa widened her eyes and mouthed, "Golly!"

Eva snorted a surprised laugh and then closed her eyes with a wince. Christine stopped speaking, then resumed. Blanche and Mathilda eyed Eva with disdain, and Eva *dearly* wished to stick her tongue out in that direction.

Christine continued her instructions, directing their attention to the supplies. They consisted of a lightweight knapsack bearing convenient straps for carrying ease, a notebook and pencil, a compass, a water flask, and two pressed, clean handkerchiefs.

"I shall lead the way there. You'll also be accompanied by a few staff who will serve lunch and tea, and, according to my dear friend Mrs. Parkin, as her rheumatism is dormant, the weather should be clear." Christine smiled. "Are there any questions?"

"No simple fox hunt during this holiday?" John Smythe dubiously examined the supplies.

"I have a tender heart for foxes and, as such, we shall substitute the traditional hunt with something less brutal. Besides, other house parties make use of the hunt to segregate the women from the men. That entirely defeats the purpose, in my opinion. Any other questions?"

Eva stole another glance at Nathan, who was now standing at the door with Stafford, his security man. He did not seem unduly alarmed or upset, and she breathed a partial sigh of relief. Perhaps they might survive the day without danger or drama.

While the others gathered supplies, Eva hurried with Louisa up to her bedchamber. They spied Mary in the hallway carrying a stack of clean sheets, and the girl's eyes lit up. "Miss Caldwell! Can I help?"

"Actually, you may be more efficient than I am, and we must be quick about this."

"Yes," Louisa agreed. "I do not want to be the reason the entire party is delayed."

Mary laughed, but quickly cleared her throat. She set down the bedding in the sitting room and followed Eva and Louisa into the dressing room. Eva showed them a few options, and Mary made quick work of getting Louisa out of her dress and into the new outfit.

"A pity we haven't time for Jane to do your hair," Mary said, and then looked at Louisa, stricken. "Not that your hair isn't lovely, miss!"

Louisa brushed it aside. "No insult at all. I've been hoping to grab this Miss Jane—everyone looks like a princess under her gifted hands."

Mary nodded, tying and buttoning as she continued. "*Certain* guests insisted they needed more help because I couldn't get to them soon enough, so then Turner brings on Jane and Mattie. Now, there apparently isn't a problem anymore and we are able to manage just fine without the new girls. I did tell Turner that Jane must stay—the guests are very happy with her, even if she is idle part of the day with nothing to do." She patted Louisa's collar down over the necktie. "I told Turner I'll keep her busy helping me. There's always something needs doing."

Eva nodded as Mary continued her stream of chatter, but lately, her mind snagged on anything even tangentially related to Blanche or Mathilda. They had run the staff ragged after the first day of the party and now had no need of extra help. Why the sudden change?

On impulse, she broached a matter that had lingered in the back of her mind since the night Nathan had shown her the secret passageway behind the panel in her room. "Mary, do you and the other maids use the servant passageways?"

Mary frowned and shook her head. "No, miss, not at all. Far as I know, nobody goes in there." She shuddered. "Too many spiders and such, and too narrow to carry trays."

Louisa's eyes widened. "There are secret passageways? How delightful! But not the spiders." She commiserated with Mary, and the two laughed together.

Eva frowned in thought. Why had the passageway to Eva's room shown evidence of activity? She chewed on her lip and remembered the open jewelery pouch in her vanity drawer, the black feather placed deliberately in her skirt—possibly in more than one.

She regretted sharing her concerns about the passageway with Nathan. He maintained an air of calm, but she knew he was strung tight. Perhaps she was making something out of nothing. Her own nerves were strained, and she jumped at her own shadow when alone or in the dark.

She shook her head and took a breath, slowly letting it out. She would enjoy the day. What could go wrong with everyone together?

When Mary was finished, the women gave her a quick thanks and made their way out of the guest wing and around the corner to the ballroom, where conversation and a bustle of activity continued.

"Excellent," Louisa breathed when they entered. "They're only now packing." She smiled at Eva and thanked her for the third time before hurrying to Inez, who held out a knapsack.

Nathan finished speaking with Stafford and joined Eva. "This is truly not a strenuous outing," he said quietly. He opened his mouth to continue but, at a sharp look from Christine, mimicked locking his lips with a key.

"Well, either way, I had best pack up my supplies." As Eva placed one of each item in her bag, she looked around at the others. Everyone was present except Burton Handy. She straightened, shaking her bag to settle the items as she looked closer around the group, thinking maybe he was behind someone.

"Who's missing?" Nathan asked.

"Mr. Handy?"

He nodded. "Haven't seen him yet this morning."

"Odd. Is he ill?"

"According to his valet, he is still abed. Perhaps supper did not sit well with him."

"I am suspicious of every shadow," she murmured, putting

her arm through one of the knapsack straps. She eyed Nathan with suspicion. "Where is *your* knapsack?"

He looked down at her with a grin. "Do not worry, Miss Caldwell. I wouldn't dream of allowing you to explore the caves on your own."

"Here you are, good man," Franklin Frampton said, smiling and handing Nathan a packed knapsack.

"Much obliged, Frampton!"

"Anything for my fellow three-legged partner."

"Mr. Frampton?" Inez Shelton poked her head into the conversation. "I wonder if I might ask you some questions about your music lessons."

He brightened. "Of course!" He offered Inez his arm and the two of them followed the stream of people now exiting the ballroom.

Eva looked at Nathan silently, chewing on the inside of her lip.

"Do not look at me that way!" Nathan's voice cracked. "I received a telegram, and he saw me leaving. Offered to pack the bag for me."

"What telegram?"

He glared. "This one." With a flourish, he whipped a paper from his pocket.

It was a message from Michael Baker, stating that barring trouble getting to the house from the train station, he would arrive just after breakfast.

She looked at Nathan in surprise. "He's coming here today?"

He nodded and shouldered his pack. "I sent word to him last night, requesting his presence. Unable to bring Amelie, however. I am sorry about that. Late notice, and she'd already committed to help Director Ellis for the day."

Eva noted the time. "Will we have to leave without him, or should we wait?"

"I believe he's just arrived—Jansen is making his way over here at his usual, rapid pace with a message for me. Seems urgent."

She raised her brows high as the butler took his time. "How can you tell?"

"It's in his eyes."

Eva snort-laughed again for the second time that morning.

As Nathan had guessed, Jansen told him that Detective Inspector Baker was in the parlor.

"Please inform him we shall meet him in the hall—" Nathan began. "Never mind, Jansen, I'll tell him myself."

"Very good, sir." The butler turned on his heel and made his way back at his same, steady pace.

Nathan grabbed an extra knapsack and motioned to Eva. They passed by Jansen and made their way down the stairs to the others who were gathering in the hall. Eva waited while Nathan went in the direction of the parlor.

Delilah lifted her hand and made her way to Eva's side. She wrinkled her brow and said to Eva, "He has called Inspector Baker?"

"I think he must be concerned," Eva said quietly. As she looked carefully around the crowded hall, she noted several footmen standing at attention. Two subtly shadowed Mrs. Winston's movements as she directed the symphony of bodies out the door. "I've not seen some of these footmen," she told Delilah. "Are they new?"

"They arrived this morning from the country estate." Delilah looked at Eva, her eyes troubled. "Grace mentioned that one has gone missing. Knowing Nathan is worried makes every-thing more troublesome."

Eva nodded. She'd seen Nathan at work; she knew of his steady demeanor, his tendency to avoid dramatics or over-reaction. That he was quietly marshalling the troops in addition to the measures he'd already put in place spoke to his state of mind. And still he managed to tease with her, helping her feel as though all was well.

"He's a good man," Eva said, almost to herself.

Delilah looked at her and smiled, putting her arm around Eva's shoulders. "Everything will be fine."

Eva wondered which of them Delilah was trying to con-vince. "Yes." She nodded, hoping she looked reassuring. When Delilah chuckled, she knew she'd failed.

Nathan emerged from the corridor with Michael Baker. Eva smiled and clasped his hands when he reached her, welcoming another familiar face.

"Amelie sends her love and regrets. Director Ellis is putting her talents to good use. Claims his files are a disastrous mess." He glanced at Nathan, adding, "I think he's glad to see me gone. Knows I won't be there to interrupt her work."

Nathan smiled, and while Eva wouldn't define it as his most carefree moment in days, it was close. He handed Michael the extra knapsack, and while Michael eyed it dubiously, he put it on his shoulders.

Mrs. Winston guided the crowd out the front door and around the side of the house. They passed by the portable dark-room, which Eva had instructed Sammy to avoid until she re-turned. With recent mishaps and "accidents," she didn't want him anywhere near the combustible materials.

As they continued to the back lawn, Eva noted several sets

of curious female eyes apprising the newcomer. When she intro-duced him as "Detective Inspector Michael Baker, my cousin's husband," the flashes of interest quickly waned. For the gentle-men, however, Michael was a potential repository of fresh crim-inal anecdotes.

Michael and Nathan fell back a few paces and conversed in an undertone. Seeking to give them privacy, Eva quickened her pace and caught up with Alice and Olivia, who chatted with Ann Parker. Blanche and Mathilda progressed just ahead, and when John Smythe circled around to catch Blanche's attention, Mathilda was alone for the moment.

Wondering if she might draw conversation from the woman without her sidekick present, Eva quickened her step again to walk alongside her.

"Mathilda—"

The other woman jumped and glared at Eva.

"Oh! I did not mean to startle you—apologies." She realized in that moment, she'd never seen what appeared to be a genuine smile on Mathilda's face. Perhaps it was that a genuine smile had never been sent in Eva's direction.

"I feel we've set off on the wrong foot since our arrival here, and I was hoping to remedy it."

Mathilda eyed her quietly. Hers was an understated beauty, as opposed to Blanche's, which was painfully overt. Eva imag-ined one wouldn't have an easy go of it when the bosom friend was Blanche Parker.

"It is 'Miss Dilworth,' Miss Caldwell."

Eva did her best not to gape. "Oh! Of course. Forgive me."

Mathilda's voice dropped to a near whisper. "I suppose that is unusual for you? That a person does not simply fall prostrate at your feet?"

Eva carefully considered her response and, in the end, remained silent.

"*My* apologies, of course, for being the first." Mathilda eyed her evenly, her gaze traveling from Eva's hair to her face. Without another word, she stepped away, joining Blanche.

Eva watched the pair as John Smythe moved forward to walk with Jens Sorenson. Mathilda whispered something to Blanche, who looked over her shoulder at Eva with a scowl. Peter Meyer hung back to wait for Mathilda and drew her arm into his. Mathilda's quick glance at him seemed a confused mix of pleasure and uncertainty. She wondered if Mathilda was rarely the friend who drew gentlemen's attention, and when Meyer offered Blanche his other arm, Mathilda's expression tightened.

Eva shook her head—mostly at herself. Why had she simply assumed Mathilda would be amenable to conversation when Eva had so clearly become her best friend's enemy? Grace jogged up from behind to walk next to Eva as they continued across the acreage, nearing the forest. "What on earth was that?" she asked.

"I thought to make friends with someone who has absolutely no use for me." She paused. "That's not entirely true—my intention was not to 'make friends.' I was searching for information."

"And did you find any?"

"Not a bit, other than to say I am not at liberty to address her by her first name."

Grace's eyes widened, and she laughed. Lowering her voice, she said, "You're in good company; last year at an intimate soiree where Olivia deigned to perform a number, she afterward attempted pleasant conversation. Mathilda told Olivia her voice was an assault on her eardrums."

"Now that is absurd. Why would she say such a thing? Not only as a matter of rudeness, but it's ridiculous."

Grace eyed the trio, who had moved farther ahead to walk with John and the other gentlemen. "Probably because Blanche is jealous, and whatever Blanche does not like, Mathilda detests doubly." She paused, observing the interplay ahead of them. "Are they each casting a net for our German guest? That sort of competition between friends never ends well."

"What do you know of Jens and Peter?" Eva asked.

Grace shrugged. "Jens's father is the Swedish ambassador, and the Meyer family are old friends of the Sorensons, from what I understand."

"And have either of them a profession?"

Grace smiled at Eva. "They have money, each of them."

They walked for a moment in silence, entering the forest on the property's edge. Eva thought back over the morning to something that now tickled the back of her brain. "What of Burton Handy—what is Blanche's opinion of him?"

Grace frowned in thought. "She has little use for him, I know that."

Eva reviewed the conversation she'd had on the balcony with the man the night before. He had been mistrustful, wary, and then finally deeply apologetic. Before he had abruptly left, he'd seemed mortified. "Did you hear word of him this morning? I'm curious about why he's absent."

"Ill, my mother said." Grace shrugged. "Perhaps he has grown weary of Blanche's constant rebuffs."

Or perhaps he was embarrassed about giving Eva the reticule in such an odd manner and, now that he'd admitted as much, felt self-conscious. Truthfully, the man hadn't done anything horribly wrong, certainly nothing criminal. He had gone very red in the face, however, and Eva had pitied him his clear discomfort.

The forest, for its small size, was surprisingly thick. Little light managed to filter through the trees from the sky above, and Eva stumbled over roots and branches. Grace caught her elbow to keep her from falling, but Eva was relieved to see she was not the only one having trouble navigating the terrain. Even Jens Sorenson, ever light on his feet, tripped and landed on his knee.

Eva felt a strong arm hitch under hers, and she looked up to see Nathan smiling down at her. "Perhaps you need a horse, milady?"

"Ha. I have been managing just fine with the help of your able-bodied sister, thank you very much."

Grace offered a mock salute, just as her own foot caught on a root and she stumbled. She shrieked as her feet tangled in her dress and she went down, taking Inez Shelton and Franklin Frampton with her.

They landed in a heap, and as those around scrambled to help them up, Grace stood and brushed herself off, her face red despite her laughter. "I am so sorry!"

Franklin, ever equanimous and amiable, smiled as he helped Inez to her feet. "No harm done here. How about you, Miss Shelton?"

Inez laughed a bit shakily and brushed at her skirt near the knee, where she'd made contact with the ground. It was dirt-stained and would require a fair amount of laundering treatment to come clean. Eva winced and noted similar expressions on most of the women present. Jens shook his head. "It is salvageable, Miss Shelton, but a few prayers would also not be amiss."

Alice now smiled at the man. "Mr. Sorenson, do you know of a product that will do the trick?"

He nodded, all seriousness. "I shall have my valet speak to your maid immediately upon our return. He's developed an excellent cleansing paste that works wonders." In an undertone, he added to Franklin, "One can participate in only so many horse races along the Serpentine before needing an extremely powerful scrubbing agent. Do I have the right of it?"

Franklin looked at Jens for a prolonged moment before finally nodding. "Certainly, certainly." After Jens returned to the front of the pack again, Franklin told Inez, "I certainly do not condone ill-conceived horse racing."

They continued their journey, and Eva took a moment to walk beside Nathan. "Tell me, what is the nature of this 'cave exploration'?"

He sighed. "I promised my mother I'd not give away the secrets of the cave."

"As I'll see them soon by myself, do you suppose you might educate me now? I do like to be prepared, you know."

Nathan looked ahead, probably to be sure his mother was not in earshot. "The cave is a source of drawings and a few random dinosaur remains."

Eva's mouth fell open. "But that—"

He shushed her.

"But that," she whispered, "that is incredible! Has the Natural Museum of Science visited? Is it carefully guarded?"

He shook his head, a smile threatening. "The drawings and bones are the result of my mother and her friends' efforts. They created the cave for us as children, shortly after my father died."

"Oh!" For some reason Eva didn't understand, the revelation struck a chord in her heart. "That is the loveliest thing I have ever heard. Were you all astounded when she showed it to you?"

He smiled. "I was too old to be fooled, but my sisters were just young enough to enjoy it."

"I hope you did not call your mother out?"

"Of course, I did not. What sort of son do you take me for?" He winked and clasped her fingers for a brief moment.

She glanced behind them to be sure nobody was there, and he chuckled.

"We are at the end of the pack, not to fret." He offered his arm, a much more suitable gesture and practical, as she tripped a few more times despite lifting her long skirt out of the way.

"Charlotte has breeches, you know," Eva said. "I've always thought it crass but am beginning to see the benefits."

"She does?" He looked confused. "When does she wear them?"

"When she visits home and works in the orchard. Or climbs into the tree house. Or is obliged to put her brothers in their place."

"What sort of brothers would harass their sister so that she felt compelled to wear breeches to defend herself?"

"There are six of them, and she is the youngest. My aunt died when she was young, and I'm afraid that except for the occasional periods of time she spent with Aunt Sally, Charlotte was left mostly to her own devices."

"Breeches, hmm." He glanced at her, and she suddenly felt warm all over. "A notion to consider. Ah, here we are."

Eva noted the edge of the tree line, beyond which lay a path that wound down to the beach. "Does this portion wind around the alcove below on the other side?"

He nodded. "This part of the beach is technically on the very border of the property, and nobody really lays claim to the caves to the exclusion of others. Through the years, my mother has notified families in the area of the 'cave of treasures,' and many people know of its existence."

They stepped out of the trees, and while the light increased considerably, Eva heard a rumble in the air over the water. "Mrs. Parkin's rheumatism gives faulty readings, it seems."

"Now," Mrs. Winston was saying, "a bit of thunder does not equal rain. Besides! We shall be covered!"

They followed her down the path, and the staff accompanying them to set up tea, in addition to the extra footmen and security Nathan had hired, more than tripled the number of invited guests. For Eva, the numbers provided an extra sense of security. What could possibly go wrong with so many people about?

CHAPTER 23

Mrs. Winston had, apparently, planned for contingencies in the event that Mrs. Parkin's rheumatism was feeling playful. She directed the staff to erect three large canopies under which the guests could still enjoy their picnic tea even if it rained. While she was engaged with the details, she waved the guests toward the seaside wall.

"Explore! Draw pictures, take notes, and remember to make use of your compass, should you get lost." Christine smiled and blew them all a kiss.

A smattering of affectionate applause, accompanied by a few low grumbles of discontent, followed her remarks. Eva looked at the wall and the trail leading down from the forest. "Somehow it looks steeper from here," she remarked.

"This is the least enjoyable view of the trail when one is a child having spent a long day exploring the caves and running up and down the beach." Olivia smiled. "Exhausted, hungry, and usually weepy—and there is the trail leading back up to the property. When you are small, it seems like the tallest mountain in the world."

Nathan smiled. "I usually ended up carrying one of you on my back."

"Or mother sent for a carriage, and we rode the long way around to the house." Grace laughed. "If we complained loudly enough, she occasionally relented."

Eva followed the rest to the mouth of the cave, where footmen were stationed and handing out small lanterns. Nathan took two and gave her one, and said, "Follow me, and watch your step. Those breeches might not have been a bad idea."

"What a wonderful idea," Alice exclaimed, following Eva. "When we were young, we wore bathing dresses or shorter skirts. This is ridiculous."

Eva glanced back at her and smiled. "Have you not been here as an adult?"

"I confess, I've not. I usually find something else to do when Mama takes her groups here. This year has been so much more enjoyable—it's the first time since I have attended as an adult that the majority of guests are my age."

The cave wound up slightly and back into the hillside, and the multitude of lanterns gave plenty of light. The cave floor was swept clean, with rocks and dirt shoved to the sides to provide an easy pathway. Only twice did Eva's footing slip, and the second time, Nathan reached back and clasped her hand. He smiled at her as he pulled her along, and they quickly reached a large cavern where, when lanterns were held high, evidence of "ancient" drawings could be seen on the walls.

She put her hand to her chest, her eyes burning at the thought of a young mother and her friends creating an adventure for her children who had lost their father. "This is splendid," she whispered, walking along, smiling at some of the images that were clearly nothing close to ancient.

When the guests realized what they were seeing, many *oohed* and *aahed*, and several exclamations of delight for the charm of it all echoed through the room.

"Over to your left, ladies and gentlemen," Nathan intoned, "please take note of . . . a pile of ancient dinosaur bones. Dating to the . . . the . . ."

"Mesozoic," Michael murmured in a stage whisper.

"The Mesozoic Age." Nathan gestured to a series of three large rocks that resembled plaster of Paris reliefs set in sturdier concrete. Inlaid were large "fossils" that looked impressively like some Eva had seen in museums.

"How did she do this?" Eva whispered, charmed.

Grace leaned in. "Hired a science student from Cambridge." She looked at the Winston girls, all gathered close. "This must have been so magical for you."

They nodded, tawny and green eyes bright with nostalgia. "It truly was," Olivia said. "This place was magical."

The cavern marked the end of the cave exploration, and rather than block up the space, Eva stepped aside to allow others to enter. She ventured back onto the main walkway and turned to the right, noting a small branch that continued by curving to the left. Nathan was behind her, and she lifted her lantern high, wondering aloud, "What is up this way?"

He put his hand at her waist and pulled her back subtly against him. She closed her eyes for a moment, wanting very much to turn around and kiss him. "That," he said, his low voice close to her ear, "is the 'supply room' where my mother keeps her extra paint for touch-ups."

Eva laughed softly. "Does she do it often?"

"Usually in the spring when visitors will soon arrive in town."

"She is exceptional, Nathan. She has a very generous heart."

"She does."

He rested his chin on her head and then she felt him release a sigh. He placed the softest and quickest of kisses on her neck before stepping back. As she turned to go, her light swung into the blackness of the supply room and caught on something that struck a dissonant chord. Something glaringly wrong in such a charming place.

She leaned back against the cool stone and closed her eyes. She must have been mistaken, surely. She didn't want to look again, though.

"Eva?" Nathan was again beside her, shielding her from view of the others.

She licked her lips and swallowed. Clutching his jacket with a shaking hand, she raised her lantern again and leaned forward, shining it fully into the entrance of the smaller cavern. It was as she had feared: a man's body lay prostrate against the wall, dressed only in underclothing that was stained red on the chest. Sightless eyes stared back at her, and to her horror, she realized he must have been there for some time. She recognized the face, and her heart seized.

Nathan cursed under his breath and pulled her against him, holding her head to his chest. It was absurd, really, that she should be such a ninny and he should be so quick to try to shield her from the image. The two of them had been together in the same room with dead bodies on several occasions, and more often than not, he adjusted lighting for her so she could get the best possible photograph for the case files. She'd long ago lost any sense of shock at the sight of a lifeless body.

The difference was, of course, that she photographed scenes that were being investigated when she arrived. She walked into situations where crimes had been committed and already discovered. She had never found one herself, and she had never been surprised by a dead body. She usually had the luxury of steeling herself before she walked into the room.

"Be still for a moment," he whispered.

She nodded, folding her arms in tight and leaning against him. "I know who it is," she whispered.

"Collins?"

She squeezed her eyes closed and nodded. "I had hopes for a moment it was a natural death."

He paused. "I do not believe it was."

She lifted her head and looked at him in the low light. "No, I would say the blood on his chest precludes any other assumption."

He sighed and gently rubbed her back. "We do not want to cause a stampede," he whispered. "I'll fetch Michael, and then we'll send for local authorities. Are you steady enough to stand here and say you're blocking the supply room to protect the magic of the cave?" He smiled grimly.

"Of course."

He released her and stepped back, and she caught his arm.

"Nathan, I do not want your sisters to see this."

He nodded and threaded his way back into the main cavern, leaving her to stand watch over the tomb.

CHAPTER 24

Michael stared at Nathan. "There is a what? In the where?"

Nathan motioned to him and led the way back up to his mother's supply cavern where Eva leaned against the wall, blocking the entrance. She stepped aside and, after he and Michael entered the small room, resumed her post. The smaller cavern was up a small distance from the main room and most people didn't realize the path threaded up any farther. With any luck, nobody would realize what was happening.

"No odor," Michael said quietly. "A commentary on the time of death, I believe Dr. Neville would say."

Nathan massaged the back of his neck. "Clearly not so advanced that someone wouldn't recognize him."

"We do not want people traipsing in and out of here, though," Michael said.

"Agreed. I'll quietly inform my mother, and she can make an excuse about the rain threatening. I want everyone back to the main property before we proceed."

"Send for the locals, though, and a coroner." Michael looked at him, the corner of his mouth ticking upward in the barest hint of a grim smile. "Seems I arrived just in time to help you."

Nathan nodded and turned to inform his mother that her cave exploration day was about to be cut short.

"Oh, no, you cannot come up this way," Eva was saying quietly to someone just outside.

"Mrs. Winston sent me, miss; you needn't worry. She's asked me to collect two large buckets from the supply room. I've been here many times. I know just where to look."

"But no—" she said and cut herself off with what sounded like a curse.

Nathan stood face-to-face at the cavern entrance with a footman who clearly had now seen what lay beyond Eva's slender shoulders. The young man put a hand over his mouth and fell back against the wall with a muffled gasp. Rather than allow him to attract more gawkers, Nathan pulled him into the room and stood in front of him, blocking his view.

"It's Collins!" the man cried out. "I know him—that's Collins!" He closed his eyes and gulped. "Turner hired him in Town before we came here for the holiday. George Abernathy shared a bedroom with him. He disappeared the day after guests arrived, and then Jansen had to hire someone new."

Nathan and Michael both shushed the man. Eva touched his arm and said, "Please, sir, we mustn't sound the alarm. Not yet. What is your name?"

"Henderson." He swallowed, and his Adam's apple bobbed. "What's happened to him?"

Nathan nudged him to sit down on the floor. "We will all leave in a moment, but we must clear the other guests first."

"Eva," Nathan said, "did you notice George Abernathy outside on the beach?"

She nodded. "Shall I fetch him? Someone else will need to stand guard."

"I will," Michael offered. "Eva?"

"Yes?"

Michael rubbed his chin and smiled ruefully. "If local constabulary lack access to a photographer, might we avail you of your services?"

"Of course." She exhaled. "This promises to be a long day."

Alarm bells rang in Nathan's head, but as if far in the distance. Collins had gone missing the day after the guests arrived . . . The black feathers, the mischief, inconsistencies . . . He knew Toole's signature, could sense his involvement. He'd always considered himself observant, but he'd not ever spent time with Toole and had seen him only from a distance. Even then, Toole had sported a full beard that all but obscured his face. He could have been under Nathan's nose this whole time.

Eva returned with George Abernathy and led him past Michael. They all looked at the footman, who appeared stunned to see the dead man. "Collins?" His face paled.

"Did you know him well, Abernathy?" Michael asked.

George shook his head. "He was new—hired for the London townhouse a month ago." He swallowed. "What on earth's happened? Who would do this?"

Nathan shook his head. "I do not know yet. I'll speak with Jansen and Turner—someone must know more about the man and his history. George, I would like you and Henderson to alert the local authorities; please run back up through the forest and take a carriage from the carriage house. Transport the local authorities here if they wish it. Did Mrs. Winston have a wagon brought round the long way for ease in returning the tents and tea supplies?"

"Yes, sir."

"Good. Once you've finished your task, please find me for further instruction."

Henderson got to his feet and followed George out of the cavern.

Nathan looked at Eva. "If only we'd have gone to Gretna Green when we'd had the chance."

Eva laughed, startled, and Michael looked at him with brows raised sky high.

"Is that the lay of the land, then?"

"Michael Baker, allow me to introduce my affianced, Miss Evangeline Caldwell. I have yet to ask her father, and so we are obliged to pretend we are not in love and knocking loudly at the chapel door."

"Perhaps not the best setting, but congratulations to both of you. Shall I wait before informing Amelie?"

Eva nodded. "Please. I want to be the one to tell her."

Michael smiled and extended his hand. Eva stepped in for an embrace, and Michael hugged her. He looked at Nathan over her head and said, "So all you needed to come up to scratch was a few days at a house party?"

Nathan chuckled. "My friend, this took planning I wasn't even aware I was doing."

Eva now regarded Nathan with an arch look. "'Come up to scratch'?"

Michael laughed. "You haven't noticed him mooning after you like a puppy? For months?"

"He maintains as much, but I don't believe I saw it quite like that."

Voices sounded just outside the cavern, and Nathan pulled Eva with him to cut off at the pass any curiosity seekers. Michael resumed his position at the entrance, and Nathan directed traffic in what he hoped was a lighthearted, jovial manner.

"You mustn't sound so gruff if your aim is to allay suspicion," Eva murmured behind him and poked his back.

As they passed the entrance to the main cavern, he saw that only a few guests remained; thankfully, most appeared to have exited in favor of tea. He grabbed Eva's hand and they maneuvered their way out of the cave and stepped onto the beach, into a stream of rain that was gathering by the moment and would soon be torrential.

"Oh, very good." He smiled grimly as he watched the tents, which were not built for gale force winds, bend and lift free of their shallow moorings in the ground. Half of the guests and staff ran up the path to the forest, and the other half ran around the bend to where his mother had at least one carriage waiting, probably two. His sisters ran with their mother, Mrs. Larsen, and Mrs. Parkin to the carriages, and the few remaining maids and two footmen who had ventured inside the cave appeared now at the threshold, staring at the weather in shock.

"If you run around the bend, you might catch the carriages," Nathan told them, raising his voice to be heard over the clap of thunder that boomed overhead.

With a shriek, they were off, and Nathan stood at the cave entrance with Eva, alone. "Well," he said, considering his options, "not exactly how I envisioned it coming to fruition, but I'll take what fate sees fit to hand me."

"What do you mean?" Eva shivered at a gust of wind that blew in a sheet of rain.

"I have been searching for an opportunity to do this." He smiled and took her face in his hands, lowering his head and kissing her. At first, he captured her shocked gasp, and then a smile, and finally a sigh as she wound her arms around his neck. In the deep recesses of his brain, he realized that his friend and partner was in the cave, standing watch over a dead man.

Eva pulled back, apparently thinking the same thing. "Poor Michael is back in there. We must get moving."

"Michael has been married for nearly three months now, one of which was spent traveling the continent and eating pastries. He can grant me two minutes of bliss at the mouth of a cave."

She tipped back her head and laughed, giving him the perfect opportunity to nuzzle the side of her neck with his nose and lips.

He registered the sound of footsteps pounding on the rocky shoreline in time to release her and straighten his jacket. It was George Abernathy, winded and white as a sheet.

"What is it?" Eva asked, her hand grasping for and clutching Nathan's sleeve.

"Mr. Handy, sir," George gasped. "He's dead."

CHAPTER 25

Eva wandered, stunned, from Mr. Handy's bedchamber. Several hours had passed since her mad dash in the rain with Nathan. She kept telling herself it must have been a mistake; she'd only just spoken with the man the night before. Guilt threatened to settle in, and she barely held it at bay, telling herself repeatedly that she'd done nothing wrong by asking him if he had been involved with Blanche's activities.

Suicide? The local coroner indicated that he would know more after an autopsy, but his initial opinion, given the empty teacup and bottle of laudanum beside the bed, was an overdose. Whether it had been accidental was uncertain, but preliminary interviews with some of the guests verified that Mr. Handy had been morose the last two days.

She walked slowly down the guest wing, still chilled from her run—nearly a mile across the property—in the pouring rain. She'd changed her clothes and gone directly to Mr. Handy's suite where Nathan awaited her in the sitting room. He'd asked her again to repeat exactly what Mr. Handy had told her the night before on the balcony, and she and Nathan had shared with the local chief of police, Chief Harlan, everything that had happened beginning with her camera mishaps and the odd encounter at the haberdashery. She'd been reluctant to implicate Blanche Parker but had answered honestly about Blanche's odd confession where she described finding the plates.

Nathan was still in Mr. Handy's suite, along with Michael, who had returned from the cave after Chief Harlan assigned constabulary to stand guard over it until he finished at the house. The more Harlan heard about the threads tying to Nathan's former case with Toole, however, the more he seemed inclined to turn the whole of it over to the CID. While they deliberated, she had finally left the room.

She considered going to her bedroom, but she didn't want to be alone. Deciding to head downstairs to the parlor instead, she walked toward the landing and past her room.

"Miss Caldwell!"

Eva stopped in the hallway and turned to see Mary, who rushed toward her with red-rimmed eyes. The girl looked back over her shoulder twice before reaching Eva; making a quick decision, Eva pulled Mary into her sitting room and closed the door. She nudged the young maid onto the sofa and sat beside her.

"I'm afraid I have no warm tea in here, Mary, but I shall send for some. What is the matter?"

Her eyes filled with tears that spilled over. She clutched a handkerchief that seemed to have served its purpose, so Eva handed her a fresh one from her pocket. The girl's shoulders shook with an effort to muffle her sobs. Eva's heart broke for her—had she carried a soft spot in her heart for Mr. Handy?

"Will you tell me what's wrong?"

Mary finally collected herself, wiping her nose and tears. Regrettably, her tears continued to fall, but she was able to speak. "I am afraid, miss."

"Oh, Mary. I understand how upsetting this is; please believe me when I say you are not alone."

Mary shook her head. "I know something." She looked at the floor and closed her eyes.

Eva's heart beat faster. "What do you know, Mary?"

"I am afraid for my life. She will know it was me who talked."

Eva exhaled quietly. "I will protect you. Mr. Winston will protect you."

"Beggin' your pardon, but Mr. Handy is dead! Nobody is safe."

"Nobody will be safe if we don't put a stop to it right away. If you know something, you must tell me." She reached for her hand. "I will do everything in my power to keep you safe. If you wish, I will make a bed in here for you until this mess is resolved."

Mary blew out a quiet breath between trembling lips. "Mr. Handy rang for tea last night while everyone was still in the ballroom. I carried it up on a tray and was prepared to knock when Miss Dilworth came around the corner."

Eva blinked. Mathilda? That was not what she had expected to hear.

Mary swallowed and continued. "She was headed for Mr. Handy's room. When she saw me there, she stopped, kind of flustered, and then smiled. She never smiles at me."

Eva nodded.

"She said she was meeting with Mr. Handy and would deliver the tea. She took the tray right from my hands." She sniffled and wiped her nose. "She told me if I said anything about her visit with the gentleman, she would have me fired and ruined."

Eva's brain spun. "So, when last you saw Miss Dilworth, she was preparing to enter his room?"

"Last I saw her she *did* enter his room. I hid around the corner and watched." Her eyes welled up again. "He is a nice man—was a nice man—and I couldn't imagine what she wanted with him. She knocked on the door, he answered it all surprised-like, and he let her in." Mary shrugged. "And that's all. And now, he's dead. Turner said he drugged himself."

Eva tilted her head and pursed her lips. Word traveled fast in a full household.

"We do not know exactly how he died yet, Mary."

She nodded. "Yes, we do, miss." Her voice broke. "Yes, we do."

CHAPTER 26

Eva thought she would go mad if she wasn't able to do something, anything. On the other side of the plateau was a crime scene she could photograph, and here in the house was a crime scene she could photograph. Mr. Handy, however, she wasn't certain she could manage. For all that she considered herself hardened to the task, he was too close for her to remain objective.

She had taken Mary down to Mr. Handy's room and waited with her while she repeated to the detectives everything she'd told Eva. Chief Inspector Harlan had immediately sent for someone to bring Miss Dilworth to the room, and Eva had ushered Mary out.

She took her via the servants' staircase down to the kitchens, a place Mathilda or Blanche were unlikely to go, and told Mrs. Snow, Turner, and Jansen about the situation Mary had bravely put herself in. She did not try to protect Mathilda; instead, she broke a cardinal rule that guests or family did not gossip about others of the same status with the domestic help. She finished her statements by saying, "Mary believes her life may be in danger, and I believe she may be correct. She can remain in the Blue

Room if she chooses, or she can stay here with you instead of being alone."

The consensus was that she would remain with them until Eva was prepared to turn in for the night. She hugged the girl, praised her for being brave, and made her way down the corridor. She passed the parlor and saw a few people seated within—Blanche Parker, John Smythe, Ann Parker, and Davis Jacobson. She paused and turned back, entering the parlor and making her way to Blanche, whose face was ghostly pale. She seemed to have aged a lifetime.

"May I have a word in private, Miss Parker?"

Blanche looked up at her, eyes narrowed. "Why?"

"We've some things to discuss. I believe you are in trouble, and I may be able to help."

She scoffed and looked at the others. "I am not in trouble, and you would be the last one I would turn to for help if I were."

Eva sat on a settee across from her. "I can say what I am going to say with the others in here or to you, alone."

Ann Parker stood, and Davis Jacobson rose with her. "For once, Blanche, do the right thing for someone other than yourself."

Blanche stared at her sister, her mouth open. "Who do you think you—"

Ann lifted her chin. "I think I am the sister who is free to leave the room. Mr. Jacobson?"

He offered his arm, and she took it. In her heart, Eva applauded the younger sister as she walked with her gentleman out of the room.

Eva turned her attention to John Smythe. "If you have had

nothing to do with Miss Parker's activities of the last few days, you may also wish to take your leave."

He seemed torn, but, in the end, met Eva's steady gaze and finally left the parlor as well.

"There are detectives upstairs, a director is on his way from the CID in London, and local constabulary are currently guarding a body in the cave. Your best friend was witnessed entering Mr. Handy's room last night with a tea tray, and now he is dead of an overdose."

There was a prolonged pause. "It was suicide," Blanche said through clenched teeth.

"Suppose it was. Why do you believe he might have taken such a drastic measure here? Last night?"

"He was in love with me; everybody here will attest to that." She tightened her lips. "I told him yesterday that I would not entertain his suit and that he needn't apply to my father for permission."

"Was that before or after you enlisted his help to give me the ruined photography plates? And why did you do that, I wonder? Why did you need him?"

She stared at Eva, mouth closed. A knock from the large handle at the front door reverberated through the front hall and into the parlor.

"That would be Director Ellis," Eva said quietly. "Tell me what happened, and I will help you speak to them."

"You're hardly an attorney, and you are of no use to me."

Eva studied her face, the cornflower blue eyes that were shadowed and bore traces of tears. "I do not pity you, Blanche," she said quietly. "You have beauty, a devoted family, lineage of which you are proud. I cannot fathom why you behave the way you do. I do not offer my help out of a sense of compassion or a desire to lend aid to a fellow woman. I believe you are spoiled, selfish, and cruel, and you have built your successes thus far on manipulation and lies.

"I do, however, care very much about the Winstons and about Mr. Handy's loved ones who will be looking for answers they may never find. There is a dead man lying in a cave we all traipsed through this morning, and I have a feeling deep in my heart he is tied to you as well, if only circumstantially. Perhaps you can correct your course now before you continue a life on this path and then try to explain yourself to your Maker at the end."

Blanche exhaled and looked away.

"Have you killed anyone this week?"

Blanche's eyes flew back to Eva. "Of course not."

"Then help yourself and tell me what you know before someone else dies!" Eva's temper flared. "If you are associating with the man I believe you are, *your* life is forfeit the moment he no longer has use of you. By my best guess, that hourglass will run out when we all leave this house, which will likely be sooner than we think."

Blanche rolled her eyes and took a breath, shaking her head as if disappointed in herself for giving in. "When you set up your camera the morning of the three-legged race, you went back to that carriage-thing of yours. Nobody was looking, so I shoved your camera over. Someone saw me do that." She swallowed, then continued.

"Mathilda has knowledge of photography through her grandfather. She knew that the plates would be ruined if exposed to light, so when everyone was later distracted watching the race, she grabbed one and I grabbed the other. We closed the holders and figured the blame would fall on the boy." She sighed. "Someone saw us do that, as well."

Eva's heart thumped. "Bernard Toole?"

Blanche scowled. "I do not know anyone by that name. I am speaking of someone else, but I am not obliged to tell his name to you. He approached me later after tea when I was outside near the labyrinth with Mathilda. We had decided to toss the plates there, make it seem like someone was playing a prank."

Eva wanted to ask why, but she remained silent.

She pressed her lips together. "He told us he had seen us do it all, but that he'd stay quiet about it if we helped him. He pulled out the reticule, had us put the plates inside, and then asked if I didn't want to at least smash them, take out my frustration since I couldn't do it to you." She lifted her chin, but eventually broke eye contact. "So, I did. I took a rock and smashed them inside the bag."

"Did you feel better?"

"Yes! Yes, I did." She leaned forward. "Here you are, plying your trade, making eyes at Mr. Winston, sucking his attention away from everyone else." She sat back. "Ann told me he was interested in you. She heard it from Olivia and Alice. I thought that was ridiculous. Decided to prove her wrong, but then you just kept charming him, and he didn't see you for the charlatan you are. He does not see you for who you are, but I do."

"What do you see?"

"Someone of mediocre birth who imagines a life far above her station."

Eva felt a smile lift one corner of her mouth. "You're not the first person to say that to me."

Blanche appeared momentarily nonplussed. "Well. Perhaps you will someday realize the truth of it."

"Why did you have Mr. Handy deliver the reticule to me in such an odd way? Was that also this mystery man's idea?" Eva's mind raced as she tried to divine a method of tricking Blanche into revealing the man's identity. Was it a guest? One of the servants? Her heart beat quickly, and she rose from the settee and paced behind it.

Blanche huffed out an irritated sigh. "The man insisted I put the thing on your bed, and then move things about in your bedchamber. I was to also report to Mrs. Winston that my room had been rummaged, as though someone unseen was lurking in the shadows. It was the first of several 'deliveries' he wanted me to make. It all made no sense to me, but by then he was witness to things I had done that would . . ."

"Would make you look very bad."

She scowled but nodded. "Every time I tried to get into your chambers, Mary was there. Mathilda and I insisted we needed her help more so that when you were out of your room, one of us could slip in unseen."

"You didn't use the servant passageways?"

"I would not even know where to find something like that. Nothing worked because there are maids all over this blazing house. I tried to buy some time before we went shopping in town, but I could never find a moment alone."

Eva considered saying Blanche had exacerbated the maid profusion herself but refrained. And this new information shed light on why Blanche had caused a thirty-minute delay heading into town earlier in the week.

"I knew he would find out if you hadn't received it. He has a timetable, he says. So to avoid further trouble with him, I told . . ." She swallowed, for the first time pausing, seeming to finally process something beyond herself. "I told Mr. Handy if he truly sought an opportunity to court me, I needed him to deliver the reticule to you. I couldn't trust anyone else to keep it a secret."

Eva pinched her lips together. She tried to maintain a bland expression, but she couldn't help but think about poor Mr. Handy, who could be trusted because he was besotted with the conniving young woman.

"I couldn't have him simply hand the reticule to you in person, though, since it contained the broken plates. If you knew it was him, I knew you'd eventually convince him to admit who had asked him to do it, which you did."

She shook her head and looked away again. "I watched him bumble and try and fail all morning long in town, trying to leave it where you would find it. When I realized he finally shoved it in your hand in the crowded shop and ran away, I hoped that would be the end of it." She met Eva's eyes, her lips thinned. "How did you know it was him?"

Eva fought again to keep her expression bland so Blanche would keep talking. She paused, though, swallowing a lump in her throat. "I watched him. Watched him as he watched you and became sadder and more disillusioned. I didn't know for certain, but he was a good man. He wanted to unburden himself. He had later realized the plates had been inside the reticule and felt horrible to have been part of it."

"How did he know that?"

"Nathan chatted with everyone he'd seen in proximity to the store. I believe he even asked you."

Blanche smiled without mirth, laughing quietly to herself. "Of course. 'Nathan.'"

"Did Mathilda poison Mr. Handy last night?"

Blanche's eyes clouded—not with tears, but, Eva realized, with fear. "Mathilda insisted he would break and admit to Mr. Winston he had been the one who had the reticule, which would then lead back to us. I do not know what she had planned to keep him quiet. She said she needed time to think; she only intended to make him ill for today. It had worked once before."

Eva stilled her restless pacing. "Sammy."

Blance looked away. "We were encouraged by this person to find ways to bring stress upon you."

"So you poisoned an innocent child?" Eva couldn't keep the icy fury from her voice.

"It was the man's idea, not mine! And Mathilda did it. I did not." Blanche shook her head and continued. "She got anxious we would be ruined if . . . the man . . . kept blackmailing us to do his bidding. We had four more bags to deliver for him, but with all the maids running around, we couldn't do it until yesterday." She shook her head. "As if we had access to the family wing without arousing suspicion. There's one more box for Mrs. Winston, but I ran out of time." She picked at a thread on her skirt. "He said to give it back. That he had someone else to deliver it."

Eva felt her heart skip a beat. "You must tell me who he is."

Blanche's nostrils flared. "I will not."

"What hold does he have on you, even now? You've told me what you and Mathilda did—it's finished!"

"He collects secrets," she hissed. "Pays people for information on the most influential families in Town. He knows things I was . . . I was not even aware of." She flinched.

"All the more reason for you to turn him in!"

"At which point he will tell everything! It is his insurance." She looked at Eva, disgusted. "You would not understand."

"I shall tell you what I do understand, Blanche. The man behind all of this, his true name is Bernard Toole. He designed the abduction of the child of an MP two years ago and held him for ransom. The family paid the ransom, but he refused to release the child. He demanded more money and wouldn't provide proof of life. Nathan—oh, apologies, *Detective Winston*—went on an undercover assignment to see if the child was alive and rescue him.

"He eventually did free the child, and the entire Toole family were arrested, all except for Bernard, who escaped arrest." Eva paused. "You have been playing with the devil. He is a cruel man who toys with his victims. He was willing to risk the life of a child for no other reason than to upset me!"

Eva rubbed her forehead, tired. "Bernard's sister, and now his mother, died in jail. He is bent on revenge and targeting those close to Nathan as a way to hurt him."

Blanche shifted in her seat. "You were wrong about the man in the cave, though. I have nothing to do with him."

Eva looked up at her. "Blanche, I suspect Collins was one of Bernard's informants. For reasons I don't yet understand, Bernard killed him. Perhaps Collins had decided to admit it to the Winstons."

Blanche bristled. "Why would this 'Toole' go to all the trouble? Why not just have his revenge and be done with it?"

"Because his revenge is inflicting the anxiety and fear before he does the final deed." Eva eyed her evenly. "Surely you understand the allure of toying with someone, just because you can."

Blanche's eyes blazed, but she didn't argue.

Eva took a breath and rubbed the back of her neck where tension had settled in with a vengeance. "Shall I bring the detectives to you? Nathan will need to know all of this immediately. Perhaps I should take you to them; they're inside Mr. Handy's room with the coroner, questioning Mathilda. A sneaking suspicion tells me she was unaware of proper dosage when she handed him his laudanum-laced tea. How do you suppose she did it? Tip it into the cup when his back was turned?"

"How would I know?"

Eva stood. "You should speak with the detectives straightaway. I wouldn't trust her not to throw all of the blame on your shoulders—not only for Mr. Handy but also the attempt on Sammy's life. And I would think twice about protecting Toole's identity, blackmail notwithstanding. The stakes are proving to be much higher than mere ruin."

Blanche swallowed, and the fear flashed in her eyes again.

"I'll send for Nathan." Eva left the room on legs that felt wooden. As she entered the corridor, she stopped short to see each Winston sister seated on the floor, mouths agape.

Eva squatted down next to them, eyes wide. "Were you there the whole time?"

They all nodded.

"Did you hear it all?"

Grace answered. "I believe so."

The others nodded again.

Olivia looked at each of them, her eyes stopping on Eva. "Which person is Toole? Is he going to kill us all in our sleep now?"

"The place is full of detectives and an army of security outside."

Alice nodded slowly. "And the carnival man is disguised as one of them. Or us."

CHAPTER 27

The storm outside continued to rage. Eva suggested Alice find Nathan to hear Blanche's confession, and she remained outside the parlor door, watching to be certain the girl didn't try to escape. Where she would go, Eva had no idea, but Blanche had a temporary ally in Toole, and that boded no good for anyone.

"Where is your mother?" Eva asked, remembering she'd not seen Mrs. Winston for some time.

"Upstairs in her sitting room with Mrs. Larsen and Mrs. Parkin," Delilah said. "We made them promise to keep her in there until things settle down. She has run herself ragged, and now with a dead houseguest here and dead footman in the cave, she's overwhelmed."

When Alice returned with Nathan, Michael, and Director Ellis, Eva decided she didn't have the stomach to listen to the whole thing again.

"I'll stay," Grace offered. "We must be certain she tells us who 'he' is. I want to be sure she doesn't lie about anything she just told you." The other three agreed, and they all remained in the hallway.

Nathan nodded.

"Where are the other guests?" Eva asked.

"Upstairs with the constabulary. We're questioning everyone in the library and keeping them there for now until we get this sorted." Nathan stayed back and looked at Eva as the others filed into the parlor. He motioned with his head, and she followed him away from the corridor and into the front hall. He looked around at the multitudes of footmen and security he'd hired, and despite her stress, Eva fought a smile as she realized he was probably trying to find a place where they could be alone for a moment.

He opened a door behind the staircase to reveal a large cloakroom. He quickly pulled her inside and switched on a small light. Without a word, he put his arms around her and lifted her up against him. She wrapped her arms around his neck, and they held each other, still and quiet. He buried his face in her hair and he kissed her neck, once, reluctantly lowering her back down.

"I want to be alone with you somewhere for days, weeks," he said, cradling her face. "All we have are stolen moments and everything is erupting."

"We will finish this business, and then you and I will be able to breathe. Now go. You need to listen to her story; it will be one for retelling." She grimaced. "Or perhaps not. After speaking with her, I feel a sudden urge to go out in the rain with a bar of glycerin soap and a scrubbing brush."

He smiled and kissed her soundly, finally raising his head when she twisted the door handle and opened the door. "Go," she whispered, and gave him a shove. "Find me later, and we'll talk."

He left, and she waited a moment, feeling ridiculously self-conscious. When she finally ventured back around the stairs, she spied George Abernathy, who had climbed halfway up.

"George?"

He turned when she called his name and hurried back down.

"I hope Sammy has been behaving himself and not bothering Mrs. Snow for too many treats."

George's brow creased in worry. "That's just it, Miss Caldwell. I don't know where he went."

Eva refused to allow herself to climb directly to the worst scenario imaginable. "He could be anywhere—lately he's made a game of exploring the house. Or perhaps he is in Mr. Winston's rooms?"

George shook his head. "I've checked. My next place to look is the darkroom carriage, but I wanted to find you first."

Eva nodded. "Let's check out there together." She hurried back to the cloakroom and withdrew a raincoat and umbrella. Jansen opened the front door, one brow raised but otherwise silent, as she and George stepped out into the deluge. She opened the umbrella and handed it to George so that he could cover them both. They ran together, splashing through puddles, around the side of the house and into the side yard where the carriage sat.

The door was ajar, and to her relief, she spied Sammy inside. "What are you doing?" she yelled.

He poked his head out and blinked. "Meeting you! It's time to go to the cave?"

"What?" She shook her head. "No! I told you we might go later, but not until the detectives are ready. Come," she said, motioning with her hand, "let's lock up and go back inside."

He held a packet of flash powder in his hand.

"Set that down." Her anxiety grew.

"But your note says to meet you now because we are

going—now." He handed her a scrap of paper, and as she read it, her heart began pounding in alarm.

"I thought you were over there for a minute—heard you rustling around in the front." He motioned to the other side of the carriage.

"Sammy, come now," George said urgently. He handed Eva the umbrella and reached for the boy. He grabbed him quickly around the waist and lifted him away from the carriage. "Miss Eva, we must go!"

He reached back for her hand, still holding onto Sammy, and they managed two full steps before an explosion shook the world around them. Eva registered reaching for George's hand, seeing him flying far away from her as she was catapulted back through the air. Everything was blindingly white, and she tumbled slowly, imagining she must look like a leaf in the wind. She felt a pain in her head, then, and suddenly everything was silent.

CHAPTER 28

The ground beneath Eva was painfully hard. She turned, and a million shards of glass sliced through her head. She cried out, but the pain increased tenfold, so she clenched her teeth and tried to open her eyes.

"Miss Eva," Sammy sobbed. His voice was quiet, hoarse; she reached blindly for him.

"Where are you, sweet boy?" she murmured. Her hand touched rocks and then, finally, a small hand.

"You're alive." His voice broke, and he cried, breaking off with a gasp of pain.

She finally managed to lift her eyelids. It was blessedly dark—the only light seemed to emanate from a small lantern. Sammy lay not far from her, and she pulled herself closer to him. Wrapping one arm around his small body, she rubbed his back even as her head felt too heavy to keep holding it upright. She rested it on the ground next to his and tried to make sense of their surroundings.

"Where does it hurt?" she whispered.

"Ever where."

"Yes." She cracked her eyes open wider, recognizing a cave

floor similar to Mrs. Winston's, but different. They also weren't in her storage cavern. "How long have you been awake?"

"Not long," a man's voice answered. "He came to just before you did."

Eva turned her head toward the sound and blinked at the lantern light. The man sitting beside it was familiar to her. The tone was familiar. The accent was gone.

"Mr. Peter Meyer, or rather, Mr. Toole," she whispered. "Your reputation precedes you."

He smiled and held a rag to his head. Blood seeped from it, and he winced. "Hurt myself in the process," he said, and shook his head. "Explosives can be tricky things, especially in the rain."

Their only chance of survival might be if she could think clearly. The challenge to do so without blinding pain was presenting a problem.

"If it be any consolation," Toole said, "I almost regret using you."

Her arm tightened reflexively around Sammy.

"And him." He pointed a chin at Sammy. "He reminds me of myself."

"Not like you," Sammy croaked.

Toole chuckled and winced again. Blood trickled in a steady stream down his face and onto his clothing.

"Was trying to blow open the side of the house to do some damage there. The family wing is on that side."

Eva thought with sickening horror about Mrs. Winston and her friends, seated in her room directly above the area where the darkroom sat. She then realized where the parlor was, where the front hall and corridor were in relation to the carriage.

"You've killed them all."

"Oh, no."

Nathan. The thought was so staggering she could barely draw a breath.

"The hall was full of people, you—you . . . you've killed everyone." Her eyes filmed over, and her vision blurred.

"Figured since there were police everywhere, I'd swoop in and grab you in the confusion. Regrettably, my own head got in the way, and I didn't have many wits about me."

He shifted and grunted. "Getting knocked in the head is nothing compared to what will happen to Winston." He snarled the name. "Without you, he will rot away into nothing. But you are decent; I admit, you gave me pause."

She blinked, uncomprehending his stream of speech.

"You were kind to Collins, poor sod. I heard you offer him tea. That became his undoing, however. Turned his conscience back on. Told me he wasn't going to be of further help."

Her mind flipped back as though thumbing through a photo album. She saw herself talking to Collins, asking if he'd had breakfast, offering to have Sammy bring him a sweet roll. "So, you will let us go?"

"No, no. This is only the beginning. We are headed to Bavaria, my dear Miss Caldwell. Hardly makes sense to concoct a plan where I don't also make money out of it." He shifted his leg, and the sound of his foot scraping against the stone floor was loud in the small enclosure. "Been planning this one for a very, very long time. Thought it would be one of the sisters I'd take." He gave her a sickly smile. "This is so much better."

Eva shoved herself upright, gritting against the pain. Everything hurt, but her head most of all.

"You've been out for hours, the two of you. Sleeping like babies. Worried for a moment you'd die on me. Harder to provide proof of life that way."

She thought of George Abernathy and felt bile rise in her throat. Putting a hand over her mouth, she breathed shallowly, knowing her head would likely explode if she vomited. Tears now escaped and ran down her cheeks. "George?"

"Don't know. Didn't have time to check him. Another good fellow, that one."

Eva gently situated her leg under Sammy's head and tried to take stock of his injuries. She ran her hands down his legs and arms, and only felt instinctive resistance when she probed his left arm.

"I think his arm is broken," she said quietly. "I worry infection will set in if we do not treat it properly." She felt his forehead. "He's already warm."

"Don't know how we'll do that because we can't leave this cave. Not for a time." He rested his head against the wall at his back, and the hand holding the rag to his head wound slipped.

"We'll have to. You need medicine also."

"You're not stupid, Miss Caldwell. Do me the same courtesy and don't treat me like I am." He smiled. "Should have taken him up on his offer. Gretna Green is a safer place these days."

She swallowed. "Where did you overhear that?" The thought that he had been an observer of her private moments with Nathan made her angry.

"Hired a new informant to provide information. He was under the balconies. In the passageways." His smile was crooked with blood smeared across his teeth. He looked nothing like the urbane gentleman she'd come to know as Peter Meyer; she could hardly believe them to be one and the same.

Her heart in her throat, she tried desperately to remember how much room existed between the parlor and the exterior wall. There was only a small water closet and maids' supply closet. Nathan, Michael, Director Ellis, Blanche, Nathan's sisters—each of them had been in the vicinity and might now be either dead or grievously injured.

She looked at Sammy and tried not to move him. His eyes fluttered and she wasn't certain if she should keep him awake or let him sleep. A slip of paper protruded from his pocket, and she pulled it out, noting the script's feminine hand. "You didn't write this note," she said to Toole.

"Miss Dilworth is helpful."

"But she has been in questioning all afternoon."

"Had her write that days ago." He tapped his head with his fingertip. "Must think ahead. She loves me, you know, Mathilda does. Rather, she thought she did because Miss Parker fancied me first. I didn't think she had the stomach for more serious tasks, but poor Mr. Handy . . . She managed that one all on her own. Too unpredictable, though, proper ladies. Won't make that mistake again. Was all set to torment our dear detective for several more days, but Miss Blanche was beginning to crack. I am not happy with that one for cutting short my plans."

He coughed, and as Eva's eyes gradually began to focus better, she realized he was in worse shape than she was.

The entrance to the cave was to her left. It was unfamiliar, however, and she didn't know where it led or if it opened onto the beach. It must have been nestled within the same hillside, though; it was nearly identical in appearance to Mrs. Winston's, aside from the lack of human maintenance.

"Where is this cave?" she asked.

He smiled. "In the side of a big rock."

"Do you have water? Is it still raining? We can all step outside for just a moment and . . . and . . . turn our faces to the sky for a drink." She shifted, testing his reaction.

He reached down next to his leg and lifted a revolver she'd not noticed. He pulled the hammer back, and it echoed throughout the small chamber.

She slowly held her hand out and sat very still. "You can put the hammer back. Those kinds have a way of being very temperamental."

He smiled, but to her relief, eased the hammer back in place. "You shoot? My sister shot. I didn't spend enough time at the carnival near the end, too busy making plans. Might have ended Winston then and there if I had been. Undercover, he was . . . I would have known him a mile away as a copper." He coughed again, wincing. "We had a carnival, you see, and Greta, she was like the American girl, Annie . . ."

"Annie Oakley," Sammy mumbled.

"That's the one. Annie Oakley." He nodded. "My sister, Greta. She was quite the shot."

Eva realized Greta must have been the sister who recently died. The irony that he had been the one who landed his sister in trouble was frustrating, but she kept her tongue. If she could only hang on until he lost consciousness . . . She didn't know how much blood he'd lost, but judging by the dark stain spreading across his shirtfront, it must have been a substantial amount.

The trick would be waiting him out without startling him into shooting them. Sammy twitched and she looked down at him, running her hand gently along his head to check for bumps or cuts. To her surprise, his eyes were open, and he looked up at her. He then cast his eyes downward and slipped the edge of something out of the same pocket where he'd had the note.

She sucked in a breath when she realized what he had.

In his pocket.

The flash powder he'd been holding just before the explosion was in his pocket, and it was highly combustible. That it hadn't ignited when the explosion had thrown them was a miracle.

She needed to think. "Why did you lure us out to the carriage if you didn't want us dead," she asked him, more to judge his level of consciousness than anything.

"Easier than abducting you from your room, wasn't it? Carriage wasn't supposed to blow so soon. Didn't know the boy was going to get inside it . . . didn't know a lot of things."

He swallowed and mumbled, "First Greta. Then my mama." He reached again for the gun, restlessly fiddling with it as his hand slipped and the blood continued to stream.

"Greta? Are you truly German, then?"

"My mother's family. Meyer. Disowned her when she ran off with my father. Ran off to join the Toole family carnival." He chuckled and coughed again, a trickle of blood oozing from the side of his mouth. "I was meant for better things . . . been living for nearly a year with the Swedish ambassador, after all. 'Course, he was obliged to take me in when I handed him proof of his support of his mistress and illegitimate children."

Sammy slipped the packet onto the ground and Eva held her breath. Again, he reached into the pocket and pulled out a book of lucifer matches. Eva closed her eyes in horror. He was lucky he hadn't blown himself up five times over by now.

She placed her arm on Sammy's shoulder, blocking any view Toole might have of the small nest Sammy was creating on the floor. They didn't have the trough used for holding the powder and creating a flash, so she slowly waved her finger back and forth in a signal to wait.

She waited for what seemed an eternity for Toole to finally slip into unconsciousness or bleed out altogether. She tried to feel sorry for him at the turn of her thoughts, but he had wreaked so much havoc with so little regard for anyone that it was impossible to do anything but put herself and Sammy first.

A shout sounded in the distance, so faint at first, she wasn't certain she'd heard it. It repeated again, and then again, growing louder. She recognized Nathan's voice—she would know it anywhere. The explosion hadn't killed him. The relief that he was alive nearly made her swoon. She felt light-headed and was immediately disappointed in herself. Eva Caldwell did not swoon. Her eyes burned with tears, though, and she assumed that might last for a while.

The shouting, now coming from more than one voice, alerted Toole, who sat straight. He tensed, listening, and put his hand back on the gun. "Not a sound," he growled. His head slipped and knocked against the wall, but rather than put him to sleep, it seemed to have made him more alert.

Sammy also had tensed, and she was completely torn. If they lit the powder and it reacted badly, they would all die. If they lit it and it produced nothing more than a flash, she and Sammy would know to close their eyes and run for the exit. It might give them just enough time to find their way out of the cave before they got shot. The voices began to fade again, and she knew a moment of panic.

Sammy must have felt it as well because he slowly sat up, as though waking from slumber.

"Be still," Toole snapped.

"He's fine," Eva said quietly, slowly holding out her hands.

"So dark in here," Sammy slurred. "My eyes don' work."

He was convincing enough that for a moment, Eva wondered if he'd indeed gone blind.

Toole groaned and leaned back against the wall again. When he blinked slowly, Sammy struck the match. The noise caused

Toole's head to snap up, but by then, Sammy had dropped the match into the powder.

"What—" Toole shouted and grabbed his head.

"Now," Eva whispered, and she scrambled up, pulling Sammy with her. She squeezed her eyes shut as she moved them in the direction of the cavern entrance; the blinding flash behind her closed eyelids was painful enough to nearly bring her to her knees. To her horror, she stumbled.

Sammy grabbed her arm and pulled her, as behind them, Toole roared. She felt the air move as he swung his arm and she stumbled again over the cavern threshold, barely keeping to her feet.

"Run," Sammy shouted, his little voice hoarse. She picked up her skirt and tore after him, glad that he'd had the foresight to grab the small lantern on their flight from the room. The light bobbed ahead of her, and she stumbled and bumped into the walls on either side as they twisted and wound their way out of the earth.

"Almost there," Sammy panted, and she felt the air shift as the smell of rain wafted in. She followed him out of the cave and onto the beach, slipping on rocks and falling to her knees.

She saw figures in the distance through the pouring rain. Sammy pulled on her arm, and she scrambled to right herself as she heard a shout behind them, echoing through the cave.

"Nathan!"

He turned, and two others with him pivoted and ran back toward them. "Get down!" All three had their weapons raised.

She and Sammy dropped immediately, and for one terrifying moment as shots rang out behind them, she was afraid Toole had actually won. Multiple shots fired then, from all around, and she covered Sammy's head with her arms, closing her eyes tightly.

A thud sounded behind them, dull and sickening, and then everything was quiet except for the falling rain and the sound of running feet. She felt Nathan lift her from the ground and clutch her to his chest. Beside her, Director Ellis reached down and lifted Sammy like a small child.

"His left arm is broken," she managed.

"I have him," Ellis said, and rested Sammy's head on his shoulder. "Let's get them to the carriage."

Eva did her best to walk but fell hard to her knees. Nathan bent and lifted her into his arms and carried her, and she put her arm around his shoulders. Her head tipped forward and rested against his cheek, and she heard the sound of his harsh breaths.

She registered Ellis directing people as the sound of horses and carriages clattered along the path near the beach.

Nathan climbed into the carriage and then settled her onto his lap. The world was again a blur as the carriage moved, but she heard Sammy cough and she reached her hand across to the other seat. Her fingers brushed against his arm, and it was enough.

She dropped her hand, rested against Nathan's shoulder, and slept.

CHAPTER 29

Nathan walked wearily from the Blue Room's sitting room, where he had set up a makeshift bedroom for Sammy, and into the bedchamber, where a chair sat beside Eva's bed. He'd kept vigil at Eva's side for nearly eighteen hours, sleeping little. Sammy was more alert; the doctor had set his broken arm, and while he still looked exhausted, it was a chore to keep him still. He did not want to be abed and reminded Nathan of that fact each time he woke. Nathan had assigned the maid, Mary, to stay with the boy and keep him from getting up until the doctor gave his approval.

Eva had not awoken since Nathan's frantic return with her to the house. The white bandage at her temple and scratches along her chin, arms, and hands, were reminders of her close proximity to the explosion that had destroyed her precious darkroom carriage and a portion of the home's exterior wall.

He settled into the chair and rubbed his eyes. The sleep he'd managed had come in fits while sitting beside her bed; every time she moved or groaned in pain, he'd been instantly alert. He now rested his feet atop the foot of the bed and leaned back, closing his eyes.

When the explosion had rocked the house, everyone in the

parlor, the front hall, and his mother's suite above, had been tossed about but, miraculously, saved from serious injury. Once he'd gotten his bearings, he'd rushed outside to view the cause with a sneaking suspicion that the carriage had been the culprit. The danger in keeping the volatile chemicals together in a confined space was always paramount in Eva's thoughts, and he'd assumed her worst fear had finally come to fruition.

He'd been frantic, trying to tear into the smoke and fire to be sure she wasn't inside. Michael and Ellis had held him back as he shouted and lunged; and the longer it took for Eva to run from the house to see what had happened, the more convinced he'd become that she had been inside the darkroom.

As the dust settled and the fire was contained, he'd been momentarily relieved to learn there were no bodies inside the carriage. It hadn't been long, however, before Ellis had found evidence of intentional sabotage outside the vehicle, followed by shouts as George Abernathy had been found some distance away. He was alive, but barely conscious, questioning repeatedly about Eva and Sammy. From what Nathan could gather, they had both been lured out to the carriage.

If they weren't inside the carriage, though, and they weren't in the house, where were they? Toole, of course. He'd known the answer before he'd asked it. His next step had been questioning Blanche and Mathilda, who finally admitted Peter Meyer was Toole. He drilled them about where Toole may have taken them. They had been belligerent until he'd lost his temper, at which point Michael had physically removed him from the informal interview and Ellis, in his calm way, had then instilled the fear of God into the young women. They couldn't say for sure where Toole might have taken Eva and Sammy, but he had mentioned something about caves.

He sighed, wondering why he even bothered to sit in the chair next to the bed. He couldn't get comfortable, couldn't relax, but wouldn't leave her side. He leaned forward, elbows braced on his legs, and rested his forehead against the mattress. His eyes burned and he shut them tightly, wondering what he would do if Eva never fully recovered. He couldn't bear the thought, and as his mother had told him earlier, it was best not to borrow trouble.

So, he continued to wait.

Bernard Toole was dead, and if there was one bright spot on the horizon, that was it. He'd come out of the cave staggering and firing his weapon, and three shots, one each from Nathan, Michael, and Ellis, had found their mark. Toole's inside hires had been responsible for lurking in the passageways and delivering black feathers, while Toole had been systematically trying to wear down Eva's nerves and undertake his plan for revenge against Nathan.

As much as Nathan had wanted to burn the cigar boxes containing "messages" for his mother and sisters, he'd turned the evidence over to Director Ellis instead. A series of mistakes on Toole's part—his new "hire" among Nathan's security crew who admitted Collins had threatened to tell all, and Toole's enlistment of help from a pair of women with selfishly conniving tendencies but no real criminal acumen—had led to his downfall.

Nathan had to amend the thought about criminal acumen—Burton Handy's body had been removed only a short handful of hours earlier, and Mathilda Dilworth placed under arrest and taken to jail. Ironically, Blanche Parker's tendency to take first place in attention and focus was more bark than Mathilda's covert bite. Because Mathilda had always been quieter, more reserved, and less demanding, Nathan had never noticed the utter lack of compassion residing behind her eyes.

Blanche Parker had finally succeeded in ruining her own good name. According to Ellis, word was already spreading furiously around London about the events at Christine Winston's House Party Benefit in Seaside. The elder Miss Parker was disgraced, and Mrs. Winston's house party was gaining such delicious notoriety that invitations to donate would be more rabidly sought-after next year than ever before. He felt only pity for Blanche, and even that would fill but a thimble. Ann Parker would weather the storm, helped in part by a potential betrothal to Davis Jacobson; the pair seemed equally charmed with each other, and Davis was determined to protect the younger sister from scandal associated with Blanche.

A soft knock on the doorframe brought Nathan's head up, and he managed an almost smile for Grace.

"No change?" she asked. "She hasn't awoken at all?"

He shook his head. "Every now and again she mumbles something in her sleep, so I hope that signals eventual recovery. I've sent for her cousins; will you alert me when they arrive?"

"Of course. Nathan," she paused, her brow creased with worry, "you must get some sleep. You're of no use to Eva or anyone if you continue like this much longer. I—or one of the other girls—am happy to sit with her while you rest; I promise to awaken you the minute she stirs."

He shook his head. "I'll wait a bit longer. I just . . ." He looked at the still form, lying on the bed and looking lifeless except for the even rise and fall of her chest. "I do not want her to wake up and not see me here."

Grace smiled and walked over to him, placing a soft kiss on

his forehead. "She will be just fine, I am certain," she whispered. "Gentle but fierce, that one."

He clasped his sister's fingers in gratitude and then, as she left the room, he was again alone with his thoughts.

He heard a mumbled whisper from the bed and jumped to Eva's side. He sat on the edge of the bed and took her hand. "Eva?"

"She's right," Eva said, her eyelids fluttering. She squinted against the light and winced. He hurried to close the curtains, blocking out the daylight, and instead switched a lamp on low. Clasping a glass of water from the bedside table, he put his hand behind her head and helped her take a few sips.

"Who is right about what?" he asked, heart pounding and nearly giddy with relief.

"Grace. You need to sleep." Eva gave him a weak smile and lifted her hand to hold his. "You become very curt and irritable when you're tired."

"I beg your pardon, Miss Caldwell, but that is simply untrue." He fought back tears as he lifted her hand to his lips. "I challenge you to name one time I've been even so much as surly, either rested or fatigued."

She closed her eyes, breathing deeply. Her voice was quiet, but to his relief, carried her customary tone filled with dry humor. "Detective, I can think of at least three investigations within the last year when the hour was very late, and you snapped at two constables and even Michael."

"But never at you." He placed the back of his fingers against her cheek and gently stroked.

She smiled. "Never at me, that is true. Whereas I have been very irritated with you in the past three days alone. I hope that does not bode ill for our future together."

"Never, as long as the reason for your irritation continues to be fixable with a kiss."

She laughed softly and winced, placing her fingers on her forehead. "Once you see the crazed look in my eyes recede, you may assume it is safe to kiss me."

"I love you," he whispered. "I've been so afraid."

Her eyes filled with tears. "That was truly awful, was it not?"

"It was."

"Was anyone here hurt?" She paused and licked her lips. "In the explosion?" Tears fell, and she wiped them away.

He shook his head and offered her another drink. She pushed herself into a sitting position and took the cup from him, slowly sipping the water.

"How is George Abernathy?"

"Bruised, a broken wrist, but otherwise well."

She sighed. "I am so glad to hear this."

He nodded. "Everyone is fine. Sammy is resting next door in the sitting room, and Mrs. Snow has visited him twice with pastries. She has not visited me with pastries at all."

She laughed, which had been his aim.

"My mother was admittedly shaken, but now is busying herself with contractors seeing to the home repairs."

"Oh, Nathan. I am so sorry. I knew of the danger the carriage presented; we should have moved it far from the house."

He shook his head. "That was my decision, and I've no regrets. I knew you would be out there frequently in the late hours, and I didn't want you far away. I am sorry for the loss of your equipment."

She lifted a shoulder but couldn't quite disguise the sadness that flickered quickly in her eyes. "Those things are all replaceable."

"They are, but they were also yours. I hope you'll allow me to help replace them."

"It is not your responsibility, Nathan, truly."

"Not yet, but soon." He made a show of checking the time. "If we hurry, we can get tickets for a trip north to Gretna Green."

She laughed again, this time with more of her usual internal strength.

"Aha! You've not said no this time." He rubbed her hand softly between his.

"No, Detective. We are not eloping."

A flurry of activity sounded in the sitting room; hushed voices, an exclamation of delight from Sammy, and a few moments later, Amelie and Charlotte appeared at the door. Charlotte clapped her hand over her mouth, her large, green eyes stricken with worry. Carefully, as though climbing onto a shaky tree branch, she sat on the opposite side of the bed.

"Oh, Eva," Amelie breathed.

Nathan smiled and kissed Eva's hand, and then her forehead. "I'll leave you to it."

"You sleep," she ordered him.

He stepped back from the bed as Amelie climbed on the place where he'd been, and Charlotte scooted close on Eva's other side. The three cousins leaned back against the pillows in a gentle embrace, and Charlotte tipped her head onto Eva's shoulder.

"The two of you are going to be the death of me," Nathan heard Charlotte murmur as he left the room. "Eva, you're practical; how dare you get yourself hurt?"

He paused just outside the door to listen for Eva's response. As he expected, it was accompanied by a gentle laugh.

"I cannot be perfect all the time, you know."

CHAPTER 30

Six months later

Eva laughed as she tossed the bouquet backward, high over her head. She turned in time to see it hit Charlotte in the face. Eva and Amelie cheered, as did Nathan's sisters, who had teased Charlotte that since the other two cousins were wed, she would be next.

They had all gathered for a Christmas celebration, which, thanks to Mr. Dickens, had become all the rage. The Winstons' country home was decorated from top to bottom with garlands and wreaths, ribbon and bells. The ballroom, where the large crowd mingled and danced, was full of all the people she and Nathan loved.

Sammy looked dapper in his formal attire, which matched Nathan's. His blond hair was neatly trimmed, his fingernails scrubbed, and Eva swore he'd grown an inch in a month. He clutched a puppy in his arms, and true to his word, he took it outside every thirty minutes to do its business.

Charlotte approached Eva as a woman on a mission and returned the bouquet to her with a flat glare. Amelie joined them, her belly now beginning to round, and Charlotte couldn't maintain her stern expression in the face of their laughter.

Amelie wagged her finger. "Inevitable, my dear. You may as well accept it."

Charlotte shook her head, her thick, auburn curls a perfect match for the holiday décor. "I simply do not have time," she said.

"That is what we all think," Eva told her. "And then it happens."

"Perhaps, for some." Charlotte was noncommittal. Her eye seemed to have snagged on a group of gentlemen across the room, however, and Eva believed she knew which one caught her attention.

"The ceremony was lovely," Amelie said. "And now, after months of planning and hard work, you may relax."

Eva was ready. Sammy's and her road to recovery after the business with Toole had felt long, but she was grateful it hadn't been worse. She didn't like to dwell on the fact that they had come so close to dying. It was shortly after Nathan and the others had found them—thanks to a reluctant tip from Mathilda Dilworth—that he and Eva had decided to begin proceedings to formally adopt Sammy as their legal son. Now that the wedding had officially happened, all that remained was the notary's signature.

Charlotte put her arm around Eva and pulled her close. Amelie reached around from the other side, and Eva knew a moment of true contentment. "Are you happy?" Charlotte whispered.

Eva's smile was misty, and she rested her head against Charlotte's. "So happy."

Eva lifted her head and kissed Amelie's cheek. "And you are happy?" she asked the mother-to-be.

"Very much." Amelie smiled. "Irritable, but happy." She looked over at Charlotte and asked, "When does school begin again for the next term?"

Charlotte grimaced. "Five weeks from now. Do not remind me; I am enjoying my thinking-free holidays."

Eva noted her parents and Aunt Sally in conversation with Christine Winston, Betsy Larsen, and Polly Parkin. Nathan's sisters mingled with the guests, each happy and smiling. Her worlds were blending together beautifully, and she was grateful. Her home with Nathan was less than a mile away, and she, her cousins, and Nathan's sisters, had worked for many long days getting each room just so.

She looked through the crowd of friends and family, trying to locate her groom. When she finally found him, chatting over by one of the large Christmas trees in the corner with Michael Baker, Franklin Frampton, Jens Sorenson, and Davis Jacobson, he was looking directly at her. She wasn't certain how he managed it, and he claimed he didn't spend every waking moment of every day staring at her, but each time she searched for him, he was already waiting with a wink and her favorite half smile.

"He is a handsome one," Charlotte said, following Eva's gaze. "The suit fits him like a glove."

"It certainly does." Eva smiled as Nathan excused himself from the other gentlemen and made his way across the room. When he reached her, he smiled at her cousins and said, "With your permission, ladies, I'd like to steal my bride away."

"I suppose," Charlotte said.

"If you must." Amelie smiled at him.

"I will return her. Eventually."

Eva could not wait. In the morning, she and Nathan were headed across the Channel on an extended tour of the continent as their wedding trip. She would miss her friends, and especially Sammy, but had been looking forward to the holiday with just Nathan for so long she could hardly believe it was upon them.

He pulled her toward the ballroom exit and she protested, "We can't leave without saying goodbye, and there are still the pictures to take!"

"We're not leaving yet," he said, smiling when she stopped resisting. "I have a surprise for you."

She looked up at him, bemused. They'd exchanged gifts, she had her lovely ring, so she couldn't imagine what was missing.

He steered her down the corridor with its cozily lit sconces and greenery, past the library, the parlor, and the den. At last, he stopped at a door that led to the butler's pantry. He switched on the overhead light, pulled her in, and closed the door, locking it with a firm click.

She laughed and grasped his lapels as he lifted her to stand on a step stool, raising her to his height. "What are we doing in here?"

"What we are doing, Mrs. Caldwell Winston, is slipping away for two minutes so I can do this." He took her face in his hands and kissed her for the first time alone as husband and wife.

She sighed, wrapping her arms around his neck and running her hand through his hair. She rested her cheek against his and relished the quiet, feeling the beat of his heart next to hers. After a moment, she gave a small laugh. "I was right, you know."

"About what?"

"Remember the day you encountered me on the stairs, and I was quite cross with you?"

He nodded.

"I thought then how nice it was that I could stand one step above you. Because it would make doing *this* so much easier." She smiled and placed a soft kiss on his lips. "And I was right."

He kissed her back. "And now we can do *this* all the time."

"Yes, we most certainly can."

The doorknob rattled, and Nathan called out, "One moment, please."

She tipped her forehead against his and laughed. "Almost all the time. Perhaps not in a place other people must access."

"This is our day, and if we want to spend an hour in the butler's pantry, we will."

"I love you," she whispered. "So much. Thank you."

He shook his head. "For what? I should thank you."

"For being patient."

"Sometimes I think I'm not very patient at all. I've locked you in a butler's pantry with me."

"You'd best kiss me, Mr. Detective Inspector Winston. Otherwise, *my* patience will run thin."

"With pleasure." He smiled and kissed her, and she decided there were far worse things than being locked in a butler's pantry during the holidays.

ABOUT THE AUTHOR

NANCY CAMPBELL ALLEN is the award-winning author of nineteen published novels and several novellas, which encompass a variety of genres, ranging from contemporary romantic suspense to historical fiction. Her most recent books, which include Regency, Victorian, and steampunk romance, are published under Shadow Mountain's Proper Romance brand, and the What Happens in Venice novella series is part of the Timeless Romance Anthology collection published by Mirror Press. She has presented at numerous conferences and events since her initial publication in 1999.

Her agent is Pamela Pho of D4EO Literary Agency.

Nancy loves to read, write, travel, and research, and enjoys spending time with family and friends. She nurtures a current obsession for true crime podcasts and is a news junkie. She and her husband have three children, and she lives in Ogden, Utah, with her family, one very large Siberian Husky named Thor, and an obnoxious but endearing Yorkie-poo named Freya.